COOKBOOKS & DEMONS

COOKBOOKS & DEMONS

MEGAN MACKIE

Cover by Oxford
Cover Typography and Typesetting by Autumn Skye
Editors: Jen Paquette

This is a work of fiction. All characters, organizations, and
events portrayed in this novel are either products of the
author's imagination or are used fictitiously.

Paperback ISBN-13: 978-1-965097-31-1
Hardcover ISBN-13: 978-965097-32-8
Ebook ISBN-13: 978-1-965097-30-4

To my friend, lover,
and chef, Paul

If the only thing keeping a person decent
is the expectation of divine reward, then,
brother, that person is a piece of shit.

- Rust Cohle, True Detective

Trigger warnings. There are references in this story to past acts of bullying and suicide. There is a depiction of discovering a suicide attempt that is stopped and the person saved in time. There is a murder but it is described in minimal detail on par with the expectations of a cozy genre.

Table of Contents

Chapter 1

IT STARTS WITH A COOKBOOK

Helena smiled smugly as she flipped through her grandmother's cookbook, surrounded by the smells of ginger and cinnamon from her freshly bought supplies. Her cousin had wanted the precious heirloom so badly, but Helena had prevailed. It was hers now. This hadn't been about ability or who had the actual skills to cook or not. This was a precious piece of her beloved Nana, and she deserved it as much as anyone.

Turning the pages of the old musty book, she slid her fingers past the printed text to touch on her grandmother's scrawled handwriting in the margins. The old woman should have been a famous chef; she was such a genius in the kitchen. But this was all that remained of that lost legacy. The cookbook may have started out as a church creation from the 1930s, complete with the cheap black spiral binding and laminated cover, but now it was a unique thing in its own right. Every blank page in the back had been filled with original recipes as well as every inch of margin, either adding to or correcting what had been printed.

Finding the page she desired, Helena slapped her hands together. "Alright, let's get to cooking!" she declared. There were three hours before her dinner guests came and she was going to make them a home cooked meal or die trying. "The Seven Dish Course for Eight!"

The instructions seemed straightforward at first. Chop this, dice that, stew and sauté and set to simmer.

It all should have been so simple.

"What the hell is wrong with the spinach?" Helena shouted, though no one in her empty apartment heard her aside from the cat. The smoke billowed into her face as she leaned over the book, desperately flipping the pages to get back to the one she wanted about greens. "Place the freshly washed spinach in the pan and sauté with oil ... but what the hell does sauté even mean? Doesn't it mean to just move it about? I thought that was what I was doing, so why is it burning?" She gave the pan a spin with her spatula, then tapped it three times on the edge while wiping her nose, which had started running from all the smoke, with a potholder.

Her timer dinged.

"Dammit—the buns...!" Helena reached for the hot pad to pull out the lumps of bread on a warping cooking sheet when she bumped the saucepan handle on the other burner. It went careening to the ground, slapping the white sauce in a slash across her tiled floor.

"No! Don't—Pooka!" she shouted as her black cat snatched one of the fish filets from the tray on the counter and ran off. "Dammit! You traitor!" She spun in a circle counterclockwise trying to catch the cat, only for it to make a full speed circuit twice before escaping for a corner.

Before she could give chase, more smoke billowed out of her oven.

"What now?!" She set the cooking sheet in her hands where her sauce had been and looked in the oven. When she had been distracted by the cat, a couple of buns had dropped off inside and were now igniting on the bottom into merry balls of flame.

"Oh crap!" she cried and grabbed for the fire extinguisher provided by the house's previous owners. She pulled the pin and directed the hose at the flames only for a pathetic amount of white, watery goop to plop out the end. "Oh dear, Lord!" She shook it hard, and another spurt of goop came out, a small burst that was more like what she had expected. It gave the inside of the oven a nice, if thin, coat of white film before dying almost immediately. At least it had been enough to put out the fire at the bottom.

"God dammit all to hell!" she coughed, tossing the useless fire extinguisher to the side. "Okay, you know what? No one really cares about the dinner if you have a really fantastic dessert. So just get it together, regroup, and focus on—"

Then she remembered.

"Oh no!"

The cake she had been baking with the buns now had splotches of whatever had been in the fire extinguisher. She slapped the dishtowel she had been preparing to use to pull the cake onto the open door of the oven in disgust and anger. And then she slipped on the extinguisher foam on the floor. The cake pan went skyward to land with a crash on the open oven door. Helena landed hard on her butt and bit the edge of her tongue.

Tears burned in her eyes when she slapped her hands over her mouth. She could taste the metal of blood as horrid pain pulsed. All she could do was sit there and sob a few moments. After those few moments, the pain subsided, and she spit the tiny piece of her tongue she had bitten off into the sink along with bright slaps of blood. Quickly, she went to her freezer and retrieved an ice cube from the icemaker to hold against her tongue-cut.

Taking in a shuddering breath as the cold seeped in, she grabbed for her grandmother's cookbook again. "It's okay. It's okay. Don't give up," she told herself, snuffling back her liquidy nose and brushing back the snot into her frizzing, rose-gold hair. She flipped desperately through the pages until she reached the last one before the index. At the top in bold, calligraphy-like letters read: "In Case of Emergencies."

A poem seemed to be written underneath, but if anything qualified as an emergency, this did. Tossing the ice cube into the sink, she focused on the flowery cursive words.

"Stir once and tap three times, spin widdershins, and spit your tongue, take a deep breath and say three times, 'Tribblespins, tribblespins, tribblespin,'" she read aloud. "What the fu—?"

Just then another alarm went off. "Oh! Now what!" Then all the alarms went off, including her phone, the oven timer, and her coffee machine. It was so loud, Helena had to cover her ears, letting the book drop to the ground.

On the floor of her kitchen, lines of fire appeared, etching out a circle that filled in with a pentagram. Words in a language Helena couldn't read ignited with bursts of scorching white fire and she swore she heard disembodied whispers sweep around her and down her spine as if carried on their own wind. Then a vacuum of silence swallowed all the sounds, exerting painful pressure on Helena's ears and sinuses.

Then the center of the kitchen ... exploded.

Helena screamed as she fell backward, hitting the baking sheet off the top of the stove. Her burned buns went flying.

More smoke billowed up, thinning as it rose and stinking like sulfur and patchouli. As it cleared, a demon sat in the middle of a blackened circle of what had once been white linoleum. He looked up from his crouched position, just as a bun hit him in the face. Swiping it off, he stood. He was enormous, easily six foot five with horns that added another half foot. He wore little to nothing but a gray apron wrapped around his middle that matched his gray skin. His eyes burned like twin suns, the pupils moving to look down at her with pinpricks of white-yellow light. He seemed unhealthily thin.

The demon looked down at Helena crouched terrified on the floor before him, then turned to appraise the room, his eyes going wide.

"What—what the hell did you do?!" he said.

Chapter 2

THEN CINDY
ARRIVES

When Helena didn't answer at first, the thing in her kitchen repeated himself.

"What ... the hell ... did you ... do?" He spat the words slowly like she was a stupid person.

"I... I have no idea!" she stuttered. *How is this happening? What is happening?* she thought.

Then the dishtowel she had left on the oven caught fire a mere few inches from her, which then leapt to her hair.

"Oh my God!" she bellowed, trying and failing to get away from her own enflamed hair. A hand jerked her up to her feet and a damp towel dropped over her head.

"Hold still. You're okay," the deep voice said, patting her head and hair gently but firmly through the towel. Then she found herself being escorted to her door.

"What are you...?" she tried to say, pulling the towel down to see, only to be thrust out of the door entirely.

"Just... just stay out of the kitchen. I'll fix this. We can talk terms later," the demon ordered.

"But... but..."

"Don't worry. This isn't going to cost your soul. Maybe just a blood sacrifice." His eyes roved over the kitchen disaster. He blew out a foul-smelling breath. "I don't know. We'll figure it out later," he said as if she knew at all what he was talking about.

Then he left her staring stunned as the door swung back and forth until the jamb caught it in place. All she could hear now were sounds of someone muttering and moving about her kitchen.

"What... what have I done?" she repeated softly as she stared at the scarred wood of the door.

Then the demon popped his horrifying head out again. "How many to be served?" he asked.

"Uh... eight," she replied, blinking numbly at the matter-of-factness of the question coming from the unearthly being.

"Got it," he said, then hesitated. "You should go fix your hair. Then... I don't know. Get the table settings ready."

"Oh," she replied, blinking at him and his unsettling face. "Okay."

He nodded and went back into the kitchen. More clanks and clatters came through the door.

Helena stood there in her dining room, frozen in shock. She could hear the sounds continuing in her kitchen but did she... had she really just summoned ... a demon?

Turning back to her door, she nudged it open the tiniest crack. Within, she saw the demon, still ugly and disturbing in his leather apron and nothing else, dropping her ruined pots and pans into the sink with disgust while his tail swiped along the counter with a wet cloth, sliding any spilled food scraps into her mop bucket now positioned on the floor.

Once he had discarded all her efforts, he slid the tray of fish filets, or the few remaining fish filets, onto the cleaned off counter. A knife flashed into his hands, though from where she had no idea, and he sliced along the filets. His tail abandoned the rag over the edge of the sink and stretched impossibly long to open her fridge. Almost on its own, the tail lifted the various jars stuffed into the side shelves in the door, then slowed to lift one jar then the next, one at a time. The demon glanced over, narrowing his opaque black eyes as if reading the labels. Then the tail selected one jar and brought it to him. He set down his knife and, taking the jar from his tail, unscrewed the lid. Taking an intense sniff inside, he stuck his pinkie finger in, then licked it.

"It'll work," the creature declared and set the jar down next to the filets. Then he turned back to the oven and opened it to peer inside. "I don't like to be watched while I work," he said, though he didn't glance at the door while he said it.

Helena meeped and backed away from the door, holding her hands over her mouth to contain any other scream-like sounds from escaping her.

Oh, this was bad, bad, bad.

Demon summoning, while not unheard of, was highly illegal! She would have been better off being a drug addict than summoning a creature out of hell to do a deal with!

Her grandmother's voice floated back to her out of the mists of her memory. "Ah well, you've already dropped the onions in the soup. Too late to take them out now."

The old adage calmed her, and Helena decided that washing her face and combing her hair was a sensible thing to do. The mirror agreed when she got to her bathroom, and she felt much more centered after. "What do I do now?" she asked the mirror.

"Set the table!" the demon in her kitchen answered, making her jump. Though how he could hear her from there seemed impossible.

Lacking another option, she went into her dining room and stared at the long table she rarely used. It was her mother who had convinced her to buy it, insisting that with her new job, she'd be entertaining a lot more, and it would come in handy. That had been three years ago, and no one but Helena herself had sat at that table yet. Boxes of the Fiestaware she had bought for the occasion sat on its dark surface waiting to be opened. Pulling back the flaps on the first box to stare down at the serene white plate with the "coastal sea" pattern gleaming up at her in all its blue and indigo glory seemed discordant with what was happening. She had also bought glasses that were similar, clear glass tumblers with seashells etched into the sides and a whole other box of wine glasses along with two brand-new sets of eating utensils.

She stood and stared at it all like they were alien objects dropped off by a passing space-shipping company. It had been so much fun to buy all this, but now—

Just then the doorbell rang. Helena jumped out of her skin again then turned her head toward her clock. It was an hour and a half before guests were supposed to arrive, so who could it be?

After a pregnant moment of panic, the doorbell rang again. Lacking other obvious options, Helena went to her door and looked through the peephole.

"Come on, Hel. Open up. I got wine that needs chilling, stat," her friend Cindy said.

"Uh, hang on one second," Helena said, glancing back toward her kitchen. To her shock, the demon stood right next to her, his hand planted against the door.

She meeped again, only to belatedly cover her mouth.

"Hel? You okay?" Cindy called through the door.

"Yeah, one sec. I just stubbed my toe. Hang on," Helena covered, speaking through her fingers.

The demon leaned in until he was too close to her face. "Don't tell anyone about me," he warned in a low voice. Again his strange smelling breath washed over her face. She had expected him to smell like disgusting things: rot and dead meat or at least halitosis. Instead, herby flavors accompanied the warmth of his breath, making her mouth water. It didn't make his threat any less intimidating.

"I-I won't," she said, shaking her head.

He seemed to accept that, straightening up before turning back to the kitchen.

"Helena?" Cindy called again.

Hands shaking, Helena managed to get her deadbolt and chain undone to finally let her friend in. Cindy stood on the other side, eyebrows pinched in concern.

Helena forced a smile as she leaned in to give her friend a much needed hug. "What? Did you come from the ER? You're still in your scrubs."

"Yeah, I figured I could change here; otherwise I would have been late," Cindy answered, crossing the threshold with her duffle bag and a paper bag holding two bottles of wine, lying on their sides at the bottom. Her friend wrinkled her nose. "What is that terrible smell?"

"I..." Helena glanced at her kitchen door. "I think I've completely ruined dinner, and I have no idea what to do."

"Well, let's first open some windows and/or burn some incense because damn, girl," Cindy said, dropping her duffle bag onto the couch before turning toward the kitchen. "And we still got time. How about we order some of that barbecue I smelled coming up the street?"

"Where are you going?!" Helena squawked when she realized where her friend was headed.

Cindy jerked, startled by her friend's outburst. "To put the wine in the freezer to chill," she said defensively, unsure of what she had done wrong.

"Uh, I'll take care of it," Helena tried to cover, surging forward to take the bags. "Just, uh, stay out of the kitchen. It's a real mess in there."

"God, you should see my place right now," Cindy countered, relinquishing the bag and turning her attention to the new plates. "Oh my gosh, these are gorgeous!"

Much to Helena's dismay, Cindy followed her into the kitchen carrying one of the new plates to keep up the conversation. Already in the kitchen, Helena spun around to block her friend, but it was already too late. "Cindy, wait!"

"Oh!" Cindy said, her eyes landing on the obvious someone past her shoulder. "Hello."

Chapter 3

A DEMON NAMED LARES

Helena turned, confused by her friend's calm reaction and even more confused by the young man standing behind her. He was fully dressed in black slacks and a blue shirt that buttoned on the side, like what a caterer would wear, all covered by a darker blue apron. His short black hair had been tied back with a blue patterned handkerchief. He turned from the counter when the two women had entered, small piles of chopped vegetables stacked nicely before him on Helena's large cutting board. There was not a wing, horn, or tail in sight, and his skin had become a normal human shade.

"Hello," he responded to Cindy's greeting with the same rumbling voice the demon had.

There was no doubt in Helena's mind that her demon had turned into ... a caterer.

The demon caterer wiped his hands on a clean towel and then offered it to Cindy to shake. "Lares," he said.

"Lares?" Cindy asked, furrowing her brows.

"That's my name," he stated. "Lares."

Demons had names? Of course, they did. Helena actually felt bad that she hadn't thought to ask.

"Oh, sorry," Cindy laughed, recovering from her surprise far faster than Helena did. "Just wasn't expecting a handsome man and you cook too. Double trouble." She slid a hair back over her ear in a flirty gesture, much to Helena's horror.

"Uh. Let's get out of his way. I have... I mean, he has a lot to do before everyone else gets here and..."

Lares held out his hand. "Wine."

Cindy held out the forgotten bag in her hand. "Oh, yeah. These need to be chilled before—"

"I'll take care of it," Lares said shortly. "Now if you could give me some space, ma'am."

Cindy looked over at Helena mouthing the word "ma'am" at her before rolling her eyes.

"Sorry, Lares. And thank you." Helena grabbed her friend's arm and escorted her back out the kitchen door. Once the door had swung shut, Cindy turned on her.

"Okay, who is that and what is he doing here, and can I have his phone number?"

"Um, he's a caterer. I called him to get some help after everything sort of ... exploded," Helena covered.

"Yeah, but where did he come from?"

"I... he... used to work for my grandmother. Why? What does it matter where he came from?" Helena asked.

Cindy tried to go back to peek, but Helena prevented her. "I mean, a real honest to god caterer in a private residence. You are going all out tonight. I knew you came from money, but I didn't know the extent."

"I'm not... it's not like... Look, he's doing this as a favor to my grandmother. Please don't make a big deal out of it because I think he's really annoyed by the whole thing as it is."

Cindy glanced back at the door with a thinking expression. "Yeah, I sort of got that vibe. Like he's a professional, you can tell that right off, but sort of that Hell's Kitchen kind of professional? You know, where he's going to go off at any minute if things aren't diced correctly."

The comparison caused a needle-like constriction in Helena's throat, but she swallowed it down. "You want to go ahead and get changed? You can use my bedroom," she offered, practically dragging her friend there by her duffle bag. The bathroom was across the hall to her bedroom. Once she got Cindy installed in there, she headed back to her dining room.

With the intensity of soon to be roadkill trying to outrun the car, she unpacked the new fiesta-ware from their boxes. Unfortunately, the new plates had factory dust all over them, which meant she needed to go back into the kitchen in order to get a dishtowel to wipe them to company-ready standards. And a garbage bag for the packaging.

Her eyes slid sideways to the forbidden door warily.

"Stop it," she muttered to herself. This was her home and there *wasn't* a demon in her kitchen. It was a caterer ... that had just appeared in the middle of a demonic summoning circle. *What happened to the summoning circle?* she thought.

Cindy hadn't noticed it and Helena didn't actually recall seeing it again either.

Deciding not to think about it further, she screwed up her courage and marched, practically sprinting, into her kitchen.

"Taste this."

She had barely passed through the door before there was a spoon thrust into her mouth. A burst of creamy chocolate fluffy wonder filled her mouth. "Oh my God," she exclaimed as her fingers rushed up to her lips to keep the dessert from escaping.

"What do you think?" the demon caterer asked. He still remained in a more human-like form complete with clothes, but his eyes flashed with their own eerie inner light, closer now to starbursts than anything.

"It's delicious," she said with a full mouth, trying to swallow some of it down.

"Yeah, yeah. I know that," he dismissed, waving the spoon back and forth. "But is it too chocolatey, too creamy, not chocolatey enough? Good mouth feel."

"Um, what is it supposed to taste like?" she asked.

"I don't know. I can't taste it. You have to tell me."

Her eyebrows shot up in surprise. "Oh. Uh, well." She rolled what remained in her mouth. "It's very intense. Like intensely sweet. I don't think I could do more than a spoonful."

He grunted and nodded at the feedback. "Ice cream," he muttered and turned away to his prep area. "Or maybe a semi-sweet cake with this layered in between. We have time. Yes, mousse cake. Maybe."

Helena stood there a bit confused, then amazed. The chaos that had been her kitchen had been tamed. While most of her disaster had been piled into the sink, the stove had a couple of pots simmering nicely, and it was clear there was something baking in the oven if the shadow backlit by the inner light was any indication.

"Do you... do you need help with anything?" she asked, lacking anything else to say.

"For you to get your ass out of my kitchen," he said matter-of-factly as he lifted up the pan that had her ruined cake in it, critically inspecting it.

"Oh, you can't use that," she warned, jetting forward to take the pan from him. "I got fire extinguisher all over it."

He blocked her with his arm, seizing her wrist in a vise-like grip. "Never touch anything in my kitchen. Understand?" he said very carefully. A shiver fluttered through her as her heart pounded. The illusion over the demon slipped, and Helena's throat constricted at the sight of the too-thin, gray-skinned creature before her. The stars in his eyes flared inhumanely bright into suns as he pinned her with his warning gaze, which didn't change, even as he shifted back to looking human.

"I... I'm trying to help," she said softly.

"So am I," he said. "Now get what you need and get out."

Like a startled deer, she scrambled as fast as she could under her sink, the door of which was right next to his leg and grabbed a garbage bag. Her desperate need for speed made the job take twice as long, the bag getting caught in the door as it closed. Then she had to double back for a clean dishcloth.

Helena glanced up fearfully at the demon, praying that he wouldn't do anything to her, but he just looked down his nose at her impassively waiting.

She fled the kitchen, back into her dining room. Gripping the back of a chair with both hands, she let the garbage bag drop to the floor while she panted like she had run a marathon.

"Oh, God, what have I done? How did I do it? What am I going to do?"

On top of everything, her tongue hurt from where she bit it. Rubbing the wound with a finger, she checked for blood.

Dammit, this is going to bug me all night, she thought.

"What's wrong with you?" the gruff voice from the door asked. She spun to face the demon poking his head through the kitchen door.

"I... I bit my tongue ...before."

He grunted. "Come here."

Each step weighed a ton, but she went back to the door.

Then he stroked along her cheek. She practically jumped out of her skin at his touch. "There. Now you can taste the food," he said. "Don't thank me. I'll add it to your tab."

"Great."

It wasn't.

Chapter 4

THEN THE
BOSS ARRIVES

"Helena, come on. It's just a dinner party. Don't panic," Cindy chided as she came back in from her bedroom. The ER doctor was gone and, in her place, stood a perfect silhouetted socialite in tight black pants with bell-bottoms dusted in white and a bare-midriff halter top that sparkled blackly.

"You look..." Helena tried to find the right word, but snazzy was the only one that came to mind and there was no way in hell she was saying *that* one.

"I haven't dressed up in so long I needed to go the distance," Cindy explained and flipped a bit more at her short hair, now infused with product to make the back turn up toward the sky like her hair was made of feathers instead of strands. It gave her an airy beauty and highlighted her golden blondeness.

Her gorgeous friend came to the table and surveyed the dishes, picking one up. "Oh, this is nice. Good choice."

The ordinariness of the plate helped refocus Helena back to earth. "Thanks. I thought it would be nice... you know."

"Oh, yeah, definitely. Let's get all this laid out," Cindy agreed and helped her set the table. Between the two of them, they had it looking fairly nice with the forks and knives in the right places and the crystal glasses sparkling beside each plate. Helena set the garbage bag next to the kitchen door, now filled.

"Yeah, it looks nice," Helena agreed, watching her friend pull out two tapers from her cabinet that she had forgotten she had.

Cindy held them up. "Should we go ahead and use these?"

"I uh," Helena said, distracted as she glanced down as the kitchen door opened slightly beside her. She didn't see anything, but the garbage bag whisked away, and she only flinched a little as it went. Cindy didn't see any of it as she dug around for the candle holders, setting the tapers into a crystal pair that Helena's aunt had given her and placed them in the central part of the table.

Cindy surveyed her handywork, propping her fists on her hips. "There. That looks great! Now we just need a lighter. Or should we wait to light them when everyone gets here?"

"Oh, let's wait until everyone..." and then the door cracked open again and one of her long, stick-like lighters appeared. "Or I'll do it now," Helena amended, taking it from the demon. "Uh, thank you," she added softly.

The door shut again in response.

Cindy grinned and leaned forward to pitch her voice down. "I don't think he's surly. I think he's just shy," she said, and then giggled.

"Yeah, maybe," Helena agreed weakly, because what else could she really say, and clicked the trigger to call up a flame at the tip.

Once the tapers were lit, Cindy dimmed down the dining room lights with the slide switch, and Helena genuinely smiled at the serene space. "It's actually exactly how I pictured it," Helena said.

"And you didn't even have to sell your soul to get it," Cindy quipped.

Helena eyed her a moment at the strangely on point quip, but Cindy didn't seem to notice as she adjusted one of the cloth napkins that Helena had simply folded into a nice triangle. "Oh, I can do better than that. I know this great fold from when I worked as a server," she said and gathered up all the napkins to redo.

"Oh, Cindy, you don't have to do that." Helena tried to intervene, but Cindy waved her off.

"No, quit it," she ordered, swatting away Helena's offending hand. "Let me do this!"

Yielding, Helena glanced at the clock. It was already ten minutes past when people were supposed to be arriving!

"Oh no, where is everyone?" A panicked thought of having gone through ... everything ... she had just gone through and no one showing up to her dinner party sent a shiver of dread through her heart.

"I wouldn't worry yet. People are always late for dinner parties," Cindy tried to assure her, but even she flashed a worried look at the clock. "Who all is supposed to be coming?"

"Charles and Chris, and a couple people from work, and my boss..." She regretted the rash move even more upon saying it aloud.

Cindy's eyebrows popped up to her hairline. "Oh. That was a bold move."

"Yeah, well, they say you don't get what you don't ask for, and I thought, hey, maybe she'd... I don't know ... like to get to know me better?"

Cindy's face looked worried. "Well, yeah, that's what I said, but it's one thing to take your boss out for coffee and another to invite them into your home and feed them. Oh!" She turned her head back toward the kitchen and nodded her head at it, mouthing, "That's why the caterer." She then tapped her nose, signaling she got it now.

"That was just ... a happy coincidence."

"Hey, take your luck where you can find it," Cindy said, then turned contemplative. "Maybe I should do this for the Head of Surgery at work."

Just then the doorbell rang. A thrill of panic ripped through Helena, but Cindy, being the one with less on the line, got to the door first. Based on her squeals of greeting, Helena was relieved when Charles and Chris came in, also bearing a bottle of wine and hugs. Charles admired the plate settings while Chris worked on opening the wine, and Cindy womaned the door as Helena's guests were coming fast and furious. Soon the room was filled with happy excited people, and Helena found herself too busy making introductions and seeding conversations to continue to worry about the demon in her kitchen.

At least until *he* appeared bearing a tray of hors d'oeuvres. Her eyes grew wide as she stared down at the little deconstructed pigs-in-a-blankets all in neat little rows on what she realized was one of the serving plates her mother had given her when she moved in, which Helena had stuffed on a shelf and promptly forgot about. Her guests cooed as they swarmed to each take one, keeping the demon from needing to enter farther than three steps into the room. Half the tray was gone before it occurred to her to spur forward and take it. She met the demon's eyes as her hand touched his cold one under the tray. His eyes flashed from the hypnotic black pits to starburst fire before returning once more to the intense black as if warning her once more about blowing his cover.

"Uh, thank you," she said, and he nodded once before returning to the kitchen.

As soon as the door swung shut, the women from her office and Cindy all let off a chorus "oooooooo la la," that of course ended in giggles. One of them even fanned herself with her hand.

Helena's cheeks burned. "Oh stop. He's just doing this as a favor … to my grandma," she said, trying to not let the lie stick in her throat. What the hell was her grandmother doing with a demon summoning spell in the back of her cookbook anyway?

A thought to ponder later … if there was a later.

"You see, I've had a little bit to think about this," Cindy said, pointing at Helena's nose with a finger from the hand currently wrapped around a half-drunk wine glass. "I don't think he's just doing this because he owes your gramma. Because from what we just witnessed there…" She didn't finish the sentence, instead blowing out a breath and shaking her opposite hand like she was at a Chippendale's show and it was all too hot to handle.

That set off another chorus of giggles, not just from the office women, but the men in the room as well. Charlie even gave her a thumbs up. Helena's cheeks burned hotly because all she wanted to do was scream at them to all run: there was a demon in the house! She had no idea how she summoned it, but they were all in danger, and she was probably going to be arrested because while demon summoning wasn't unheard of in the world, it was definitely punishable by three different authorities, and even if she didn't get caught, the thing in her kitchen would probably eat her soul and—

Her panicked train of thought was cut off by the doorbell ringing one final time. The laughter stopped as everyone noticed Helena's terrified expression.

"My boss," she whispered.

Everyone scrambled then, feeling the same urgency that she did, mostly out of an abundance of care for her, but while she left her coworkers to tell the rest the low-down concerning Helena's boss, Helena rushed to the door.

Opening it, she about had an additional heart attack.

There stood her boss, an elderly woman with silver hair professionally coifed by an expensive salon to emphasize the "silver vixen" look that was so vogue right then. The lady was dressed down for her, which meant that everything she wore probably individually would cover Helena's mortgage payment for a month.

"Scarlet," Helena greeted, offering what she hoped was a welcoming smile. She opened the door and gestured an open hand of welcome. "And Yosef, welcome, both of you."

Scarlet's arm crutches chinked as she placed one then the other inside the door before crossing the threshold herself with so much painful dignity that always made Helena flinch and admire her at the same time. Behind her followed Scarlet's gorgeous assistant Yosef, carrying her bag with one hand out in readiness should his boss fall.

Helena had forgotten to include Yosef in the count for dinner.

As she continued to step back to let the dignified socialite through her door, she glanced back over her shoulder at the table. The rest of her guests had all moved forward in a poor attempt of appearing like a nonchalant crowd in order to be ready to greet the unofficial matriarch of their city but not look like they were waiting to greet her. This had left the table more or less abandoned, and to her amazement, the demon was there, already adjusting the table settings for another person with smooth crisp motions. By the time Scarlet had finished her entrance, the table had been reset, and it looked like it had always been that way.

Then he was gone again into the kitchen.

Maybe tonight wouldn't be so bad after all?

Chapter 5

THE
CONVERSATION
TURNS TO DEMONS

"**O**h my gosh, I'm so full. I'm stuffed!" Cindy declared to everyone else's cheers and agreements. Various empty plates were pushed back, and more than one belly was being rubbed with satisfaction.

"Okay, spill it. Did you sell your soul for your caterer tonight?" Chris laughed.

"Oh for God's sake, Chris! That is not appropriate," Charlie chided, slapping his husband with the end of a napkin.

"Do people even do that anymore?" one of Helena's office workers, whose name was completely escaping her at the moment, asked.

Helena felt like she would throw up at any minute.

"I knew a guy from high school who apparently summoned a demon so he could get a promotion at work," Charlie said to which Chris laughed. "It's not funny.

He went to jail and everything just for attempting to summon one."

"Yeah, but that's like going to jail for marijuana use or something. I mean, sure it's illegal, but everyone does it, right? I mean, in college?" another office worker asked.

"And now we all know more about Cheryl than we did before," someone said, and the table laughed again.

"We sometimes get people in the ER for demon summoning," Cindy said soberly. "It is very serious. All kinds of things can go wrong, not just with the summoning itself which usually involves blood, but if you don't bind the demon correctly... people have died from being disemboweled. It's horrendous." She took a sip of her wine.

Helena couldn't help but glance over at her kitchen door. Binding? She hadn't done anything of the sort, and she felt sweat at the lower part of her back tickling. An image flashed through her mind of the demon bursting forth through the door, picking Cindy up by the neck, and chopping her head off with an enormous cleaver.

It didn't happen, and the conversation pulled her attention back.

"So you've really seen someone who's been attacked by a demon?" someone was asking Cindy.

She nodded. "Yes. Some asshole summoned one to get revenge on his girlfriend who dumped him for another man. It killed both her and the new boyfriend, then turned on the guy. Tore his arm off before it could be sent back. Guy died on the table from shock and blood loss."

A pall fell over the table.

"Well, that was a scintillating conversation. Let's never speak of it again!" Charlie intervened, and this time everybody listened to him.

26

"Sorry, Helena. I didn't mean to imply that you would do such a thing. The caterer seems very nice and very human," Chris amended, nodding toward Helena.

"Oh! No, it's fine. It was just a compliment, right?" Helena agreed, relieved to be getting off the subject.

"I saw a demon once."

The statement froze the table, and all eyes slid over to Scarlet. Yosef sitting next to her paused as well, his wine glass halfway to his mouth before he dropped his head and shook it in despair.

Scarlet didn't seem to notice or care if she did. With a tricky, conspiratorial smile, she leaned her elbows onto the table, lacing her fingers together in front of her. "He was gorgeous."

There was an intake of breath around the table. "An incubus?" a voice asked in awe.

"The most dangerous demon known to woman, yes," Scarlet said, relishing her command of the room. Her eyes grew distant as she stared into the past. "And he was everything they say. Tall, dark, otherworldly. 'Beautiful' wouldn't capture what he was. Still a man in shape. In every shape. And he smelled..." Then Scarlet seemed to wake up from the dream she was building, seeing her captive, breathless audience. "There is a reason incubi and succubi are the most commonly summoned of all the demon-spawn," she purred.

Chris licked his lips. "And ... what was he like?"

Scarlet blinked once. "Like?"

Chris shifted in his seat and Charlie planted his head in his hand.

"Yeah," Chris continued since no one was going to bail him out. "You know."

27

Scarlet smiled predatorily, looking a bit demonish herself. "Why dear boy, I wasn't the one who summoned him, of course. But let me assure you, demonic sex is just as tragic as the rest of it. It robs your self of the energy of life, and nothing is ever right again. Nothing ever tastes right, touch from normal humans feels like numb pawing, and it spoils any other delight the world has to offer. All the victims are left with an insatiable craving for their lover, and they will do anything to get it."

"Like having sex on ecstasy?"

"Worse," Scarlet assured. "They destroy everything you were and everything you could be and leave a hollow shell screaming out for a memory of what they had done. Incubi kill just as effectively if not more cruelly."

Just then the kitchen door opened as the demon caterer backed into the room, carrying a tray laid out with several bowls of chocolate mousse cake. He paused when he encountered the tension in the room.

"What's wrong?" he demanded. "Did something happen with the food?"

"No! The food was delicious," Helena said, jumping in and chorused by her guests, who also agreed with her sentiment, all worried they had offended him. "That's the... uh problem. We all thought it was too good to be ... earthly made," she said adequately, if awkwardly.

The demon sniffed at that, the human face he wore truly hiding his secret beneath it.

Just imagine he's real. Just imagine he's human. He's human. He's human, Helena repeated in her mind as she stood up and came over to him as natural as if he *had* been human. Because he was. He was human. Totally.

"Let me help you with that," she offered and took up two of the small bowls with cake upon it. They were beautiful sculptures, chocolate cake layered with mousse cream, each cut into different shapes. They were all proportionally the same size and topped with lattices of chocolate that were already sweating condensation.

"These are beautiful," Cindy chimed as Helena set plates before her and Scarlet simultaneously. Her friend turned back to the demon. "Really, this is just gorgeous. It just got us talking about demons and demon summoning, you know, because your food is honestly too good to be true."

Again, the demon sniffed at that. "Demon summoning is a stupid practice," he declared.

Helena almost dropped a plate of cake onto Chris.

"Yes, I think that is the conclusion we have all reached this night," Scarlet declared and everyone nodded. Yosef held up his glass for more wine, and everyone dug into the dessert, turning the conversation to safer topics.

The conversations lingered long after the plates were cleared and the last sip of wine was drunk.

"Well, I don't know about you youngsters, but while I have had a lovely evening, I must be the first to make a graceful exit," Scarlet declared, standing up from the table. All the males leapt to their feet in a surprising show of old-fashioned manners, and Yosef came around to offer his arm to his employer, which she took with the grace of a Duchess. "All of you, sit, sit! Enjoy the rest of your evening. Our host seeing me out is more than enough."

Everyone offered good-byes and platitudes. Chris even raised his empty glass in salute and Helena did just that: escorted her guest of honor to the door. Yosef went and fetched the arm crutches she had brought from next to

Helena's coat rack while Scarlet turned to Helena, setting her hand on the younger woman's arm.

"Come talk to me in the morning," Scarlet said softly. "I have an idea I'd like to discuss with you."

A flutter of excitement tickled inside Helena's chest. Was this it? Were "big things" going to happen for her at the office?

"Absolutely, I would love to," she said effusively.

Scarlet nodded, satisfied by her barely contained reaction. "You did good tonight, my girl. I've had my eye on you awhile, and I think it's time we did something useful with you."

She gracefully took her crutches then and turned as Yosef opened the door for her, exiting without anything further. Yosef, for his part offered Helena a wink and a brief, "Thank you for dinner," and then he was gone right behind her, reshouldering his bag of mysterious things. She made sure the door was shut behind them.

Helena floated all the way back to the table.

"Well?" Cindy asked as soon as she came into sight. All the faces turned to Helena expectantly.

"I think I can ... cautiously say," she paused for her own dramatic effect, letting the smile take over her face, "that my first dinner was a success."

Cheering went up around the table, and Helena let herself giggle for the first time that evening.

Shortly after, everyone else left, the dam already broken by Scarlet. Her coworkers didn't seem jealous, only speculative about what the meeting with their mutual boss could be about. Charlie dragged Chris out, who didn't seem to really feel the effects of the wine he'd consumed until he stood up and it all went to his head. Cindy lingered the longest, insisting on helping with the dishes, but the demon had already whisked them away to the kitchen and so a quick argument about how tired she really was after doing so many shifts without a weekend convinced her to get going.

The quiet felt thunderous as soon as the door shut behind her friend and her duffle bag.

The night was over, but *it* wasn't over yet.

Chapter 6

DO YOU KNOW HOW DEMON DEALS WORK?

Taking a deep shuddering breath, Helena steeled herself and marched toward the kitchen. The dishes had already been cleared from the table and all that remained was the cloth and various crumbs.

Just before she pushed her kitchen door open, bile came up at the back of her throat and she paused for a moment to swallow it back. On the other side of the door, she heard the clinking of glass bumping glass. He was definitely still in there. Gently, she pushed the door so it opened a slight crack.

There he stood, still wearing the catering outfit, his back to the door. His hands were dunked into her kitchen sink, washing pans, while her dishwasher next to him hummed away on what she presumed were all the plates and glasses they had just used.

He looked so normal.

From this angle, she could see more of his hair from under the blue kerchief he wore, which was dark. No horns, no tail. Just a guy, who then turned around holding the baking sheet she had tried to use for her fish filets.

He moved to set the clean version on top of her stove when he paused. Lifting his head, his burning eyes stared at the doorway.

He caught her spying on him.

Deciding to face the inevitable, she pushed the door the rest of the way in.

He jumped, dropping the baking sheet. It bounced off the edge of the stove and would have hit the ground except he caught it with his tail, which manifested into view. "Hell in a handbasket!" he shouted, which startled her back in return. "You scared me!"

"I... I scared *you*?" she challenged, trying to process that statement.

"Where the hell did you come from?" he said, turning away, then he snapped his fingers multiple times in the air while he blew out a shaking breath. It was a surprisingly human gesture for him. "Why are you sneaking around like that?"

"I... but you saw me?" Helena pursed her eyebrows as she gestured at the doorway where she had been peeking.

He blew another breath and turned another circle, calming himself down, then set the baking sheet on the stove top with his tail.

"Is everyone else gone?" he asked, throwing a towel over his shoulder.

"Uh, yeah," she said, still standing there perplexed.

The demon caterer reached into the sink and pulled the plug, the water making a *glub-glug* sound as he did it.

He ran the water and rinsed it out while she stood there watching him. "For the record, I didn't see you. I just had that creepy feeling like I was being watched and was trying to figure it out when you opened the door," he argued.

"But we made eye contact?" she pushed.

"Okay, we made eye contact," he said, irritated. "I'm not going to argue."

Now she felt bad. "Do you... do you need any help in here?" she asked.

"No, just go sit down at your table and drink your wine. I'll have this finished in a minute," he said as he ran the water again, this time dipping wine glasses into the stream to wash. Once more, his tail manifested, appearing after a brief shimmer in the air, like a heat mirage, before wrapping itself around one of the used glasses. It carried the fragile thing over to her as far as it could reach. "Here. This one was yours."

Helena had to take a step in to grasp the glass. "Uh, thank you." But she didn't leave. Instead, she screwed up her courage and brought the glass back, stepping up beside the creature in her kitchen.

Heat, or some sort of wrong energy, seemed to radiate off of him but that also could have been her imagination. She couldn't say. "I'm actually all good with the wine drinking," she said and set the wineglass into the water to disappear under the fresh suds.

He grunted, then retrieved it back out of the water. His hands had changed, reverting back to the dead-grayish skin and long black nails he had before. She gasped again, realizing she stood next to the demon in all his glory once more, no longer glamouring himself as the caterer. His black nails clicked against the glass as he turned it over to go at the inside with her rose pink bottle brush.

Fascinated, she watched him rinse the glass out under a fresh stream of water and then set it upside down on one of her dishtowels on the counter over the dishwasher. The juxtaposition of the supernatural creature doing a perfectly mundane thing seemed to keep her mind from cracking into a million pieces.

"Are you going to watch me the whole time?" he asked, his voice rumbling next to her. She looked up his bare arms to his head with the elegant black horns arching like ram's horns.

Swallowing, she backed away and went into her towel drawer to get a dry one. Turning back, she took in his full body, now no longer covered with anything resembling clothing. Just his full moon and the string of the front leather apron. The crack down the middle was covered by his tail, which maintained that strange grayness of skin until about a foot down it when it morphed into blackness. The tip of his tail had the typical triangle devil tail ...thingy, and it swung back and forth in a little contented arc near the ground, like a cat. His wings were tucked tight against his back so he could move easily. Otherwise, the other disturbing aspect to him was his too thin frame, highlighted by what she could see of his ribs with their deep grooves.

She commented on none of this but came up on the other side of him this time to grab one of her wine glasses and start drying it. He didn't comment on her helping him or do anything to stop her.

"Thank you," she said, three dry glasses later, "for such a good meal."

"It tasted good?" he asked, a longing in his voice.

"It tasted amazing," she confirmed.

He nodded, not looking at her, a complicated expression on his face, like a mix of satisfaction and regret.

"So... you do this a lot?" she asked.

"I'm not going to take your soul," he said instead of answering.

That made her flinch, like she had been caught sneaking a cookie. "Oh, well that's good," she said.

"I mean, not unless you want me to," he added. "I don't know how much you know about demon summoning, but there are other ways to deal with the cost."

Her mind jumped to a million things that she had either heard or imagined. "Honestly, I don't even know how I did it this time. Don't suppose I can just return you without paying since I didn't mean to?"

He shook his head. "Sorry. I performed the service, and it's not me that gets paid, but the cosmic debt. I used as little of it as possible, though. Tried to make what you already had work. So it won't be too bad."

"Cosmic debt?"

He sighed. "You can think of it like magic, I guess. Demon magic. I used as little as possible."

"But you did have to use some?"

Now he looked down at her with narrowed eyes into slits of starlight. "I made a three course dinner with dessert on no notice. For nine. Believe me, I performed miracles tonight."

She giggled at that, which surprised her. But it also made him less scary, so she leaned into it. "I guess I did leave you with a disaster."

He's just a normal caterer who helped me out of a jam. This is fine. This is fine. This is fine. Some part of her started to believe it.

For a moment at least.

Beside her, he drained the water, rinsing away the suds again, having finished the last wineglass. He then plucked up the one she had finished drying, reaching around her with his long arms. He picked up all but the one still in her hand, spacing each between his equally too-long fingers.

A tremble rolled down her spine, the same wrongness she got from licking a battery. Then he was gone, moving to her cupboard where she kept her liquor and the various glasses required for proper liquor drinking. When he opened it with his tail, she saw that the inside had been organized.

Shocked, she opened another cupboard where she kept her pantry items. Instead of the different series of cans and glass bottle thrown in haphazardly, they were stacked neatly with the labels facing out. She opened the cupboard below it, and the boxes where she kept her cereal along with one sad box of oatmeal and her various sides that she never made were lined up as well and ordered.

"How did you... when did you have time to do this?" she asked, opening her dishes cupboard to find the same thing, bowls and plates sorted and rearranged so that everything actually fit properly.

"Don't worry. I'm not charging you for it either. I just couldn't stand it," he said, grabbing up the dishcloth to rub at a spot on the last glass before putting it away.

"So you used ... demon magic as well?" she asked, looking around at the deeply spotless counters and the floor devoid of the standard pile of dirt in the corners that she could never quite get.

"Like I said, I couldn't stand it," he said, an edge of growl in his voice.

It wasn't directed at her, but she pursed her lips at it. "Thank you," she said.

"Yeah," he answered, sighing as he flipped the towel back over his gray shoulder and folded his arms across his chest, surveying the domain he had been master of until that moment. "Okay, I guess it's time. How do you want to do this?"

A small, worried half-whimper escaped her throat.

He turned to her, his imposing form bearing down on her even from across the room.

Then he sighed. "You don't know how any of this works at all do you?"

Her throat had closed up, so she shook her head while tears burned at the bottom of her eyes.

He sighed a second time and gestured a hand. Immediately his form changed, reverting back to a normal man's with burning ethereal eyes. "Is that better?" he asked, obviously annoyed.

She nodded, swallowing her tears. It was better, even if only marginally because she still knew what he was underneath. "I'm sorry," she said. "I don't know how I did this, I don't know what it all means, and I don't know what I would have done if you hadn't helped me—"

"Okay, okay. Calm down," he said and gestured toward her dining room. "Let's go sit down, and I'll give you the full rundown on how this works."

Chapter 7

THE BEST CAKE
EVER... I THINK

Like a martyr walking to her execution, Helena crossed into her dining room and sat down. Only half an hour before, it had been filled with the laughter and conversation of her friends.

But maybe that was a good way to go out? Her last night on earth had been lovely. Isn't that what people most wished for?

"Nope," she said, shaking her head to herself. This was not what she had wanted at all. She wanted to live.

A plate appeared before her, holding one of the pieces of cake. It was followed by a full glass of milk clunking onto the table. "Eat this. It'll help you feel better," the demon said, and he took the chair around the corner next to her and sat.

She eyed him and the cake with mistrust, even though she had already consumed a piece at dinner. He still wore the human face and clothes as he sat down. She hated to admit it, but that helped somewhat. Thinking of him as human made him less scary. But still, there had been two pieces left in the kitchen, and he didn't have the other with him.

"Aren't you going to have one?" she asked, picking up the fork on the plate but not intending to use it on the cake. Even if it was a pathetic weapon, and she didn't even know if she had the will to use it that way, it was better than nothing. Would the tines even penetrate his skin if he attacked her?

"I can eat if you want me to, but it won't taste like anything to me," he stated matter-of-factly, crossing his arms over his chest. He didn't look at her when he said that, instead letting his strange eyes drift off into the middle distance. With his human face on, he looked so ... tired.

She furrowed her eyebrows. "It won't taste like anything?" she repeated, incredulous. "But you were... oh." Her eyebrows shot up as she put it together. "That's why you had me tasting for you."

He nodded, but the long-seeing eyes had shifted to her cake, now filled with hunger.

"But how do you know if your food is good then?" she asked, glomming on to a safe question. After all, she didn't taste everything.

"I can smell it," he said in a low voice. "Chocolate, frying fish, buttery savor. I can smell all of it. But the second I put anything in my mouth, ashes." He touched his lips with his fingers in a mockery of a chef's kiss.

"That's horrible," Helena said, forking a bite of the chocolate into her mouth. It sat on her tongue, heavy with the prospect of it too turning to ash in her mouth. It didn't. It remained the decadent symphony of flavor it had been from that first spoon lick. She hadn't even realized she had started eating it, and already the plate was half gone.

"Yes," the demon said, his eyes following her motions with the fork from plate to mouth and back. "It's horrible, alright." Then he blinked as if remembering himself. "Alright. So... based on what I've observed, I am guessing that you've never actually done any of this before?" He gestured at the kitchen. "The summoning and the payment and all."

"I'm still not sure how it happened."

He waved a hand. "It's fine. Don't worry about it. I'm going to tell you what you need to know to settle this."

That raised her alarm bells again. "But how will I know it's the truth, and you're not trying to trick me or something?" she asked before wondering if asking such a thing would anger him. She had flashes of being tied to an old-fashioned spit and roasted with an apple in her mouth while the demon basted her with a paintbrush.

Instead, he just cocked one eyebrow at her. "You're just going to have to trust me," he said, amused. "And if you don't ever do it again, everything should be fine." He cleared his throat and repositioned in his seat. "Alright, what you need to understand is this: there are three things you can give a demon to pay for their services." He ticked off three fingers. "The shorthand for it is mind, body, or soul. And before you freak out, it's not what you think," he warned, holding up a hand as Helena reacted to the list.

He plowed on. "Body is the easy one—everyone knows it. We consume something from your body. I'm sure you've heard of blood sacrifices. It doesn't have to be blood; it's just the most sensationally known thing people offer. Soul is... well, really a misnomer. It's life energy, usually taken

41

from you via sex and is the go-to of most succubi or incubi. They've perfected getting the most out of that."

He paused to see if she comprehended. "Do you have a question?" he said, probably noting her expression.

"Well, I mean..." She sighed, deciding to let her caution go a bit. "It's just... all the movies and documentaries out there about the dangers of demon summoning. You're making it sound so ... normal?"

"Look, don't let me mislead you. Demon summoning is really dangerous. I'm not kidding," he stressed, crossing his arms over his chest as he leaned back. "But it is determined by scale. Like having a drink of wine at dinner, mostly fine. Having a case of wine at dinner, probably going to kill you."

Helena thought about that as she took a drink of her milk. "What? So, for little things you can just cut your finger, but for big things like..." She tried to think of an example.

"That's where you get into the human sacrifices, yes," he said, nodding. "It's all to pay the... let's just call it demon magic. It pays it back. And demons always get paid back."

And just when I start to feel comfortable, he says something like that, she thought. "Okay, then. What do *you* want?" she asked, steeling herself. "What would be a fair compensation for dinner?"

He held up his thumb with the other two fingers. "The third thing. Mind. Mind usually means I can consume a memory, thought, dream, something like that."

"You want one of my memories?" she asked.

"Yes, please." He nodded effusively.

Helena scraped at the plate, gathering up the mousse frosting onto the edge of her fork. "Will it hurt?" she asked, bringing it to her mouth.

"No," he said, then leaned forward and thumped his hand against her forehead.

The world tilted sideways. The lighting in the room went wrong and sounds echoed sharp and painful, all while echoing hollowly. There was no illusion around him now. The demon sat across from her in all his emaciated horror. The ground seemed to be opening up through the boards of her floor, letting in sulfurous smoke and waves of heat, along with cries of pain and suffering which no one would be able to assuage. Coldness pressed against the inside of Helena's skull, like an ice cream headache but sharper and physical as she felt something leaving her through the palm of the demon's hand.

And then it was over.

Helena sat there stunned as the room returned to her soft dim lighting. The floorboards were normal and flat, and there were no other sounds except the ticking of her clock on the wall.

Then the demon next to her moaned.

She jumped a little bit as he leaned forward, once more hiding behind a human facade. His fingers were pressed to his mouth, his eyes closed in pure ecstasy. Then he leaned back, tilting his head, breathing hard as if he were going to orgasm or something. Helena found herself recoiling in her seat but unable to look away.

Then he sighed, letting his arms drop to his lap while his face morphed into pure bliss. "Oh damn, that was good," he said, then added. "Too much butter though. I didn't need to overcompensate so much."

"What... what was that?" Helena demanded, rubbing at her forehead where the ice cream headache faded but left her feeling disturbed.

"My payment," the demon said, opening his eyes to look at her. "I just ate your memory of eating that chocolate cake."

Her eyes went wide, then she glanced down at the finished plate, before going back to him. "You ate my memory of me eating the cake. I can't remember what it tastes like at all." It was a disconcerting feeling.

He nodded, drunkenly sitting up in the chair. "See? I told you. Not so bad. We're square now."

"I really wish you had asked first before you..." she gestured at her head when the proper nouns for it just wouldn't come to her, "did that."

"If I had, you would have tensed up, maybe even fought me about it, and made it harder on both of us," he said simply.

She wrinkled her nose. "You still should have asked for permission."

He looked at her askance. "I'm a demon. Sue me." Then he slapped his hands on the table "And we're done here. You can send me back now." He stood up and moved back toward her kitchen.

"What? That's it?" Helena asked, rushing after him as he spurred himself away.

"Yup," he said, changing back into his demonic self the second he crossed the threshold. "I got what I want; you got what you want. Never summon demons again, and we can call this a win-win. Hurray. I rarely get those."

It all seemed too abrupt. He hadn't even tried to upsell her for her soul with promises of more power. "But what if—"

He spun back to her, pointing a black nail straight at her nose. She managed to stop half an inch before it sank into her skin, her eyes crossing as she stared down at it.

"No," he said. "No, 'buts.' No summoning me again. Do you understand me? Like you said, this was an accident. Don't become just like every other human being in the world and suddenly get greedy because that path *will* cost your soul and the destruction of everything that you love and care about. Are we clear?"

Helena carefully backed up. Then nodded. "Yes, I understand," she said.

He lowered his finger. "Good. Now send me home."

"Okay," Helena agreed. "Um, how do I do that exactly?"

Chapter 8

A DEMON NAMED RAFFERTY

He sighed, the bat-like wings on his back drooping. "Where's the cookbook?"

She scurried over to fetch it while he took position in the middle of the room. The summoning marks from before flared to life, and Helena realized that they had gone invisible before when her guests had been there. But she supposed since he could hide his appearance, he could have hidden the marks of her demon summoning as well. She hugged the open book against her chest, not knowing what page she needed to go to next and waited.

Her ... guest took up position in the middle of the circle, down on both knees and tucking his wings comfortably behind himself.

"Before I forget," he added, and his tail whipped out to snatch at a piece of torn paper on the counter. His prehensile appendage held it out to her to take. "I wrote down a formula that you need to use to cleanse this circle after I'm gone. Mop once will take the initial mess out of your floor as well as the remnants of demon magic and then again for a year to *thoroughly*," he leaned forward to make her meet his eyes to stress his emphasis, "thoroughly clear out the magic so no one else can 'accidentally' call me again. And you should be fine. I checked. You got all the ingredients there, but if I make it for you, I'll corrupt it, so you got to do it yourself."

"And then go to church every Sunday and get blessed or something?" she asked. She sort of meant it as a joke—she had seen it in a movie once.

The demon just shrugged. "I mean, if you want to. If it'll make you feel better, sure. Now turn to the spell you used to call me and read it backwards." And then he resettled back, wrapping his tail around himself. The pose he assumed looked so very ... zen-like and peaceful. He even had his eyes closed as if preparing to accept his fate.

A new sensation cut through Helena, watching him, one that had nothing to do with herself, just him.

"Um, are you going to be alright?" she asked, hesitating with her grandmother's cookbook in her hands.

"Am I going to be alright in hell?" he asked wryly, again that eyebrow cocking up in amusement as he peeked his eyes open.

"Well, yeah," she said, not knowing how else to express the feeling creeping in.

A look of almost tenderness warmed his star-burning eyes. "Yeah. I'm going to be fine."

"But how can you? It's hell?"

He flicked his wings in surprise and confusion. "Look Helena, you're clearly a very good person, but you have to understand, it's where I belong. I did plenty to earn my place there. That's not your responsibility." But his hand did something else contrary to his words. Where he had had his fists balled and resting against his thighs, his right hand uncurled and lifted. The clawed fingers stretched toward her as if asking her to take it. Then he closed it again.

"You'd better get reading," he said softly, resolutely.

Helena pursed her lips together, then pulled the book away and looked at the spell her grandmother had scrawled in her clean perfect cursive. "Thank you, by the way," she said before reading.

His strange, alien face smiled sadly. "It was lovely to meet you, Helena."

"It was lovely to... wait. What is your name? I know you said it earlier..."

"I ate it. Don't worry about it," he said, waving a hand.

She blinked once. "Why would you do that?"

He sighed. "Like I said, I clean up after myself. And because if you know my name, you can just summon me again without the spell, so forget it." He narrowed his eyes in warning.

"How about Rafferty?" she asked quickly. "Can I call you Rafferty? That won't summon you, right?"

He cocked his head at that. "Why Rafferty?"

"Rafferty Jones, *Food Emergencies*? He's a famous TV chef?"

The demon chuckled and shook his head. "Sure, you can call me Rafferty."

"Thank you for everything, Rafferty," she said. Her heart twisted as she said his new name. His presence still disgusted her, but he had been nothing but kind. "It was nice to meet you."

"Okay, that's enough," Rafferty said, waving his hand at her. "Get on with it."

Helena nodded, then lifted up the book and read the words of the spell one at a time backwards. She didn't sense or smell anything, there was no shift like there had been before, but when she looked up, Rafferty was gone.

The world seemed so normal the next day. She got up, got ready for work, and even took the train—all normal, all the same. But she felt like she was only seeing it all for the first time.

Once the demon had been sent back to ... where he had come from, and she had mopped up all the traces of the summoning with a mix of baking soda, lemon, vinegar, and allspice, for some reason, from the recipe the demon instructed her to use, she had been sure she would never fall asleep. After all, what had just happened had been terrifying, hadn't it? It should have kept her up all night with worry and fear, knowing demons existed for sure and that she had made a deal with one.

Instead, she fell asleep immediately upon her head hitting the pillow.

Sitting on the bench of the train, she stared out at the trees passing. The train was elevated in this section and zipped through the carefully pruned branches of the trees lining each side, making the light dance and sway within the car. The late fall colors and the gentle rocking added to the peace and fulfillment she enjoyed. She wasn't sure anyone else felt it, but there was a connection inside her that seemed to permeate everything around her. She was alive and whole and safe. And happy. It made her feel like she floated as she got off the train and walked the three blocks to her office building, then up the eight floors to Scarlet Promotions, Inc.

"Well you look sunny today," Yosef noted when Helena walked through the clear, tempered glass doors of the office.

He stood near the reception desk with a set of folders tucked under one arm, looking perfect in his business khaki pants with the soft violet shirt. They were the casual, warm colors everyone in Scarlet's office wore as the boss tried to foster her "garden of talent." Everything in the office itself reflected that theme. There were flowers and potted plants everywhere, even some hanging vines in planters interspersed among the natural, not fluorescent, lights. Everyone was allowed to wear business casual with as many colors as they desired unless there was a formal business meeting of some kind with outside clients. There were no cubicle walls to separate everyone, just open concept desks that switched between sitting and standing with a hand crank. Small tables of refreshments sat at every end. Lunch was also catered every day. When privacy was needed, there was a row of silent booths installed along the one wall with round, ship-portico windows set in the doors so those within could be seen, but not heard.

It was a little kumbaya, but as far as office cultures go, there were far, far worse, if the life section of most major newspapers were to be believed. She had only been there three years, and outside of two coffee shops and a short stint in a box chain bookstore after college, it was the only place she had ever worked professionally.

All of this was tucked back behind a long clear wall that cascaded in a magic waterfall fountain that made the moving colors beyond it shimmer and shimmy. Faces were hard to make out, but Helena realized that several of the blobby faces were looking through the wall at the little exchange happening in the reception foyer.

The first feeling of unease slid through Helena as she glanced from the watching eyes to Yosef. "Hi. What's ... going on?" she asked carefully.

He sniffed at her, breaking his neutral face as he thrust out the folders to her. "You're in charge of the McCater account now."

Helena stared at the folders before her. As one of five event coordinators, she would have been less shocked if he had presented her with the Oscar and Publishing Clearing House Check.

"You're serious?" she asked breathlessly as she reached to take the folders.

"Scarlet wanted to tell you herself, but she's having a slow morning, so go over these, and she'll meet with you at ten. Her office."

"Alright, I'll be there," she agreed, hugging the files to her chest as happiness burned through her chest in happy little fireworks of joy.

Yosef nodded once and turned to walk around the waterfall wall to Scarlet's office.

Helena exchanged a glance with the receptionist, the only true witness, who had been fielding calls the whole time. She excitedly gave Helena a dual thumbs up while continuing to talk to whoever was on the other end of the phone. Stunned, Helena allowed herself to grin back, and then moved to go around the glass waterfall wall.

"Congratulations!" the office erupted the second she cleared it, stunning her again into a standstill. Everyone there started clapping along with their cheers and more than a few people came forth to pat her on the back or give her hugs.

"Couldn't have happened to a better person."

"You absolutely deserved this."

"Invite *me* to dinner next time!"

The cheers and well wishes followed her all the way to her desk, where she numbly dropped her purse and messenger bag, while not daring to let go of the precious folders she had been given. Finally, Yosef reappeared and chased everyone away and back to work. She set the folders down on the desk like they were holy relics and pressed her fingers to her lips. Everything she ever wanted.

"Thank you, Rafferty," she whispered. He may have been a demon, but in this, he had been an angel.

She hoped wherever he was, he could hear her.

Chapter 9

BUT I STARTED THINKING...

"Do you think hell is real?"

"You've been thinking about it ever since we mentioned it at dinner the other night?" Cindy asked and Helena nodded. It seemed a strange topic to bring up on the sunny late afternoon at the outdoor café, probably one of the last for the year, but it had been weighing on Helena's mind. It had been a week since getting her new projects, yet something in her newly perfected world felt off. So when Cindy had invited Helena for a belated celebratory dinner before the good doctor's next shift at the hospital, Helena jumped at it. She needed to talk it out.

She hadn't even meant to bring up the question, but there it was, like a smelly fish flopped on the table. She was just on the brink of taking the question back when Cindy waved her hand before she could speak.

"If I'm honest, I've been thinking of it too. It just gave me this heebie-jeebie feeling that night, you know.

53

I haven't been able to shake it off. A lot of funny dreams and everything." She met Helena's eye. "How about you?"

"No, no funny dreams per se," Helena said honestly while shaking her head. She had actually never slept better.

Cindy shrugged. "Okay, then it's just me. It was just such a weird thing to bring up at a nice dinner, you know? But yeah, I guess so? I mean, if demons are real, and that is a confirmed fact, then the place they come from must be hell, right?"

"You think it's as awful there as they say?" Helena took a sip of her water as if washing the bad taste of those words away. Her heart pounded, but it wasn't like there was anyone actively investigating her for demon summoning connections, right? The FBI had more important things to do than that.

Cindy chuffed a dry laugh. "Well, yeah. I would think."

"But I mean, how would they know if we've never really been there?" Helena asked. "I mean honestly, if everyone who has ever gotten themselves dragged into hell never leaves, how the freaking ... well, hell, do we know what hell is really like?"

"Well, hypothetically..." Cindy paused and rolled it around in her head a moment. "I guess, if it isn't so bad, why are demons always trying to get out of there?"

Helena nodded at that. "Yup, that's it, isn't it? It's got to be as bad as they say."

"I mean, best not to dwell on it?" Cindy offered. "Don't get me wrong: I've certainly seen enough people pass through the emergency room that definitely were headed that way." She blew out a breath. "Most definitely bad mama-jamas."

Helena cocked her head. "But if you knew they were bad ... you treated them anyway?"

"Well, yeah." Cindy shrugged. "After all, they may have done something bad, but *I'm* not going to do something bad by not helping them. That's on me then. I mean, how can they have a chance to redeem themselves if I don't try? It's what I figure anyway."

Helena smiled and put a hand over her friend's on the table. "You are a very good person, Cindy," she assured.

"Ha, I try. Some days I succeed. Now can we order some chocolate cake? I'm going to need a dose of endorphins after that."

"Absolutely—on me," Helena said as she raised a hand for the waiter to pause and take the dessert order. Soon enough they were cutting their forks through a delectable slice of chocolate mousse cake, topped with fresh whipped cream.

"Oh my God, Heaven," Cindy declared. "Not as good as what your caterer guy made the other day, but still Heaven." Helena paused at that statement. Rolling the chocolate around in her mouth, she had to agree.

Yosef caught her at the top of the next day. Since it was Friday, Helena had already debated about taking one of her allotted half-days off, but she knew that plan had just been squashed when she laid eyes on him waiting for her.

"Scarlet wants to talk to you," he said, thrusting the notebook that she kept at her desk at her. In one smooth motion, he traded it for her purse and briefcase. "I'll drop

these off for you. Scarlet is already in the conference room."
And then he was gone without another word.

Lacking anything else to do, Helena proceeded to the conference room.

Like the rest of Scarlet's "garden," the conference room was filled with greenery and light with one wall entirely made of glass looking out onto the city. It made the room feel more like a porch than a contained space. Today it was raining, however, and the splats of streaky rain made it feel closer to a greenhouse to Helena. Scarlet sat at the head of the only conventional thing in the room, the table. She was seated in her mobile chair today, which she zipped around the table as soon as Helena entered the room.

"There she is, there she is. Come in, and feast your eyes," Scarlet declared, stopping midway of the table before a folder laid out with papers and brochures.

"What's all this?" Helena asked, coming up beside Scarlet to look where her gnarled fingers indicated.

"This is a good day is what this is." Scarlet eagerly slid the brochure over to Helena pre-opened. The glossy paper showed a large ballroom with a glittering chandelier filling it with fairy light. There were elegant, circular tables everywhere draped with creamy white cloths and the chairs around them were all gold-painted and upholstered with matching cream cushions. And there were people, all equally elegantly dressed, like from a modern-day version of a fairy tale, dancing and laughing as only people in fairytales can. The whole image filled Helena with an acute longing to be there and be a part of it.

"I was so beautiful," Scarlet said wistfully.

That was when Helena realized the foremost woman in a striking red dress that folded around her like a rose was in fact Scarlet. A slightly younger, more mobile Scarlet, whose age only enhanced her beauty, like dust on a precious wine bottle. Only those who were truly cultured could understand it.

Helena almost said so but doubted such an observation would be received in the manner it was intended.

Fortunately, Scarlet didn't wait for her to respond. "This was my crowning achievement and now I bequeath it to you."

Helena practically jumped out of her skin, much to Scarlet's cheeky amusement. "I'm sorry, Scarlet... I don't understand..."

"The Winter Rose Ball is in six months, and I want you to organize it." Scarlet turned her wheelchair back to the head of the conference table. "I have organized the Winter Rose Ball since its inception, and officially I will this year as well, but time does not agree with my desire to do it. If I want this to exist beyond me, I must pass the torch while I am still able to. Therefore, you will be my deputy in this endeavor, but in all practicality," Scarlet laced her fingers together leaning her elbows on the table as she grinned wickedly at Helena, "you will be the one in charge, with Yosef's assistance, of course."

Helena stared at her employer in utter shock, almost dropping the brochure she held.

"All this because of one dinner?!"

Horrified, Helena did drop the brochure to slap her hand over her mouth, but it was too late to take those imprudent words back.

Scarlet broke out laughing so hard she practically cackled.

"Yes and no, of course. Like I have said, I have enjoyed your work so far. I saw a lot of talent in you, but that dinner cinched it for me. I like you and I like your style. I believe I can pass what is most important to me to you, and if I am right, I will possibly be passing more things." She arched an eyebrow at Helena, whose mind raced.

Could she mean ... passing the company to her? While Helena had admitted to only Cindy that she wanted more than anything to own and run her own publicity company, Helena never thought...

She looked Scarlet straight in the eye. The thought did occur to her that there had to be dozens of people more qualified than her, more people in line for such a gift. She had a passing thought to say exactly that because it would be the humble thing to do.

"Thank you, Scarlet. I will not let you down," she said instead.

"Excellent." The older woman sighed. "Honestly, I'm relieved. I thought I was going to have to coax you a little bit. Assure you that you were qualified for this task."

Helena gave a lopsided grin, then shrugged one shoulder. "Yeah, but ... I *want* it. So I'll figure it out."

Scarlet's grin morphed into a smile that made her seem ten years younger. "Take anything you need from these materials. You will also be working from my office. I've had a desk put in for you. God knows I have enough space for one or ten. You make all the decisions and I will give you final approval. It's a big job so Yosef will be your partner in this, but I want to see what you do with the creative side of it, so think of it as you are the director of the show and he is your assistant director. And don't worry about me stealing credit. This is going to be an open secret, and I have plenty of things I will need to teach you in the interim."

Helena nodded, already deciding her next move would be to race to her desk, grab her phone to call Cindy, and tell her everything.

"You'll also be getting a raise and an upgrade in title—"

"Thank you, ma'am!" Helena cried, too excited to stop herself—she was already grabbing up all the materials Scarlet had laid out for her.

"Slow down, young thing. Slow down, I need you to take notes on this. You're going to want to figure out flowers, and negotiate with the venue, and the catering, the decorations and invitations—"

"The caterer?" That made Helena pause, the word making her flinch a little. Though there was no good reason it should have. Of course she would need to hire a catering company.

Scarlet winked. "You may hire whomever you want. I know you have at least one ace up your sleeve."

Helena hated to do this, but she knew what her answer had to be. "I'm sorry, Scarlet. But I can't ... do that. It was a one-time thing..."

She could see her whole future burning up right then and there.

No one ever told Scarlet no.

"Ah yes, I understand," her boss said instead, then waved a hand at Helena. "Don't make that face and don't worry. I've worked with plenty of 'artists' before, trust me. I was just saying if you want to pass the opportunity to that extraordinary talent, you are free to do so. It isn't your fault if they don't want to make any money doing what they love. Now take a seat. We have plenty more to discuss today."

Chapter 10

IT GOT WEIRD

Helena stared at her to-do list in frustration. She had a dozen caterers waiting for her to make calls and start setting up tastings, but she had been avoiding this task the most. She looked at their portfolios, flipped through their websites, and checked out their online videos. Perfect credentials and prideful mission statements.

And there on her kitchen counter next to where she had propped up her computer sat her grandmother's cookbook.

She hadn't been able to make herself put it away, nor could she dare to cook anything else out of it. Like she had a dozen times before, she laid her hand on the stained cover. After a minute of that, she flipped it open slowly and fingered her way to the back pages. There in her grandmother's script was the spell to summon Rafferty.

Don't ever summon me again. She could practically hear his stern voice warning her.

She closed the book firmly and picked up her phone.

"You're just setting up appointments. It's no big deal," she assured herself. Yet, she only got three numbers in before she canceled the call.

Moving so she didn't have time to stop herself, Helena picked up the book, turning to face the middle of her kitchen. It had been two weeks since she had first summoned the demon. Two weeks of washing her floor according to his instructions with the vinegar, lemon, allspice, and soda. There wasn't a trace of the summoning circle left that the naked eye could see. There was no way this would work.

"Stir once and tap three times, spin widdershins, and spit your tongue, take a deep breath, and say three times, 'Tribblespins, tribblespins, tribblespin...'" She waited with a held breath.

Nothing happened.

"Okay, I suppose I needed to do the things in the poem, too? I think I did bite my tongue the first time..." she said, looking down at the pages.

The smell hit her first, then a crackling sound called her attention back to the floor. To her amazement, the blackened lines of the circle re-emerged from the floor, burning upward as if someone was holding a million cigarettes to a piece of paper all at once, reburning a pentagram and other symbols into her tile. Soft, eerie whispers seemed to dance among the hissing crackle and then the whole thing flared. Helena wasn't sure what happened next because she had to close her eyes and look away, but then the overwhelming burning was gone. Slowly, she lifted her face from the crook of her arm where she had shielded her eyes and looked at the uncanny form kneeling in the circle.

Oh crap. She did it again.

Immediately, she felt revulsion for the thing there. Everything about it felt wrong, but she ignored the feelings. She knew what she was doing, and it was too late for regrets now.

Slowly, the creature lifted his head. His eyes seemed to struggle to focus on her at first, but then they narrowed to hardness before closing entirely. The creature sighed and flexed his wings in a show of irritation. "How can I serve you, mistress?"

"I'm so sorry about this. I know what you told me, but—"

"How can I serve you, mistress?" he growled out, his eyes flashing hot with anger. Then he closed them, his face going still, as if he were mastering himself. "How may I serve you, my mistress? State what you desire me to do, and I will state the price for that service."

"I... I don't want anything from you," Helena said.

He wafted his wings in irritation. "It is pointless to demur now. Just state what you want."

"I... Well, I wanted to thank you."

"You would have thanked me best by never summoning me again."

"I know that's what you said, but I mean, just hear me out, okay? I was just sitting here, and I'm supposed to call all these caterers for this new job I have, and I kept thinking—"

"That you want me to cater this big important event for you. Yes, I see," Rafferty said, clearly exasperated.

"No!" Helena held up her hands. "No, I don't want you to do that. I can hire another caterer. It'll be fine, seriously. But I just... I just kept thinking about you still in hell, and here I'm sitting with everything I've ever wanted in the world—all because of you. What you did for me was a miracle."

He stood there stunned a moment, his hands loose at his sides and his face relaxed as he took in what she was saying. "I'm not a good ... being, Helena. I deserve to be where I am."

"Yeah, but ... can't you take a vacation?"

The sound that came out of him alarmed Helena at first; it sounded like gravel grinding in a blender. Then she realized it was laughter. He lifted his great hands tipped with black nails and covered his face as if he couldn't bear the humor of it.

She chuckled herself a little bit.

Finally, the noise died down as he dropped to sit on the ground, his wrists resting on his upturned knees, his apron covering exactly enough. "A vacation? From hell?"

"Yes," she said, latching on to his opening. She sat down on the floor as well, crisscrossing her legs. It was only when she settled that she realized that she had dropped just outside his circle. She didn't know if that meant anything, but she ignored it.

He leaned forward to fold his thin, long legs underneath himself, mirroring her. "I can't stay here. Even just being summoned comes with a cost. It's just often baked into our final price of service."

"Well, okay, how much does it cost to have you here?" Helena asked. "We can work this out."

He leaned forward and dropped his face into his hand. "Why are humans always such idiots? You always think you can just trick the system. The system is designed for your tricks. It counts on you believing you are smarter than it."

"Will you just answer the question?" Helena was getting exasperated.

He reached his opposite finger and tapped his nail against his head. "This takes energy to maintain."

"What does?" she asked, getting frustrated.

"My body!" he growled. "This body on this plane–"

She held up her hand. "Wait, slow down. Your body... why would your body cost anything to be here?"

"I'm trying to tell you!"

"You're not explaining it very well!"

"It's because... because..." He flicked his wings out, and she wondered why this was such a struggle for him to talk about. "The dead are not supposed to return to this world once they've died. It's a fundamental law of this plane of existence, and my very presence violates it. In order for me to be here, this circle made a body for me to inhabit, and it's a twisted one from one like yours that was created naturally."

Helena blinked at the implications of that idea.

"So you're ... actually dead?"

"When I became a demon, yes, my mortal body died." Rafferty nodded.

Helena blinked at that. "You were a man?"

"I was an idiot who thought he could trick the demon he made a deal with, and now I am one of the infernal creatures, which is why I didn't want you to get involved."

"But I'm not involved," Helena protested. "I don't want anything from you. I just want to help you."

"Look you want the whole laid out truth—here it is." He leaned forward to look her directly in the eyes. The fire in them hypnotized her, and she couldn't move. They were like pools opening up to swallow her, and the eerie, wrong feeling crawled along her skin, urging her to tear it off to stop it. "The only way you can keep me here for any extended amount of time is to make a contract with me. What I'm supposed to do then is get you to sign away yourself to me in exchange for something you think will make you happy, and then when I do that, I pull you down into hell with me, in order to move up in the demonic hierarchy. Okay? Then you get unleashed to do the same, all the while suffering for your sins here on earth. Is that what you want, Helena?"

Helena wanted to scream.

She could feel every horror he described, the deep terror of an existence that was nothing but pain, nothing but unreality. If only she could scream!

He closed his eyes, finally releasing her from his hold. She found that she could move again. Terrified, she pushed away from him, sliding across the floor until her back hit the front of her oven. Desperately she rubbed at her arms to chase away the creepy crawling sensation. For a moment, she thought she would throw up.

"What did... did you do to me?" she choked out, her tongue feeling too thick.

"Gave you a taste of what you're asking for because apparently you need the point spelled out. Now send me back and don't ever summon me again." He settled back from her and pulled his knees up against his chest. His wings framed his form, making him seem like a dark shadow sitting in the middle of her kitchen.

She felt a powerful urge to attack him. To destroy this unholy thing that had violated her. It was terrifying, and she knew he was there to harm her.

The primal instincts dragged her to her feet, and she scrambled for the dirty frying pan she had left on her stove from breakfast. She lifted it up, feeling mighty and righteous with her weapon, prepared to smash it down onto the demon before her.

The demon closed its eyes and waited.

Helena battled with herself. It would be so easy to give into it. She wanted to so badly, and it would feel so good to hit him with her weapon.

"This isn't... no!" she shouted and threw the pan. It soared through the air and crashed through the glass doors leading out to her back porch.

She dropped to her knees, panting, struggling to make sense of what had just happened. "That's *not* who I am!" she shouted.

Chapter II

THEN HE MADE ME TEA

Rafferty looked over his shoulder at the destroyed door, eyes wide with amazement. Slowly, he stood up, his back to her as the cold wind blew the wisps of his hair. A piece of glass holding on at the top wavered in the night wind a moment before losing its grip and gloriously crashing to the ground. Both beings in the kitchen flinched at the sound.

"Oh crap," Helena said as she stared at it. "That's going to be expensive to fix."

Rafferty grunted, then turned, finally stepping out of the circle. Helena didn't realize what he was doing until there was a clink of metal bumping metal. Looking over her shoulder, she watched as the demon filled the dented kettle she kept on her stove from her sink. The fire on her stovetop made her flinch again, and she dropped back onto her backside to press her hands against her face. She couldn't hold it back anymore and started crying softly.

She didn't care what else the demon did around her. And she didn't lift her head again until something warm pressed against the back of her hand. Startled, she scuttled back too fast and banged her elbow against the cupboard.

"Ow," she whimpered meekly, grabbing the elbow.

"It's okay. Just drink it," Rafferty said, squatting down where he had been standing so he was on the same level, well the same level-ish, as she was. He held out one of her large mugs, steam rising from the top.

"What is it?" Helena asked, eyeing the mug.

"Something to undo what I did," he said. There was no hint of apology in his voice.

"*What* is it?" she asked again, narrowing her eyes at him.

He sighed. "The black tea with a dollop of honey and a sprinkle of nutmeg and cinnamon. Chamomile tea with peppermint or lavender would be better, but you don't have any. Black tea will give you an immune boost. Cinnamon for health, protection, and happiness... nutmeg is for luck usually, but in this case it just goes well with cinnamon."

He stretched his arm to its full-length to hold the cup out for her to take. Her hands shook as she did. It smelled warm and wonderful. She knew she shouldn't trust it, but she drank down half before she began to feel like the person who could make that sort of call.

The first thing the demon did was walk back to her shattered back door. He held out his hand toward it. A weird, unearthly, glassy sound slid over her skin, giving her goosebumps, and then the glass reformed itself in the door. He opened the door and retrieved her pan, then came back to drop it into the sink. Beside her, he resumed a squat, his wings wrapped around him, like he was trying to shield himself from her view.

She licked her lips. "What happened to me?" she asked.

"I showed you what I am fully."

Helena shuddered with the memory. "I'm going to feel that in my nightmares forever, aren't I?"

"Probably, but I don't know," he admitted. "I am an unnatural thing trying to force itself into creation." He dragged his black nail along her kitchen tile. The nail left no trace but seemed to be drawing something, or maybe he just liked the feel of the semi-smooth surface. "We all crave it. Being here in creation."

"But you can't be here?"

He shook his head, which meant shaking his horns. "You feel it even if you don't know what to call it. We just don't belong here."

"What's wrong with where you are?" She took another sip of her tea.

"It hurts to be there, like all the time. We can never get comfortable in our own skin. That uncanny feeling you get around me. I feel that about myself every second. And there is no reprieve except..."

She didn't want to prompt him to continue, pretty sure she understood, but she did need to confirm. "Except when you consume the essence of another."

"From one of creation, yes," he said. He stopped his tracing and set his chin on his arms, wrapped about his knees. His wings hovered behind him now, as if he intended to fold them all the way around and hide. "You should send me back."

Helena shook her head. "This isn't fair."

"I did this to myself. I sold my own soul to another demon and got dragged into the darkness for it. I have no one to blame but myself, and you are not responsible for me," he said resolutely. "As it is, I'm not really sure what we're going to have to do to fix this current summoning without payment from you. I fudged the rules last time."

They fell into silence for a minute.

"I have an idea," she said and stood up to go to her fridge. While her legs were still wobbly, they held her. From inside, she pulled out a three-quarter wheel of brie and an unmarked jar. Then she grabbed some crackers from her cupboard and her charcuterie board. She set it all down on the floor between them, then knee-walked over to her silverware drawer to retrieve a butter knife.

The whole time, the demon watched her from within his little wing cave.

She uncapped the jar, spread some of the contents onto one of the crackers, then sliced off a thin piece of the brie to set on top of that.

"You should have done the brie first, then the jam on top of that," Rafferty commented in a low voice, like it pained him to watch her assemble the snack.

"Noted," she said dryly, not really caring for being told how to make her own snack the way she liked it. When she finished her preparations, she held the whole mess before her. "This is really tasty. You're going to love this."

"It'll taste like ash," he replied bitterly.

"No it won't," she assured, forcing herself to smile. Then she popped the whole thing into her mouth. She held it there and leaned forward, beckoning him to do the same.

"What are you doing?" he asked warily.

"Do that thing you did before where you pull the memory of this taste from my mind," she instructed.

His wings actually recoiled away an inch. "You are crazy. You want me to touch you again?"

"I'm giving you permission to touch me," she stressed. "Big difference. Now do it. I'll be fine."

He hesitated, but she stared him down, meeting his starburst eyes with determination. Then he shifted, the eyes dimming to plain darkness, but instead of the uncanny demon sitting before her, it was the man-form he wore before. She had to admit it made it easier to be close to him, not because of the unnerving appearance, but it felt like his demonic aura had lessened considerably. Like a dimmer switch just before it clicked off.

He then leaned forward like she wanted and set his forehead against hers.

Helena chewed the snack in her mouth and continued to breathe through her nose as the cold sensation rolled through her mind, leeching away the taste even as her brain registered it. There was less drama to it than before, no strange sideways feeling or whispers accompanying flashes of what she assumed had been hell. Just the ice cream headache, which actually lessened as she gave the memory away.

"Oh hell," Rafferty moaned in his throat. Helena kept her eyes on him the whole time, and she smiled for real as his face turned to pure bliss. As soon as she swallowed, he sat back, his eyes still closed in ecstatic bliss. "Apple, raspberries, blackberries, but not too sweet. Almost savory and that paired with the creamy brie... you're right. It's perfect."

She prepared another one.

Just before she brought it to her mouth, he peeked open his eyes. "What are you doing?" he asked.

"That was payment for summoning you. Now this one is your gift," she said and set the cheese and jam cracker in her mouth.

He looked like he would protest again, but she set her jaw and arched an eyebrow at him. His lips thinned, but he obeyed, leaning forward again so they could repeat the process. This time the moan was even greater and his fingers came up to clasp her face.

"Ugh, it's too much! It's too much!" He leaned back and those same fingers went to his mouth as if the food could not be contained there. It struck Helena as sad as she chewed, now tasting it since he had stopped pulling the memory from her. Tasting it was one thing, but...

"Do you actually have to eat at all?" she asked, setting up the crackers for another round.

His chest heaved from the sensations he felt, and he dropped his hand there as if it could help contain his emotions. "We don't eat on the other side, but we feel hungry nonetheless."

"But you can eat here?" she asked, chewing up one of her snacks for herself this time.

His eyes finally opened, and he watched her hungrily. "Yes, I *can* eat. It just means nothing."

"Hmm," she said and picked up two of the prepared crackers now, holding one out to him. "Let's try something. We both eat these at the same time while you pull the memory, okay?"

He only hesitated a moment, taking the cracker from her and looking at it as if he couldn't trust it. She set hers to her lips and waited. He yielded to her pressure and copied her action. Together, they slid the food into their mouths and then leaned forward to touch.

This time it was different.

Helena's whole world exploded into a symphony of flavor and taste. It felt strange and exhilarating. She had heard of people describing fine dining experiences as if they had been better than sex. Was this what they had been referring to? She whimpered a little as he moaned. His forehead pressed into hers, but it also felt like they had gone past the physical bounds of their bones to merge together. Such a thing seemed like something that should scare her, but she didn't resist, and it gave back as much as she offered. At last, they had to swallow, and she was aware of him gently pulling away.

Breathless, she opened her eyes, surprised that she had actually closed them. The being sitting before her stared back at her in wonder.

"What... what was that?" she asked.

He touched his tongue with his fingers. "I... *tasted* that," he said, mystified. Tears beaded on the edges of his eyes. "Thank you," he whispered, voice wavering as the rush of emotion overwhelmed him. "Thank you."

Tears responded in her own eyes as she smiled. "You're very welcome, Rafferty. I'm glad I could do this for you."

He couldn't respond to that, other than to cry some more, and she moved to wrap her arms around him. His face planted in the crook of her shoulder, and he sobbed for a long, long time.

Chapter 12

AT LEAST HE MADE ME BREAKFAST

Helena woke up in her bed with no sure memory of how she got there. She lay under her warm covers, feeling like if she just stayed still enough, she'd go back to sleep and right back into the delicious dream she had been inhabiting.

Her bladder had other plans. "Oh hell," she muttered and dragged herself out of bed. Just as she crossed her hall to go toward her bathroom, however, she heard a *clink*ing in her kitchen. She froze in place, her heart beating rapid-fire tattoos. Someone was in her house!

There were more *clink*s and the sound of frying.

Someone was cooking?

Helena held still, desperately trying to remember. Did she bring someone home last night?

She had!

The memory of the previous night rose from the depths of her sleepy brain. Cautiously, she crept down her short hall to peek into her kitchen. Just as she pressed the door free from the jamb, it jumped open. Rafferty, still looking like a human, stood on the other side.

"Good morning!" he said formally, bowing his head once to her.

"Hi," she returned lamely, feeling terribly awkward, especially in the face of his good humor.

"I have breakfast for you," he said and presented her with a beautiful plate. It looked like it had been pulled from a photo session for a food magazine. Picture perfect, sunny-side-up eggs lay next to several strips of bacon and five dollar-coin pancakes. There were even little drips of syrup dotting the edge of the plate as artistic decoration with a single raspberry perched on top of the pancakes.

Her mouth watered as all the smells wafted up into her nose.

"Go sit down," her house guest said, pushing her toward the dining room table. "I'll bring you something to drink in a minute." He thrust the plate at her and disappeared into her kitchen again.

Lacking other options, Helena shrugged and sat at the table. But the needs of her bladder still hadn't been addressed, so she picked up one of the mini pancakes to stuff into her mouth as she scurried off to quickly take care of business. By the time she came back, fully relieved, a glass of milk sat waiting by the plate.

"Rafferty?" she called and peeked into the kitchen to see the demon washing the dishes in her sink. Now he was back in his demonic form, and it almost made her laugh to see him standing there, wearing one of her clean aprons over his dingy one, his triangular tail flicking back and forth like a contented cat while he worked away in the suds.

There was still a wrong feeling emanating from him, but maybe she was getting used to it because it didn't bother her as much that morning. He hummed to himself contentedly, so she let him be and went to enjoy her breakfast.

Or at least she tried for two bites, then stood up and went back to the door.

"You don't have to clean, you know," she said, pulling the door open just in time to see him hanging her apron back up.

"It's alright," he said. "It's all done." He turned back to her and had... well, it wasn't a smile on his face, but so freaking close to one she didn't know what else she would call it.

"Oh!" she said, looking at her tile beneath his black-shoed feet as he shifted back to fully dressed human caterer. "The circle..."

He looked down, having thrust his hands into the pockets of his slacks. "Yeah, well. Don't get too excited. It's still there," he said. The circle had completely vanished again. "I mopped away the majority of it, but the essential particles are still embedded into the tile at this point. And will remain so as long as I'm here."

"Noted," Helena said, determined now to have no other house guests over for the next two weeks, just to be safe.

"How are you feeling?" Rafferty asked, eyeing her.

"Fine. Why?" she asked. She glanced down at her plate. "Did you do something to breakfast?"

"No," he said, unable to keep his eyes from glancing over at her plate hungrily.

Helena grinned. "Would you like to taste it?" she asked teasingly.

A small pucker of worry appeared between his eyebrows. "I just want..." Then he closed his eyes and took a step back. "Never mind. It's a bad idea."

"I feel fine. We can do this," Helena assured him.

He shook his head. "You're out of eggs. That's all there is."

"Okay. That doesn't change anything I said," she stated and made herself reach out to take his hand to lead him back out to her dining room. He followed behind her demurely as a little boy, the puckered worry still between his eyebrows.

His concern made Helena wonder if there might be long term consequences to what she was doing, but if there were, she gave it the same amount of regard she gave drinking alcohol or eating too much sugar. This was still in moderation.

"Sit," she ordered him like a dog she was very affectionate with, and he did so while she took her place and positioned the plate between them. "What do you want to taste first?"

He stared at the plate, then dragged her eyes back up to her. "You're really going to willingly keep doing this?"

Helena shrugged one shoulder as she plucked up some bacon and broke the crispy thing in two. She held one out to him, but when he went to take it, she pulled it out of his reach and instead directed it straight to his mouth. He snorted a moment, obviously consternated by the idea of eating from her hand, and she just grinned at him. Finally, he opened his mouth and let her feed him the bacon while she quickly put her own half into her mouth. Then she leaned forward and set her forehead against his forehead like they did before.

Again, like last night, flavor burst over her tongue, crispy, warm, salty, and meaty. She had never tasted bacon like this before in her life.

"How are you doing that?" she breathed out as soon as she swallowed, leaning back to open her eyes.

"Doing what?" he asked, echoing her breathy voice. She noted the tears leaking down his cheeks unheeded. Gently, she wiped them with a thumb, and he let her as he breathed through his nose, clearly still overwhelmed to taste so much after so long.

"You know," she insisted, then gestured vaguely to her mouth. "It all tastes better when we..."

He shook his head, clearly struggling to focus on what she was saying. "What?"

She studied him for a moment, trying to detect some trick or lie in him, but he just kept licking the inside of his mouth, savoring. "Why?" he finally asked. "What are you tasting?"

Just then, Helena's alarm went off on her phone.

"I guess just amazing bacon," she said, picking it up to look at the screen and tap off the alarm. "Okay, I'm sorry, but I've got to get dressed for work."

She grabbed up the fork and shoveled one of the perfect eggs whole into her mouth. She tried to repeat the process with the other egg, but it dripped with yolk because her tines pierced the underside. Quickly, she held it out to him. He obliged her, but this time she stood to lean in, which wobbled her off balance in her rush. He grabbed her hand to help steady her and the flavor intensified like before, like someone had upped her tastes buds from normal to eleven.

Keeping her eyes open this time, she watched his face.

Rafferty's expression was all bliss, letting the drizzle of yolk leak down his chin. It brought Helena's heart happiness to see it. *It's not being kind if it costs you nothing to do it,* she thought, remembering one of her grandmother's aphorisms. Once they swallowed, she let go and went to her bedroom to get dressed.

"I have to work today, but since it's Friday, I won't work the next two days. I figure you can just stay here for right now. You know, rest, watch some TV until I get home... would that be okay?" she said, shedding her pajamas.

"That would be fine," he agreed from her doorway.

"Geez!" she cried out, startled as she whirled naked toward him. "Get out!" She scrambled quickly to grab a used towel off the floor to cover herself.

Rafferty continued to stand there, cocking his head amused. "You've seen me in as little," he commented.

"When were you last alive—the Stone Age? Get out!" she shouted.

"1672," he said simply, grinning. "The Age of Absolutism."

"Yeah, well this is 2022, and this age requires absolute consent. Now get the hell out of my room!" she ordered, pointing to the door.

He backed away, disappearing down the hall. "How's this?" he asked.

"That's good, but you know what would be better?" Helena crossed the few steps to her door to slam it shut.

Chapter 13

IT WAS A TON OF FOOD

"**D**id you get a chance to call and make the appointments with the caterers?" Yosef asked. He was leaning over her new desk in Scarlet's office, looking down at his clipboard of to-dos.

"I've called three of them so far," Helena said, tapping her pen down on her notes. "I'll do the other five here before I leave." She glanced at her clock. There were two hours to go before the end of the day.

"Leave? Where are you going?" Yosef asked.

Helena cocked an eyebrow. "Home? At five? Like we normally do."

Yosef pursed his lips. "Do you really think that is wise at this time?"

She noted his warning. "Well, so far we still have time to get everything done, and if we start pulling all-nighters before we need to, we'll burn out too close to the finish line."

Yosef continued to stare at her.

"I also have a friend visiting this weekend," she said.

He narrowed his eyes.

She narrowed hers in return. "And last I checked, I am the deputy for this project."

He blew out an exasperated breath and straightened to swipe his clipboard off her desk. "Fine. Do what you want," he said, whirling to go back to his own desk on the other side of the office.

With his back turned, Helena felt free to sigh herself before passing a glance over at Scarlet's desk. It stood empty. Scarlet hadn't even come in today, but that was the privilege of being the boss. No one to hold you accountable except yourself. Still, Helena wondered if she needed to talk to Scarlet about Yosef or if it was something that would only backfire if she tried. It was getting frustrating. Ever since Helena had taken over this project, it seemed like Yosef had challenged every one of her decisions, and she really wished he would stop.

I suppose this comes with the job, she thought as she picked up her office-designated landline and started dialing the next caterer.

"Hello, City's Best Catering. How can I help you?"

"Hello, I'm calling on behalf of Scarlet Promotions..."

Just then Helena's personal mobile lit up, silently alerting her that Chris was calling. She flipped it over so she wouldn't be tempted to answer her friend.

"Okay, what can I do for you?" The woman on the other end sounded annoyed.

"I would like to set up a tasting with you."

"We don't do tastings. We're a catering service," the woman said impatiently.

"Yes, we are looking to hire a catering service," Helena said through gritted teeth. She was too tired for this.

"For how many people?" the woman said business-like.

"Fifteen hundred."

"How many?!" the woman said, finally perking up.

"Fifteen. Hundred," Helena said slower, now getting annoyed and letting her voice show it.

"Who are you again?"

"Helena Rhodes. I represent Scarlet Promotions. We are interviewing caterers for the Winter Rose Ball. Can I please set up a tasting appointment with you?" Helena said, trying to sound moderately civil as she spelled it out.

There was a long pause on the other end. "Our Executive Chef will have to call you back," the unhelpful woman said, very unsure now. Helena left her contact information and thankfully got off the phone.

"Ugh," she grumbled under her breath. "Only four more to go."

Helena didn't know what to expect as she wrestled her keys into her house's door.

Just before she turned the key, she stopped as a thought hit her.

I left a demon at my home, alone. All day.

She didn't know why that reality was hitting her then, but she turned to look around at the quiet street she lived on. Her house was a small one bedroom, a forgotten relic from an earlier era. The majority of the houses like hers had long been knocked down and replaced with three-story apartment buildings or three-flats that made her house seem like someone's kid sister tagging along with the older kids.

She didn't see anyone else on the street or hear very much outside of the usual city noises just a street away from this fairly quiet oasis. No one suspected that a demon was so close.

Taking a deep breath, Helena fortified herself. "It's alright. He isn't going to be here forever."

Just then her phone rang out, playing "Dancing in the Streets." She almost dropped it when she picked it up, catching the sight of "Chris" written across the screen again.

"Oh, dammit," she said as she hit the answer button on the phone, then wedged it between her shoulder and cheek, so she could use her free hands to try to get her door open.

"Hey Chris, sorry about not calling you back. I was on other calls all day at work," she said into the phone as she turned her key, then paused as the faintest smell of something hit her nose. She supposed she shouldn't have been surprised that her houseguest had cooked dinner. What else was a food demon left to his own devices going to do?

"Yeah, that's okay," Chris said, sounding tired on the other end of the line. "I just need to talk to someone about a thing I'm wrestling with."

"Here, just give me a few minutes to get into my house…" Helena said when she finally got the door popped open. A richer wave of food smells enveloped her, drawing her into her home with its enticing aroma.

"Yeah, yeah, I'm okay. Just take your time. I can wait," he said, sounding tired and sad, which concerned Helena since he was usually the most jovial of people.

"Hey, I'm home!" she called as she stumbled through the doorway only to be greeted to quite the sight on her dining room table. It was covered with dishes, more than enough to feed a dozen people, all plated like they were ready for their close ups. On her TV, mounted to the wall in her designated living room, a cooking competition of some sort was playing.

"What is all this?" she cried out but got no response. "Rafferty?"

"Helena, is everything okay?" Chris shouted from the phone.

She pressed it back to her ear. "Hey, I'm sorry, Chris. Can I call you back? I have a ... thing I got to take care of first," she stated as she stared at the feast on her table.

"Yeah, sure. Just whenever. Thanks," Chris said and then was gone before she could say good-bye. Normally, she would have thought that strange, but nothing beat what she was witnessing right before her.

"Rafferty?"

Walking past her overladen table, she went to the kitchen.

Within, it looked like a cooking storm had blown through.

Grocery bags leaned on and against the counters, many of them partially empty. Her garbage was overflowing with discarded food containers. There were even more completed dishes lining her counter. And in the middle of it all stood the demon responsible.

He was in his human form, one hand still holding her flat frying pan on the stove, the other holding a spatula. He looked up, blinking at her sudden presence. Then he turned and surveyed the wreck of a kitchen. He seemed to be taking in the same enormity of it all as guilt flooded his face.

"I ... didn't realize until you came home just now that I might have gone a little ... overboard," he confessed softly.

The pan continued to sizzle, puffing up a burning smell, and he quickly used the spatula to pry up the toasted sandwich he had been in the middle of making. He set it on a waiting casserole dish that he was using as a plate since apparently all the others had been pressed into service, turned off the burner, threw down the spatula and backed up, running both hands over his head. While he was still human, Helena got the impression of Rafferty's tail flicking behind him in agitation.

He straightened, going all formal like he had on the first night he had cooked for her. Helena could feel the wall he put between them reform as his face went impassive. Then he bowed his head with dignity.

"What are you doing?" Helena asked, bringing her own head down to try to make eye contact with him.

He sighed exasperatedly. "Despite your words from last night that this is a 'vacation' for me, the truth of the matter is that I am a demon under a contract to you, even if that contract is dangerously ill-defined. Therefore, certain rules still apply."

"Yeah, okay," Helena said cautiously, not liking where this was going. "And those rules are?"

The outer corners of Rafferty's eyes squinched like her ignorance pained him. "The rules are that if you do not lay out specifically what I can or cannot do with your energy, it is in my best interest to ... 'run up your bill' as much as possible."

"Oh," Helena said, her eyebrows shooting up to her hairline. She looked from the demon to the piles of groceries, then leaned back out the swinging kitchen door to take in the feast on her dining room table.

"Uh... I can't eat all this."

Chapter 14

THE FOOD NETWORK IS DANGEROUS

"So you do this on purpose?" Helena asked, leaning back into the kitchen.

"I..." Rafferty hesitated, looking at the door into the dining room piled with the dishes he'd made. The outer corners of his eyes squinched even more, like he wasn't sure if he was in pain. "No. I didn't intentionally go out to do this to you on purpose, but it just sort of ... happened."

"How much is this going to cost me?" she asked.

Again, he looked around at what he had done. "I'm not sure," he said. "I tried to use as much real food as possible."

"Still, the point of this was to get me on the hook for a meal that I can't possibly eat all of?" she asked.

"That ... is the strategy that could be used in this instance, yes," Rafferty said.

She arched an eyebrow at him. "Are demons not allowed to lie? Because I would think this would be something that would be beneficial for you to lie about."

"We can lie," he said defensively. "But I'm not."

"Okay, so if I got this straight, you were just acting like a demon does without really thinking about it, and now I owe you a cosmic debt for your labor because I didn't say you could not do what you did. But you didn't do it on purpose. You just weren't thinking about it and it just came naturally?"

Rafferty pursed his lips together, like he was debating something. "Most of the cooking I've been exposed to is either what I already knew or what I can glean when I'm here. Since you left me for the day to my own devices, I did what I usually do." He gestured over to a pile of books at the end of her extra counter below where she kept her dishes. They were all opened and stacked haphazardly on different pages, some with things stuck in between for quick flip backs, like spoons and her can opener.

"And then..." he continued, once more hesitating.

"And then what?" Helena pressed.

He squared his shoulders to face his judge and confess his sins. "I discovered the Food Network channel."

Taking a step forward, he pulled out one of the celebrity chef books Helena bought in college. She had burned two things she tried to make from it and had never opened it again. On the lower part of the cover over the smiling chef's face was the printed tagline: "As seen on the Food Network!"

"Oh my dear lord," Helena breathed. She went back into the main room, passing by the dining room to go into the living room section where the TV continued to broadcast its latest offering, You Think You Can Macaroon?

"Oh my God. It's like I left a drug addict at home and forgot to lock up my cocaine stash," she stated, then glanced over at Rafferty as he followed her into the room. "I don't have a cocaine stash, by the way."

"I wasn't going to say anything if you did," he replied.

"But what I still don't understand is... how did you get all this food? I know for a fact I wouldn't buy..." she glanced over at the table, trying to pick out what she was seeing amongst the cornucopia of options, "pomegranates or seaweed or whatever that purple stuff is."

"Purple cauliflower rice."

"Yeah, you see. I know for a fact I do not have any purple cauliflower rice."

"Well... you don't buy the rice. You get the cauliflower and then you—"

"Not the point!" Helena said, torn between anger and amusement at this bizarre situation. It was just so much food! "How did you do all this? Is it all demon magic?"

"I..." He hesitated, then reached into his pocket and pulled out a black mobile smartphone. He held it out to her. "I saw you have one of these and while I was watching this show about dive diners in the Southwestern Americas, there was this commercial for an app on a phone that can allow you to order whatever groceries you want and so I made a phone and then made the numbers go up in the wallet thing and..." He looked around again at the groceries. "I got carried away."

"Yes, we've established you got 'carried away.'" she said, attempting to make sense of what he was telling her. "So you magicked a phone into existence and then basically magically hacked it to give yourself enough money to order all this food."

"And give a generous tip, yes."

"Uh huh," she acknowledged. "Therefore, you stole all this food?"

He froze at that. "I... yes. Technically, as far as human laws are concerned. Though the authorities would have a difficult time proving that I did," he agreed. "I didn't want to use demon magic to cook with because then I wouldn't know how it actually turned out, like if the dish worked or not."

She didn't think her eyebrows could furrow harder, but she surprised herself. "What? Why?"

He cleared his throat. "Demon magic can make anything seem tasty, even garbage. I wanted to know if the dishes actually worked, so for that ... I needed real food."

"Oh. Wow." Helena nodded, practicing radical acceptance. "Okay, that made sense. Well, I guess I should be relieved it's not all made out of children and dogs or something." She hooted and retreated back into the dining room to look at it all. "It's ... not, right?"

"No," Rafferty said, bringing the casserole dish with his grilled sandwiches on them as he followed her into the dining room.

Helena's stomach growled. Despite the issue at hand, it had been a long day, and she couldn't quite remember what she had for lunch. She looked down at the pile of grilled sandwiches he had made. All but the last one had been cut into triangles. They didn't quite look right, yet she couldn't put her finger on what was wrong.

"What are those?" she asked.

"French Toast Turkey Sandwich," he said.

Her stomach insisted she try one. It was getting too hard to think with all this food around. Still she hesitated.

"Is anything more going to happen to me if I eat one?" she asked.

"No, these don't have any demon magic in them, like I said. I wanted to know if the recipes actually worked," he said, holding the casserole dish out to her. She took one and dared herself to take a decent bite.

"I mean don't get me wrong, I—my God..." was all she got out before she stopped as the pillowy delight of the sandwich hit her mouth. She had had turkey and cheddar cheese sandwiches before, but this was something entirely different.

"When you said, 'French Toast,' I thought this was going to be sweet," she said as she took another mouthful. "But it's not! It's amazing." Mustard with mustard seeds bursting in her mouth added tanginess and the whole thing was gone before she realized it. "That was inspired," she complemented. "Did you come up with that?"

Rafferty averted his gaze. "I saw it on Diners Vs Dining."

"What's that?"

"It's a show about diner cooks and high-end restaurant chefs competing to make the most original, high-level cuisine. I saw one of the diner cooks make this, and I felt compelled to try it."

"Hmm," Helena said, looking down at the casserole dish of remaining sandwiches, wondering how something so delicious could be the cause of so much drama.

"I don't know if it's price-of-my-soul good, but it's really good," she added, reaching for another triangle. Still, there was no helping it. "Alright, so how are we going to do this?"

Rafferty flinched at her question. "What?"

"Your payment. I mean, I simply can't eat all of this food in one sitting and then have you eat all my memories like we normally do. I don't even know how many memories you need. I mean how is this even quantifiable? How much do I need to pay back energy-wise?"

Rafferty chewed his lips a little more aggressively, and it was only then that she realized he was getting angry. Looking at him, she noticed that his wings were appearing and disappearing behind his back, along with his crest of horns. The tail just remained, flicking back and forth. A low-level growl rumbled from his chest.

Helena felt the instinctual tug to back up from a dangerous animal, but her higher functions told her doing so would be a mistake. Like prey triggering a predator.

"Look, um. I'm sorry I don't know, but please don't get upset at me for asking questions," she started to say, but he dropped the casserole dish onto an empty chair, the only remaining available surface, with a loud thunk. Thankfully, the casserole dish was quality and resisted breaking. Then he spun on his heels and marched himself into the kitchen. Beyond the swinging of her kitchen door, she heard the thumping and clanking of dishes being moved vigorously around.

"Great," she sighed, popping the last bite of that gloriously delicious sandwich into her mouth. "I invited a demon into my home, and now he's pissed off, and I don't really understand why." But it wasn't like googling this issue wouldn't get her some red flags with certain government agencies. "Maybe I should send him back?" she asked herself softly.

The swinging door banged open again. "Yes! That is exactly what you should do!" Rafferty shouted as he re-entered, moving around like an aggressive leopard with nowhere to go. "You need to send me back!"

Chapter 15

ALMOST GOT SUCKED IN

Helena blinked at him, completely surprised. "How... you could hear me from all the way in the kitchen?"

He threw a hand at her. "This is why you should never have summoned me to begin with, for hell's sake! You have no idea what you're freaking doing. Of course I can hear you. I can hear your voice anywhere in the universe; that's how you can summon me. You call for me, and I have to come trotting like a good little show pony and make you tea and crumpets while you bleed your damn soul out for something as stupid as a good meal!"

"I... I don't even know what a crumpet is," Helena said in a small voice.

"That's not my freaking point!"

Helena held up a hand. "Okay, what I'm hearing is you want to go back?" she said carefully.

"What?! No!"

"Then why are you screaming at me?"

"I don't want to go back!" he said, pacing back and forth in front of the door to the kitchen.

"Okay, then... what are you saying?" she said, struggling to stay calm.

"You're not stupid. I can see that you aren't stupid, so why are you acting so damned stupid?" he growled, pressing his fists into his temples.

"Rafferty, stop pacing," Helena ordered, realizing something.

He stopped mid-pace, his body calming as he obeyed her command. He wasn't happy, but there seemed to be a "rightness" to his expression, like he was a little bit relieved that she had finally figured out something.

"Okay, please don't get mad while I work this out," Helena said. "Alright?"

His eyes slid over to her so he was looking at her askance. Then he crossed his arms and grunted.

"Am I correct in saying that when a person summons a demon, that demon must obey whatever commands they are given by the summoner, including rules about what they can or cannot do?"

"Yes. Or they incur more cosmic debt."

The implications of that rang out for Helena and why so many people would be tempted into doing what she initially had done accidentally.

"So... are there people who just summon demons for the power trip of having someone else under their control?"

He dropped his gaze, basically confirming it.

"Wow, demon magic is messed up."

"Exactly what I have been trying to establish with you since the moment we met," he said, now lifting his eyes as if invoking the higher powers to give him strength.

Though since such a thing was probably not possible, Helena assumed it was an old habit of his from when he had been human.

"See, this is why you are so confusing," Helena said, pulling out one of her dining room chairs so she could sit down. "You're a demon—I get that. Your job is to try to rob me of soul, life energy, and whatever the third thing you said was so you can improve your own situation. I get that. But then you keep trying to save me from all this, even though it is completely against your best interests, and as a demon, you seem to be insisting that a 'demon' would never do such a thing."

He paused for a moment, then pointed out, "Unless that was part of my scheme to get you to actually trust me, by making a big show of trying to save you and then definitely skin you for all you're worth."

God, she hoped he was being metaphorical. "Is that what you're doing?"

"No," he turned and started a slower version of his pacing. "But that is also what I would say, right? You can't trust me. You shouldn't trust me. I'm a demon."

"Like I said, you don't make a whole lot of sense."

"You know, I could say the same thing about you," he shot back. "Look, if you knew a tenth of the horrible things I've done as a human, never mind as a demon, you would not be this kind to me."

Helena scrunched up her nose at that. "Why would the things you've done have any bearing on how I choose to treat you?"

Rafferty's mouth dropped open at that question. "What are you? A freaking saint?"

Sighing, Helena shook her head. "I'm just trying to help you, and you're making it really difficult."

"You can't help me. No one can," Rafferty snarked and pulled out a dining chair for himself to sit down upon. He let his gaze drift over the myriad of dishes, then picked something off of one of the plates, a piece of pie crust on what looked like a kind of pot pie and put it in his mouth.

Curious, Helena asked, "What does it taste like?"

"Ashes," he muttered.

"And that's everything you eat? Ashes and dirt?"

He shook his head. "Just ashes. Dirt actually tastes like something and not all of it bad."

She lifted her hand to him.

He eyed it suspiciously. "Don't. Don't do that."

"Why not? You can taste it if you do," she said.

His lips thinned again. She waggled her fingers at him, temptingly. "Come on. You know you want to," she pushed with a wicked gleam in her eye.

Finally, he grasped her hand, his larger fingers lacing between hers, and they both picked up a fork from the small pile of silverware he'd stuck amongst the dishes. As soon as the bite hit her mouth, Helena squealed. And then spit.

"Oh my God! That is so awful!" she declared, her horror amplified because of her expectation that it was going to taste good.

"Oh yes," Rafferty said, chuckling as he chewed. "That is some nasty shit." He cut another bite and stuck it into his mouth. "Oh that is perfectly awful."

"Then why are you still eating it?" Helena cried, releasing his hand to go to her kitchen to get something to drink.

"Because it's not ashes," he said, laughing, and stuck the fork in again.

"Well, if it's all the same to you, I'm going to have some more of that French Toast sandwich."

"I think I added too much of something, but I can't put my finger on what yet. Definitely not enough salt," he added.

Helena shook her head unable to suppress a smile as she ducked her head into the fridge to grab a cold can of bubble water. As she turned, she spotted her cat, Pooka, whom she hadn't really seen in days. The little thing was crouched down on the ground, staring while her tail flicked slowly back and forth, her yellow-green eyes wide.

"Hey Pooka, what's wrong?" Helena asked. Then, just on the edge of her hearing, Helena thought she heard whispers. Shutting the fridge and cracking the can, she looked all around, trying to pinpoint what it was she heard. Taking a step back, the circle burst to life beneath her feet. The black lines reappeared and began to emit a stinging smoke. Helena got a big whiff of it into her lungs and immediately started to cough. The whispering became louder and painfully insistent, making her wince as she dropped her nearly full can of water so she could press both hands against her ears. It didn't help though. The whispers still got through, drowning out all other sounds.

Rafferty burst through the door as Pooka yowled past, running away for all she was worth, and stopped just on the outside edge of the circle. It affected him too as he flickered back to his demonic self. The closeness of him to the circle was like adding lighter fluid to an already burning flame. Helena couldn't stand any more. The world around them felt like it had tilted and just wouldn't right itself.

Losing her balance, she fell over. Curling down onto her side, she tried to close eyes against what was happening, but nothing she did stopped it. The whispers grew louder.

"I pay the debt!" Rafferty barked.

Instantly, the whispering and pain stopped. Everything was impossibly quiet after all that noise. The pain was gone, and Helena could lift her head again. She felt exhausted, like she had been drinking all night. The circle still burned in the tile, but it had stopped smoking, leaving only a bad taste in the back of her throat.

Beside her, a pair of knees hit the ground.

She jumped, making a small yip sound.

A hand dropped next to the knees, and a wing appeared over her.

Rafferty panted, fully back in his demonic form.

"What happened? What did you do?" she croaked out, her tongue feeling large in her mouth.

"I paid the cosmic debt," he ground out, voice full of pain. "You're going to be alright now." Then he leaned forward, resting his forehead and the curved bend of his backward sweeping horns on the ground before laying his wings over himself, like he was trying to hide.

Helena pushed herself back up to sitting, wrapping her arms around her legs. The wrongness feeling was back, but she didn't pay it any mind. She knew it was just Rafferty. She stared at his form as it pulsed with his breath.

"Are you alright?" she made herself ask.

"No," he growled.

Her vision became cloudy, and Helena rubbed the grit from her eyes. "I don't understand. How did you pay the debt?"

"If, for whatever reason, a demon cannot get someone else to take the debt for them, the cosmic imbalance will burn us away instead. Permanently. We have no bodies, no memories... all we have left is souls."

Helena's eyes went wide as she realized what that meant. "And when that is all gone..."

His wings tightened around his body reflexively.

"But Rafferty... why did you do that?" Helena asked.

"I don't know," he whispered.

Chapter 16

INVITING A
DEMON TO DINNER

"We have our own debts to pay back, and if we don't find someone else to take our places when that happens..." Rafferty said. "It's how they motivate us into joining the demonic Ponzi scheme. A small glimmer of hope that we can actually save ourselves," Rafferty said calmly.

They had returned to the dining room, and he had shifted to his easier-to-be-around human form. To Helena's surprise, most of the food Rafferty cooked had been destroyed, along with several of the dishes they had been sitting on, leaving nothing but ash in its place. Not her new Fiestaware for some reason.

"And why did it damage all the food?" Helena asked, taking another sip of a new bubble water can. The original bubble water had turned brackish.

"The imbalance doesn't really care what pays the price, just as long as it's paid. Most food is made of organic compounds, fruits, vegetables, flesh. Living stuff, or recently living stuff from creation, but has no will any more to resist. Those sorts of sacrifices can replace the body price. It was easy and nearby."

Helena furrowed her eyebrows. "So like, the ancient feasts to the gods were really this sort of thing?"

"Humans have always tried to play with these forces. More than one civilization has been destroyed trying to keep up with the price. That's why the majority of humans moved away from this sort of thing," Rafferty said. "Because it is stupid."

Helena looked down at the floor of her dining room, trying to process. The floor itself was surprisingly clean. "But my house?" She indicated the wood table and wood floor. There was no damage that she could see. "Those things are made from organic compounds from creation?"

"Longer dead, older, covered in lacquers it would have to eat through. It would consume them eventually, but it would take longer and isn't as easy. It would have devoured you first before it would start in on the floors. Even stone would eventually be crumbled into dust, turning all of this around it into a hellscape until the balance is paid."

Helena looked down at her hands, which still shook. The skin hung dry over her bones, like all the moisture had been sucked out. She had been sipping water for a while, but when she had managed to crawl out of the kitchen with Rafferty, her tongue kept sticking to the roof of her mouth. She didn't understand what any of this meant, or what exactly had happened to her, but she knew one thing—she was never going into her kitchen again.

Helena had to fight the urge to run out of her house.

"Are we safe now?" she asked in a small voice.

"Yes, the debt is paid, and if we don't use any more demonic magic, we won't incur any more debt. Except the one that I inherently already have just being here. The circle is more or less closed. If I hadn't used demonic magic at all, I'm not sure it would have gotten through now."

"I'm never going to sleep tonight," she said, shaking her head at all this horrible information.

The next day dawned sunny and bright. Helena opened her eyes and stretched deliciously. She couldn't remember the last time she slept so well. Luxuriating while she lay there, she tried to remember going to bed last night, but nothing came to her. Beside her, Pooka was curled up, eyes closed and purring.

"Man, I must have been really tired," she said to her cat, "but to be fair, it was a hard day's work yesterday. Trying to get those appointments with the various catering services had been more of a challenge than I thought it would be."

Pooka stared at her with slitted eyes. Off in the distance of her house, she heard a clinking, kitchen-y sound. The disturbance spooked the cat, who jumped off the bed to disappear under it.

"Ugh, if only it wouldn't cost me so much to get the one guy I know could do a good job," Helena muttered, unsurprised by her cat's reaction, since she usually hid from strangers, and pushed back the covers. Slipping on her bathrobe, she did her basics in the bathroom, then made her way to the kitchen.

Pushing open the door, she smiled at the demon with a man's face standing there, flipping a pair of eggs onto some toast that had green stuff smeared all over them.

"Good morning," she said cheerfully and went toward her coffeemaker, only to be intercepted by an already steaming cup.

"I don't know how you take it," Rafferty said, passing it to her.

"But you know that I drink it?" she inquired as she redirected to the fridge to get her lavender creamer that she bought from the organic coffee shop just down the street.

"Why else would you have the coffee maker?" he asked, and she had to concede the point.

Dropping a dollop of the sweet, scented stuff, she let it mix naturally as she replaced the creamer in the fridge, then turned to head back to her dining room. Before she got there, Rafferty went ahead of her, bearing the plate, which he set down at her spot like a waiter. He stepped back to pull out her chair.

"What are you doing?" she asked as she set the coffee next to her plate.

"Being of service," he said simply.

"Why don't you sit down and join me?" she invited as she sat down so he could stop doing that.

"I'm fine," he stated, backing up so he could take a spot against the wall, his arms behind his back.

"You're making me feel like I'm in a hotel," she said, looking at him over her shoulder.

"I think it would be better for both of us if we kept a distance," he stated.

Helena wondered what had happened between yesterday and that morning. Yesterday had been the first time she had felt comfortable around the demon, seeing him all vulnerable like that after he had gone a little crazy cooking all those dishes. She had loved his wide-eyed amazement at the Food Network channel.

"What happened to all the food by the way?" she asked. She remembered eating that delicious French Toast sandwich, but not really anything else from his feast.

"I made it go away. It was a foolish mistake of mine, and I apologize, mistress," Rafferty said, bowing his head like a penitent.

"Oh, that's a shame. It all looked so good," she said. "What a waste."

"It was not wasted, mistress. It was like it never existed."

"Why are you calling me mistress all of a sudden?"

He averted his gaze, resting it on the floor instead. When it became clear that he wasn't going to say anything more, Helena sighed. Two steps forward, one step back.

"Rafferty, this is your vacation. And you are creeping me out by standing where I can't see you. Come sit down."

She hated to order him to relax, but this time, the demon obeyed. He crossed to take the seat kitty-corner from her, and they eyed each other as he slid to sit, folding his hands on the table. He looked ready to spring up any moment.

Helena sighed, accepting what little victory she could and looked down at her plate. "Avocado toast?" she guessed.

"Yes, with a poached egg on top," her reluctant guest confirmed.

"Did you see this on a cooking channel as well?" she asked, picking one of the pieces up so she could take a bite.

A guilty look crossed his face, his way of confirming.

She chuckled as she took a bite. Lime had been splashed onto the avocado, just enough to make the natural brightness of the savory fruit sing even brighter. The egg capped that brightness just as it was about to be too much, easing the taste on her tongue.

"Hmm," she cooed as she chewed, then took a second bite that got a bit of the yolk. The yolk inside was still runny, and it burst into her mouth with creamy goodness. She didn't even mind the little bit of yolk that dribbled down her chin.

Rafferty's eyes seemed to devour the sight of her eating as he watched her every move, but she didn't mind it.

I'm getting better at understanding him. She contemplated the situation he was in. She couldn't imagine what it had to be like to not be able to taste anything. What was letting him devour the memories of her food really going to do to her anyway? There was a second piece of toast.

"Do you want to try this?" she asked, pushing the plate a little toward him to offer him the other piece.

"No, this is yours," he insisted.

"You looked starved," she noted, though he really didn't when he was in his human form. The emaciation of his demonic form was well hidden under the human skin. It was his eyes that looked so hungry.

"No," he said firmly, pulling his folded hands toward his chest like he was turtling up. "I cannot feed off your memories at every meal you have. You won't make it two weeks if we do that."

She mulled that over. "Okay, so then we gotta make it count. Is there anywhere in the city you would like to eat?"

That invoked an eyebrow raise. "Anywhere?"

"Well, sure. There are lots of great chefs in the city, and I need to do some tastings for work. Plus I think it's more fun if you let someone else cook for you. You get to see what they would do differently and stuff." She didn't know how persuasive she really was being, but she kept smiling at him, hoping for the best.

Rafferty flattened his hands onto the table while he thought hard. "I... I think I could do that," he said carefully. A tremor of excitement cometed through his starlight eyes.

Helena smiled even brighter. "Great!" Then she eyed his caterer's uniform. It was only then that she realized he had worn the same one every day that he had been in her presence. "Do you have anything else you can wear?"

Chapter 17

TAKING A DEMON SHOPPING

The answer was no. Rafferty did not have anything else to wear, and both of them were reluctant to have him use demon magic to conjure anything more appropriate to go to a two or even three star restaurant. She'd rather just use money.

"Come on. This is going to be fun," she said, dragging Rafferty into the high-end outlet mall. The demon looked overwhelmed, but she kept a firm grip on his arm. As far as she could tell, as long as he stayed in his human form, no one seemed to really notice anything out of place about him. Not on the bus ride over there nor as people passed them in the mall itself.

Yet, Rafferty was stiff as a board, walking in a way that would have made the Tin Man look like Gumby. "That's my favorite place." She gestured toward the *105th* clothing store. "You can get really nice pieces for really low prices because they are just trying to move the inventory. We'll go there first to get you something better to wear..."

"This is a bad idea, and we should leave now," Rafferty growled under his breath.

"What's wrong with you?" she asked, smiling politely to a mother and child trying to get by as Rafferty came to a full stop next to a very leafy potted plant.

"I don't... I don't like..." he struggled to say.

"You don't like what?" she pushed.

He dropped his voice even more, leaning forward to bring his breath to her ear. "I don't like people."

"Yeah, that's obvious," she said dryly, rolling her eyes.

"I mean, I never liked people. Not ever. It's all too much." He pivoted then, turning to head back the way they had come. "I can't do this. I'm going."

"Hey, hey, hey. Calm down. You're fine. This is fine," she soothed, running her hands down his arms. He rolled his eyes as he let her stop him, dragging him back to their semi-hiding spot. "Look, okay. I can appreciate that this is hard for you. I'm guessing you haven't really gotten out very much in the last how many hundred years?"

"Three hundred fifty."

"Right," she confirmed, annoyed, but pushed on.

"And yes, usually people summon me into a kitchen or something. Definitely into their houses, and when they're done, I'm dismissed," he conceded.

"Okay, so ... not a lot of crowd interactions. Completely understandable. But we can't exactly go into a restaurant with you looking like you're part of the staff, right?" she said, gesturing to his caterer's outfit. Then she had an idea. "I bet I can find a store in this place that you would love."

Rafferty looked around. "Look, I don't really care about how I look. I never really liked clothes, okay? They were just something to keep on your body when it was cold and to keep the priests off your back. You know? Modesty and stuff. More or less."

"Huh. Okay, well that's an extra tagline that's going to need some more explanation later, but right now, will you please just trust me and come with me? This is one hour of your life."

He eyed her warily.

She leaned in even closer, careful of the words she was about to say. "I would think spending one hour in a place you're uncomfortable in this reality would be preferable to an hour ... *elsewhere*," she said with a you-know-what-I-mean attitude. "It can't be nearly as bad, right?"

He narrowed his eyes at her, his lips pressing so hard they bulged. "Fine," he bit out, confirming her argument had persuaded. He simply couldn't argue with that. Instead, he offered her his hand, and she took it gladly, dragging him to the one place she knew he would like.

At the far end of the mall, tucked into a corner was a double-wide store. She knew the minute he saw it because he came to a dead stop, making a guy who had been going too fast behind them trip. Rafferty didn't notice him or his curses though. His eyes were glued to the display laid out before him.

Just behind a large pane of glass, someone had created a magical kitchen. On a faux counter, next to a smaller version of a kitchen table, different appliances danced about, some of them suspended by wires to convey their merry whimsy. Utensils of every shape, size, and color had been laid out on a sweeping, curving board. Someone had drawn long staff lines on it, as if it were a sheet of music and the utensils were the notes. Decorative cupcake papers had been turned into flowers, while in a flower box on the fairytale kitchen's fake window was a row of different flours ranging from Almond to Semolina.

Above it all read the name: "A Cook's Wonderland" in Miss Muffet font.

"Told you you would like it," Helena said proudly.

"How is such a store possible?" he breathed.

"Uh, the development of commercialism and globalization over the last few centuries," Helena said, thinking of what could have been available to him three hundred and fifty years ago. "You think this is amazing? Wait until I take you to a grocery store."

Mesmerized by what he was seeing, Rafferty drifted forward toward the store's entrance. He stopped at the threshold, staring inside. "What are they doing?" he asked.

"Oh, looks like cooking classes."

In the back half of the store, a line of cooking stations lined the wall with an extra-long continuous white granite counter creating an alley that separated it from the rest of the place. People were gathered within this alley, talking, laughing, and cooking while a woman dressed like Rafferty only in white with a blue kerchief covering her hair, demonstrated at her elevated cooking station at the far end.

Helena took his cold hand in her warm one. "Come on. Let's go in."

"No!" he said, urgently resisting. "No. I am... I am unworthy."

She wanted to laugh like he was joking, but his face told her he was anything but so she choked it down.

"Rafferty, don't be silly. It's just a store. For cooking supplies. Everyone is worthy. That's the point of a place like this. 'Anyone can cook.'"

He winced at that, shooting her a disgusted expression. "Who the hell said that?"

"A cartoon mouse, but it doesn't mean it's not universally and uncopyrightably true," Helena insisted.

"Let's just... just take me to that clothing shop you wished to go to, and let's get out of here." He continued to pull away, but Helena wasn't having it.

"One thing. Let's go in and buy you one new cooking thing."

"It's not like I haven't used everything that has been invented since the 1600s."

Helena glanced into the store. "Have you ever used a rice cooker before?"

"A what? What do you mean?"

"Okay, so you don't get summoned into Asia very often." She tried one more time to drag him in, but still he resisted.

"Just leave it alone!" he said. Then when she looked back at him, exasperated, he added softly, "Please. I can't."

At that, she relented. "Alright, alright."

They traced their way back to *105th*. Because it was the middle of the day, there were very few customers in the store, and those that were there were shopping through the racks on the women's side. Instead, she led Rafferty over to the men's side where several impossibly well-sculpted mannequins were frozen in "cool guy" poses sporting the latest fashions.

"So what do you like to wear?" Helena asked, clacking aside some hanging clothes to get a better look at the available colors of a lovely set of dress shirts.

"Short breeches and a toque," Rafferty muttered.

Helena paused to look at him. "Well there's a visual," she said. "Didn't they believe in shirts in 1600s?"

Her demon leveled a glare at her. "Yes, we wore shirts."

"And the little necktie thing right? Cravat?" She grinned, enjoying herself way too much. "Well since we aren't going to a historical re-enactment themed restaurant, let's find something a little more modern for you."

"Just pick whatever you want. I don't care. Just pick it and I'll wear it." He sighed.

"That sounds like an early days relationship to me," a store clerk said, a woman with big hair and an even bigger smile, her voice singing out with a small Southern twang. "Now don't tell me—let me guess." She looked between the two of them. "You are friends starting to think about dating, but you're both still on the fence, am I right?"

"No," Rafferty said, offended, "not even remotely."

"We just met a few weeks ago," Helena said. "Been on three dates so far."

"We've had three meals together," Rafferty again corrected.

Helena laughed and leaned in to the clerk. "I like them grumpy. They're just so cute when they're grumpy."

The clerk's smile didn't falter. "Well, it takes all kinds, doesn't it? Now my name is Honey, and how can I be of assistance today?"

"She says I need better clothes to go to this high-end restaurant she got reservations for," Rafferty reported.

"Well, while you cut a dashing figure, I can see why she's concerned. They might think you were one of the wait staff," Honey said, slapping his arm lightly as she laughed at her own joke.

Rafferty didn't react. For a brief moment, Helena thought he was going to flare his demon-aura or something, but Honey didn't even seem to notice.

"So do you know your size, sugar lips?" she asked, already pulling out a tape measure attached to her wrist to pull across his shoulders.

"Uh, no," Rafferty said uncomfortably.

"Don't worry. Most men don't. Or what they tell me is dead wrong." Without asking permission, she stuck her arms under his and wrapped her measuring tape around his waist. "Hmm, darling, you smell good," she declared. "Like rosemary and thyme. You a baker?"

"He's a cook," Helena corrected. "He's a self-study."

"Got a YouTube channel?" Honey asked, looping her measuring tape around his chest, then slipping it out to dance down his arms. "Hold your arm out, honeypot."

"I like this," Helena said, pointing at a dark suit on one of the mannequins. "Black suit with black shirt and black tie. Very mysterious chic."

"Fine. Whatever. Just let's get on with it!" he growled, jumping away from Honey as she knelt down before him to measure his inseam.

"Okay, okay," Honey said, holding her hands out. "We'll do the black suit. I can eyeball the rest." That last was directed at the area he wanted her to avoid, giving him a smug smile instead.

"You're wrong," Rafferty said as Honey finally wandered off to a rack of dark-colored shirts.

"About what?" Helena asked.

"There are some things worse than hell."

Chapter 18

TRYING ON CLOTHES IS HOT

Helena waited in a chair in the changing area, sitting next to the tri-fold mirrors. Changing rooms like this always seemed to have a set.

"How's it going?" she called into the sizable stall where Rafferty had disappeared.

All that came back was silence. She leaned forward a little to glance under the door, and she saw his socked feet standing there, already slipped into pants.

"Raffie?" she called gently. ""Do you need help?"

"I just..." he said, sounding frustrated. "This neck thing..."

"Your tie?"

"Well, I'm trying to!" he barked.

"No, I mean, it's called a tie," Helena corrected. He didn't respond. "Do you want me to come in and help you?"

"No, I can get it ... if I just..." The sounds of struggle on the other side didn't inspire confidence.

"Raffie, just open the door," she said.

After another few seconds of struggle and several more under breath curse words, the mechanism on the door rattled and the oversized thing swung inward.

The demon man stood there in the black dress pants, his black shirt untucked, definitely struggling with the modern tie in his hands, which he had somehow tied into a confusing knot that he couldn't undo.

"Oh, I see. Okay, we're going to have to tuck that shirt in first." She reached for his pants, then stopped. "Can I touch you?"

"What?" he asked, genuinely confused.

"I'm just going to tuck your shirt in, but to do that right, I need to undo the pants to lay it flat. So can I touch you?"

"What? Yes, yeah, it's fine, whatever," he dismissed, working on the tie.

"Oh, okay," she said and undid the top button of the dress pants. "I just thought you would object."

"No, I don't care what happens to this body. You lose your sense of personal space or modesty pretty quickly in hell," he said, finding the right bit to pull as the knot in the tie finally came undone.

"It's just with Honey back there, you were very defensive." Helena reached around his waist, flattening his shirt to smooth it down his backside, trying to ignore how her cheeks were burning hot as she did it. Rafferty didn't seem to mind at all.

"Well, she's her," he muttered, holding his arms up as he waited for her to finish adjusting his shirt, the tie dangling from one hand.

"And I'm me?" Helena asked, straightening so she could bring the top of his pants together to button and zip up. As the zipper ticked its way up his crotch, her eyes drifted upward to look up into those eerie, but beautiful, starburst eyes.

"Yeah," he said, softly.

They held the breath between them for an eternity.

"You have starbursts in your eyes," Rafferty noted.

"What?" Helena asked, cocking her head slightly to the side.

"Within the brown of your eyes, there is green. It looks like a starburst," he said.

"Oh, thank you."

"I didn't pay you a compliment—just stating a fact."

"Oh. Okay."

Another still moment passed.

"Do you have the tie?" Helena asked.

He handed it to her, and she shifted back a little, partly to catch a breath, but partly to also measure out the tie in her hands. Then she looped it over his neck and focused on doing her duty, turning the silky cloth over in her hand until it tightened into a perfect Windsor knot.

"There," she said, brushing her hands down his shoulders even though they were perfectly smoothed down. "Now you look handsome."

He shook his head. "Don't. Don't do that. Don't be kind to me," Rafferty whispered, his voice growing thick. "Don't be kind to me."

Helena blinked. "Why?"

"Because it isn't going to last," he barked, backing away looking more sad and angry than afraid.

"Shh!" Helena shushed urgently. "Keep your voice down. We're not the only people in the store."

He obeyed, but it did nothing to slow down the urgency of the words coming out of him. "None of this is going to last, and then in two weeks it'll be over, and I'll be back there in a place where nobody is kind. Don't you understand?" He paced, lifting his hands up but at a loss as to what to do with them. "Don't you understand—this is worse. This makes it far, far worse, to feel someone be kind to me, knowing it'll end forever, and I can't take it with me. They'll rip it from me, given the chance. Or, even worse, I'll do something stupid and sell it off because a memory of kindness... You have no idea what that is worth there." He continued pacing like an animal as he spoke, so clearly in pain.

Helena didn't flinch away. Instead, she cornered him. His back was to the wall before he realized she was there, and he tried to flinch back as she reached out her hands. "No, don't! Don't, please," he begged, his voice pitching down into a whisper as he pleaded. "Don't do this to me."

But she didn't stop. She knew she needed to keep going as she wrapped her arms around his head and pulled him down into a hug. "It's okay," she whispered.

He could only resist a second more before he collapsed into her, his face buried into her neck, his arms wrapping around her and holding on like she was a life preserver in a vast, dark sea.

He didn't cry, but he shuddered and she just held on until it passed.

"You're right. I can't stop you from having to go back," she confirmed. "I'm sorry about that."

"It's not your fault," he said. "I did this to me."

"Listen to me, Rafferty." She licked her lips. "You're right. I don't know you really. I mean, I don't know what you've done. I don't need to. But I can't be anything other than who I am. I just want to be kind to you, and I know you've had too little of it. I like you, Raffie."

His head shook a little as if he couldn't accept that statement as true. "Why?" he asked.

"I don't know, I just do—"

"No, why do you keep calling me that nickname?" he asked.

She pulled away then, to look up into his face, which had become blotchy. "Because I'm your *friend*. You don't have to be mine, but I am yours, Raffie. And friends give each other nicknames," she said.

Now a tear did slip down his face, even though he tried to hold it still as a stone mask. "I don't deserve you," he whispered.

She shrugged. "This isn't about deserving. If good memories are currency in hell, then, let's go make you the richest demon in all seven levels of it while you're here," she said, offering him her smile.

He made an effort to return it. "You are so beautiful, Helena. Hellie," he tried. Then he wrinkled his nose. "It doesn't sound the same."

"It's fine. I like it," she said. "Hellie and Raffie."

"Hello, knock knock, how's it going in there?" Honey called from the other side of the door.

Helena took a step back to give them some breathing space. She turned toward the door. "Good, really good. I think we'll take the suit."

"Do you mind if I take a peek? I was guessing with the pants," Honey offered.

"Is it alright?" Helena asked him. He nodded and she unlatched the door.

Honey came in, holding a shoebox. Her eyes zeroed in on the cuff of his pants. "Oh, I told you, I'm good. That is going to fit just right once we get you into the right shoes." She held up the box. "Wanna see if I'm three for three?"

"Yes," Rafferty said, adjusting the tie around his neck before adding a belated. "Thank you."

Honey paused a moment, beaming at him, as if his thank you really hit her in the heart. "You are so welcome," she said softly. "I just love my job, making people look good. It makes a body feel valued, you know what I mean?"

She knelt down before him to open the shoe box, pulling out a slick black dress shoe with a square toe. "Now, these are a little on the pricey side, but they will last you forever and are built like a sneaker inside, so really comfortable. And if you buy them with the whole suit I should be able to swing you a nice discount."

"Thank you. I really appreciate it," Helena agreed. This was going to hit her in the pocketbook, but it was worth it. "We'll definitely take the whole thing."

"Helen—Hellie," Rafferty started to object, but she touched his upper arm with her fingertips and he quieted.

"My treat," she assured him. "It'll be fine."

Honey continued to beam up at both of them before offering the opened up shoe for the human-looking demon to slip into.

"Oh cherry pie, I'd give these clothes to you for free if it wouldn't get me fired. You look too good in them," Honey assured, tying the laces of the first shoe then bringing forth the second one. A few moments later, after several adjustments at cuff, seam, and a good tug on the back of the jacket, she stepped out of the dressing stall. "Oh my. Look

119

at you." She gestured over to the tri-fold mirrors, inviting him to look.

"No, that's okay. I don't need to—"

"Go ahead," Helena insisted, giving him a little push on his back.

Reluctantly, he stepped into mirrored space, rolling his eyes. Then he sighed and lifted his head to look. He froze.

Honey brought her hands up clasped before her, her smile beaming even more if that was possible. "Now, look at that. A man who has found his true self," she said.

Rafferty squinted at the three people reflected in the mirrors. "I've never been a vain person," he said.

"It's not vain to like how you look," Helena assured him. "Do you like it?"

He kept staring, then rolled his shoulders. The images in the three mirrors did the same. "Yeah. I guess it's alright," he conceded.

"Oh high praise indeed!" Honey declared before turning to Helena. "Usually all I get is an acknowledging grunt." Then she bent down and lifted up a large paper shopping bag with the store's logo on it. "Here's for his other clothes. I'll meet you both out front and then you can get on with your da-ate!" She sang out the last part with a little excited shimmy, then the store clerk disappeared out to the main floor.

"Yeah," said Helena. "Then we can get on with our date."

Chapter 19

IT'S CALLED L'APERTIF

he restaurant was gorgeous. High above the city, the place was walled with glass. Beyond the windows, the darkness twinkled with a million lights from the various buildings, streetlamps, and countless cars moving along the street. There was a little observation room by the host podium that had a glass floor, daring guests to go and stand out on apparent nothingness and get a three sixty view of the city.

"Though it's really one eighty, right?" Helena said as she crept up to the edge of the glass floor, but she just couldn't work up the courage to trod upon it.

"More than one eighty," Rafferty said. He had no problem standing on the glass floor. He even had his hands in his pockets like it was no big thing, gazing out into the city of stars.

Helena huffed at him. "Could you like, give me your hand or say something to help me have a little confidence?

I'm finding it really difficult to move my leg out there. It just won't go that way." She demonstrated her body's resistance. Granted, the dress she wore went down to her knees in a tight, slinky way that wasn't helping. In fact, it was like the short black thing with its silver threads around her bodice area was trying to tell her, "No, don't do it. You have so much to live for."

Rafferty turned to her and offered his hand. Before she could take it, he re-adjusted himself and bowed even deeper, his hand even more proffered. "My lady, if you would join me," he said.

That made her laugh, and as she took his hand, her legs unlocked for a second. Then when she took the first step, she looked down. "Oh damn, no!" she squealed and backed away. "I can't. I can't do it."

"It's fine. It looks like the hostess is back," Rafferty said, walking off the observation deck to offer her his arm in the more modern fashion.

They approached the podium just as a woman in a short black dress with a matching short black coat took her place behind it. "I do apologize for the wait," she said. "We had a mess up in the kitchen and..." She sighed and renewed her professional smile. "Sorry, do you have a reservation with us today?"

"Yes," Helena said, stepping up. "It's under Scarlet Promotions."

The hostess looked down at her list. "Yes, I do think I saw that. One second." She ticked something near the bottom before plucking up some menus. "This way, please."

She led them through the dimly lit space filled with tables set up on different levels, one table on each, to a table along the window. Scarlet's name had been recognized in this establishment, and while the *Tower Top Restaurant* didn't often cater outside of itself, for Scarlet they would bend over backward to do it. The Winter Rose Ball was a choice event.

Once they approached the table, Rafferty held her chair before taking his own seat, and the hostess waited politely before presenting them both their menus.

"A server will be by to explain the menu, but before we get started tonight, please let me know if there are any food allergies the chef should know about."

"No, nothing for me," Helena said, glancing at Rafferty, who was focusing very hard on his menu. "Raffie?"

He blinked and looked up. "Yes?"

Helena tipped her head toward the hostess. "Do you ... have any allergies?" she asked. She couldn't imagine he did, but one could never be sure.

"Allergies?" he questioned.

"No, I don't think he does," Helena quickly amended, exchanging an awkward smile with the hostess.

"Alright then, excellent," she said. "A waiter will be with you shortly."

And they were. Within two steps of the hostess leaving, the waiter swooped in to pour bubbling, clear water into their glasses from a carafe.

"Hello, I am Éliott. I will be your server this evening," their waiter said with a light French accent.

"Oh!" Helena said in surprise. "I thought we were just having French cuisine, but you actually are French?"

"Oui, madame." He nodded, smiling sweetly. "The chef is my cousin, and he invited me to have a chance to come to America and work at his restaurant while I went to school. I of course said, 'oui.'"

"Well, welcome to the states," Helena said, nodding the greeting at their authentic server. "I'm glad because I don't speak or read any French, and I need to take notes on this meal, so maybe you can help me?"

"Oui, madame, of course, but I would also like to point out..." he leaned forward to point at the menu, "that while the menu is in French, the line underneath..."

"Is written in English," Helena said, seeing what he was showing her and feeling silly for having missed it. "Sorry, I was just so hypnotized by all the pretty French."

"*Quel est votre plat de poisson ce soir?*"[1] Rafferty suddenly asked in perfect French.

Helena and the waiter's eyes widened.

"*Le plat de poisson de ce soir est bar au beurre blanc, monsieur,*"[2] Éliott responded, "*Pardonnez-moi de le dire, mais vous parlez comme un Français.*"[3]

Rafferty paused as he was about to say something else, then slid his gaze over to Helena, clearing his throat. After an awkward pause, Éliott politely said, "Is there anything else, madame?"

"No, not at this time," she said with a note of apology, her eyes still watching Rafferty, who turned his gaze out into the cityscape.

"Very good, madame. Shall I bring you the first course?" Éliott asked.

---

[1] English translation: What is your fish course tonight?

[2] English translation: The fish course tonight is white butter bass, sir.

[3] English translation: pardon me for saying, buy you sound like a French man.

"Yes, thank you," she agreed, adding an apologetic smile to her tone. He graciously nodded and withdrew.

"Rafferty, what's wrong?" Helena asked, tipping her head to try to capture his gaze.

"I'm sorry," he mumbled. "I am ruining your gift." He tried to straighten and adjust his silverware setting even though they didn't need it.

"No, not at all. It was nice to hear you speak French like that. I know you said you were from the 1600s, but you never said where. So you were French?"

"I do not wish to talk about it," he said, but even as he spoke, a French accent bled through his words. He closed his eyes as he realized it.

"It's fine. We don't have to talk about it," Helena said and took another sip of her water. "This is a really beautiful view. I wasn't sure the clouds were going to blow through in time but—"

"You don't want to talk about it?" Rafferty questioned, squinting his eyes at her.

"No, not if you don't want to," she stated.

He continued to squint at her.

"What?"

"Is this that reverse psychology thing? Are you trying to trick me?" he pressed.

"No, not at all—"

"Because ever since you've brought me up here, you've been prying away at all my secrets, and now you're not interested?"

"Do you want to tell me?" Helena said, getting a bit exasperated.

"No."

"Good! Then I don't want to hear it because to be fair, you've been moping all day since I woke up, and while I get it, you've..." she glanced around them, but no one seemed to be listening, "...gone through hell, I frankly, wanted to just have a good dinner and enjoy myself. And I thought that's what you wanted to do on your vacation. So stop being such an *ass* about it."

Thankfully, Éliott returned at that moment with a small tray bearing the l'apertif course. "The l'apertif course: Byrrh." He set one glass before each of his patrons. Each glass had a single perfectly sculpted sphere of ice. It looked like a moon set in a red pool that smelled spicy to Helena's nose. "Think of it as a slightly spicier sweet vermouth," their waiter explained to Helena, per her earlier request. "Enjoy."

And then he was gone.

"Oh my gosh, this smells divine," Helena said, bringing her nose closer so she could take a deep sniff. "You ready?" she asked, and she held out her hand to him, laying it on the table on the window side so it wouldn't be too conspicuous. For a brief moment, she thought he was going to turn her down again, but then he slipped his cold fingers over hers and picked up his l'apertif with his other hand. She extended her l'apertif to him and they clinked. "To your health," she said, cutely, then together they drank down their first course.

Helena felt Rafferty's hand squeeze hers as they tasted. To her it felt wonderful, a delightful buzz of warm mellow fruits dancing with the spices that made her think of elegant ladies and gentlemen waltzing in circles in the candlelight. When she peeked over at Rafferty, his own eyes were closed as he held the concoction on his tongue, like he wanted to hold the flavors there forever. But eventually they had to swallow and the moment passed.

"Hmm, that was nice," Helena said.

"You don't remember," her companion suddenly said.

"Actually, I do seem to be—"

"When they take you and you die."

Chapter 20

THE FRENCH CONFESSION

"I'm sorry?" Helena said, refocusing on what Rafferty was telling her.

"When they ... take you," he continued, mimicking her use of code words. "So much of who you were when you were alive is burned from you. Not just your memories, but your faith, if you had any, your desires and wants, the things you liked, your name, the basic facts of yourself, the things you prized, your triumphs, even your very language, the stories we would tell, all of it goes to pay your initial price, the debt you owe for the power you commanded from the demon you summoned. And if they did their job right, you racked up quite a bill. All any of us are left with are the terrible parts of ourselves, and those are mere scraps of the men we once were."

"Just men?" Helena asked, cocking her head.

"Women too. Everything in between. Souls," he corrected. "That's all we are when we die. Our bodies are burned away first, the living flesh, our connection to the matter of this reality, then our memories, and then all we are is this soul, exposed raw and unprotected to our pain and suffering. What most people don't understand is that this..." He held up his hand staring at it as if it were a marvel.

"Explain it to me," she urged softly.

"This flesh shelters us. It can't void the pain we all feel, but it can lessen it, can give us the tools to hide it and cover it. But when we are pulled to that terrible place, the pain that drove us to make such bargains in the first place is placed against us like living coals all around and we burn. And we cannot escape it without help. Without the few moments of reality to cloth us once more in flesh. Well, only those who have enough of themselves left to even try."

His gaze shifted away from his hand to her face.

"So no. I don't remember what it was like being a French man in the 1600s."

"But you spoke French just now," Helena pointed out.

"Yes, I did," he said. "But I don't know why. It was very strange."

Helena shifted all that information in her mind a moment. "I mean, it is very strange because most of the time when you talk, you don't have any accent either. You sound more or less like me." She laughed at the observation.

"Yes, well that I can explain. That's exactly what's happening. When you give the bite of your tongue and blood to the circle, it uses that as a template to give me a shadow of what I need to interface with this world just like my body."

"It gives you an ego?" she supplied.

His eyebrows bobbed as if he hadn't thought of that before. "Yes, essentially. What knowledge you have I can glean a piece of, along with whatever I can hold onto myself from the previous times I've come—"

"To this city," she inserted quickly, realizing that their dinner conversation was about to be overheard by the next course.

"Yes, this city. At least the pieces I don't have to trade away. It isn't perfect, but I can limp along," he said, lifting his head up to face the waiter as if he were an unwelcome intruder.

"L'entre," Éliott declared, as he presented his tray holding two small dishes bearing a small array of finger foods. Another waiter smoothly came up behind him with his own tray to swipe away the empty l'aperitif glasses.

"On this plate, we have smoked salmon canapes, an olive tapenade on a thin piece of rye bread, and a gougères, or tiny cheese puff," Éliott said as he laid the small plate before Helena, then indicated each item with a point of his finger. Then he moved to lay the second plate before Rafferty. "Usually we only serve one appetizer per guest, but because this is for a very special occasion, the chef wished for you to try a wider selection of what we can offer."

"Thank you. It looks delicious," Helena reassured, and after their water glasses were topped off, the wait staff moved on. She stared at the plate, wanting to taste it, but it felt wrong to just dive right back into the fine dining experience after the things Rafferty just told her.

"I am sorry," he said. "You're right. I am ruining this for you."

"But you remember cooking," Helena said, plucking up the olive tapenade to take a small, independent bite.

"Yes, well, I hate cooking," he said, looking down at the plate before him like he was trying to puzzle them out. "It's better to serve the gougères with a soup to dip it in."

"You hate cooking?" she asked, genuinely surprised. "But you seem so passionate about it."

"What do you think I did to get dragged to that place?" he said in a low voice. "My greatest wish, to cook for the King, became my condemnation, and ashes is all I'm allowed to taste." He held up the olive tapenade and took a bite, chewing it, but clearly not enjoying it. She tried to do the same, taking up the olive tapenade, but when she reached for his hand, he pulled it out of her way. Then he popped the rest of the l'entre into his mouth and chewed it away.

"It's what I deserve. It's fine," he said.

She set the food down. "If it's what you deserve and you are nothing but dark things, then why are you so kind to me?"

"Again, what makes you think this isn't all a part of my long con?" he said in his gruff way, but when Helena looked into his starburst eyes, they crinkled just the littlest bit.

"Well, if you are trying to trick me, I don't care. I would rather be a person who gets tricked when trying to do something kind than live my life being cold and alone," she said with an airy flippancy. This time she poignantly held her hand out to him to take. "Now, you're going to have to taste the other half of this one because I need your help judging this food, and whether you like it or not, you are the expert, so come on." She waggled her fingers at him.

He reluctantly grinned and gave over his hand before obediently tasted the second half of her olive tapenade.

"Much better when using my taste buds, right?"

"Yes, much, though I'm sorry I am marring your experience," he agreed. Then he looked down at the plate before him, his face growing thoughtful as he rolled the food he could now taste in his mouth. "I could make this better," he said.

"Oh, okay," Helena said, not sure what to do with that. Or what he meant by his "marring" her experience. "But you can't do it for the Winter Rose Ball, so do you think this will go over?"

He licked his teeth, then took a sip of water.

"Let's try the rest of them. Let me see how these three work as a group."

Helena thought the warm creamy cheese inside the gougères was delightful while the smoked salmon canapes were interesting. Soon after that, the fish course came followed by small lime sorbet to cleanse their palates before the le plat principal or main course.

"I just don't know what to do about Yosef because while he technically doesn't outrank me, he sort of doesn't have a rank, you know? Like a ronin or something. Do you know what a ronin is?"

"A Japanese samurai that serves no master," Rafferty said.

"Okay, then maybe ronin is the wrong word because he definitely has a master. The way he takes care of Scarlet, you'd think she really was his mother," she said, scraping the last bit of sorbet onto her spoon.

"Hmm," he said, having finished with his and releasing her hand so she could enjoy it. Eating with the spoons had been a bit of a trick to keep in contact so they could taste.

"What's that 'hmm' about? Do you have something to share with the class?" she pressed.

"You like him?" her demon asked.

"No, I've been just saying how much I don't like him."

"But you desire him?"

"Don't you have to like someone to desire them?"

"Not in my experience." He shrugged. "What I can remember of it."

"Wait, so you're thinking that Yosef likes me?" she asked.

"Do you think he likes you?" he turned back on her.

"No, the only person he seems to like is Scarlet." Then she stopped as she heard what she just said. Her jaw literally dropped. "No. You're saying... he and... Scarlet is..." Yet now that she thought about it, she couldn't unthink it. "Oh. Oh. Oooohhhhhh." She picked up her water glass to take a sip, but before she could, she said, "Oh, now that I think that I absolutely want that to be true. That would mean it really isn't about me at all. He's trying to protect Scarlet. I mean, this ball really is her legacy, and if he thought it was going to be her last, and I'm slacking off on it..."

She set her glass down without taking a sip, so she could press her hands to her heart. "Aw, that would mean he really loves her, and this is a sort of tragic romantic gesture."

Rafferty's eyes smiled just as Éliott returned to pour them each some red wine.

"What?" she asked, noting it.

"I love your stories," he said, taking up his wine.

She did the same, slipping her hand into his as easily and naturally as if they had been doing it for years. "I love your cooking," she said and clinked her glass to his.

As the warm, bright flavors of the wine danced on her tongue, Eliott moved away just as another couple was being seated at a table indirectly nearby. With hurried surprise,

Helena swallowed her wine and set down her glass to grab her napkin before she spilled some on herself.

"Oh my gosh, it's Chris. I didn't know they were going to be coming to this restaurant tonight," she said, then stopped as her eyes fastened onto a woman being seated with him.

It was not Charlie.

Chapter 21

THEN CHRIS SHOWED UP

"Okay, this is probably not a big deal. He's probably just with his boss or a business colleague or something—" Then she watched the two people kiss and hold hands, Chris gently rubbing his finger along her cheek.

"What the hell am I seeing right now?" she breathed.

Rafferty sighed. "He is with a woman. What is surprising about this?"

"Well, one: he's married to Charlie. It's not about women or men. It's the fact that his tongue just went into the mouth of someone who is *not* Charlie."

"Maybe they have an understanding? It is not uncommon at all. I would know."

Helena let out a worried breath. "I mean maybe? But ... I don't know. I feel like Chris would have told me about it? But I mean, it's their private life, so why would they... Oh, dammit, I don't know what to do."

"Ignore them, refocus here, and enjoy the rest of your meal," Rafferty said practically, but it didn't help the gnawing panic inside.

"It is easy to give that advice when you don't have to live with the consequences," she said levelly.

"Consequences?"

"Yes, if I don't tell Charlie, and he finds out some other horrible way... or maybe this is all on the up and up, and I don't say anything, but I'll always treat him a little differently when open communication would have solved all of this."

"You are always seeking the 'right' answers, aren't you?" Rafferty said, his hands folded in his lap.

"I..." She stopped at that. "Well, yes I suppose so."

"Let me tell you something: from my experience, nothing we do here really matters," he said before taking another sip of wine, even though he couldn't taste it.

Helena frowned at that. "I think making a deal ... like we both have, matters a lot. And no, that's not true. We are what we do. It's the only thing that matters."

Pursing his lips, Rafferty sat back just as Éliott appeared bearing plates with tiny roasted birds on it, something that reminded her of cheesy mashed potatoes, and green beans with slivers of almonds.

"We have here: Pommes Aligot, Haricots Verts Amandine, Caille rôtie et raisins," Éliott said, "which is roasted quail and grapes."

"I think I can identify the rest," Helena agreed, nodding at the green beans and cheesy potatoes.

Éliott gave her a wink. "Anything else I can do for you?"

"No, we're good. Thank you," she returned, keeping her eyes on the young man and not on the friend just behind him.

"Oh, not yet madame. I see you need more wine," he added, tapping his nose before disappearing to go fetch it.

Once their server was gone, Rafferty held out his hand toward her. This time it felt like a challenge. Like he was waiting for her to stop this game now that he had said something she didn't agree with. But she did believe it— her actions defined her, and she would not punish him for something as petty as having a differing opinion from her. So she gripped his hand, and they continued with their meal.

After the first bite of the quail, she had to release her hand to bring it to her mouth to prevent the juices from escaping. "Oh, my God, I've never... You know you hear that phrase, melt in your mouth good, but this thing is actually melting in my mouth. This is amazing."

Rafferty chuckled as he cut another bite, and it was only then she realized she let go of his hand while he chewed. "Oh, damn sorry," she said, reaching out to recapture it.

"It's alright. I'm getting as much enjoyment watching you eat this than actually eating it," he said warmly, the starbursts in his eyes dancing merrily.

"You think I'm this crazy about a tiny bird—you should watch me eat Thai food," she said.

"Yes, I want that more than anything in the world," he said. "I could spend the rest of my time here with you in this city, watching you stuff your face with every food imaginable."

She narrowed her eyes at him. "I know you're teasing, but I also think you mean that."

He lifted a bite of the quail, offering it to her. Chuckling, she bit down on his fork, making a little *grr* sound. As she chewed, it occurred to her for one heartstopping moment, *Am I flirting?*

The implications of that would have startled her, but her gaze got drawn away from their table and locked onto Chris, looking directly at her.

"Oh crap," she said softly.

"What's wrong?" Rafferty asked, following it to look past his shoulder. His own narrowed as he realized what was happening.

"Just ignore him," he repeated slowly, but it was too late.

"He's coming over here," Helena said, alarmed, and Rafferty reclaimed her hand, not to take from her but to give her strength. Strangely, a warm feeling of calm did sweep through her, and she managed to take a deep fortifying breath before her friend made to their table.

"What the hell are you doing here?!" Chris hissed at her as soon as he was close enough.

"Hey!" Helena tried to say cheerfully, like she was happily surprised to see him, but it morphed into a protest as he planted his hands around her, one on the back of her chair and one on the table, boxing her in. His sudden weight made the silverware jump and attracted the attention of the few other people seated nearby. He towered over her.

"Answer me—are you following me?" he demanded even while he turned and smiled an apology at the closest neighbors.

"What? No," she started to say, but Chris didn't even slow his roll.

"I thought you were my *friend*. I can't believe you are doing this to me." His face was so close to Helena's, she could feel him spitting on her as he spoke.

"You need to back away right now," Rafferty warned. He had stood up and seized Chris's wrist of the hand planted on the table.

"Calm down, buddy. We're friends," Chris dismissed, shaking him off, then did a double take back at Rafferty. "Wait, you're that caterer from that dinner she gave a few weeks ago."

"Yes, Rafferty here is helping me try out different places to pick a caterer for a thing at work," Helena explained quickly, not really understanding what was happening but desperate to get out of it as easily as possible.

At that explanation, Chris did back off, looking confused and unsure. "Oh," was all he said. "So... so this is a coincidence." Then his eyes went wide as if he were just understanding the implications of his actions. He glanced back at his "date," who was looking over their way with a clear expression of concern. Their table's waiter stood next to her, frozen at the aggressive display. "Okay, Helena, I know how this looks—"

"Is everything alright here?" Éliott asked, cordially, but with a clear stance of someone who was ready to do what he must to protect his guests.

"Yeah," Chris said, blinking at the sudden appearance of the waiter. "This is just one of my good friends. I didn't know she was supposed to be here today," he said, looking to Helena to corroborate it.

She nodded. "Yeah, yeah, we're old friends. It was just a shock is all."

Éliott nodded, though he clearly didn't believe it, but also wanted to restore the serenity of the dining room. "Well, your current reservations are for two couples only and all of our four person tables are spoken for, so we cannot accommodate you sitting together. Therefore, I must be the bad guy and ask you to return to your party." He smiled politely with the killer eyes of a nightclub bouncer.

Chris straightened his jacket. "Yes, of course. I'm sorry." He turned to all the neighbors, saying louder, "Sorry everyone," which was not received well as it prompted grumbling. Éliott didn't leave Chris's side until he had been walked all the way back to his seat.

Only then did Helena let out a breath, giving Rafferty a brave face. "I'm alright," she tried to assure him.

"Bullshit. No, you're not."

"Yeah, but I got to be," she said, readjusting her napkin on her lap. "We still have the salad, cheese, and dessert courses to go."

"Forget that. Do you want to leave?" Rafferty asked.

"No," she assured, squeezing his hand again. "This is your special dinner out. I'm not going to ruin that."

"You didn't," he said. His eyes were bursting with fiery stars and that was when she realized the wrong feeling was radiating off of her companion. Suddenly it hit her that she had taken a demon to a very public restaurant, which rang a klaxon inside her.

"Please, don't do this," she asked softly. "Don't hurt anybody."

His eyes widened a little bit, maybe because he realized what was happening too. The wrong feeling subsided just as Éliott returned. "How is your dinner?" he asked, his eyebrows pinched together in a genuine show of worry that was touching.

"I am so sorry, but we need to go," she said, not willing to abandon the dinner for her sake, but she would before Rafferty lost himself. "I am so very sorry."

Éliott leaned forward. "If you would like me to have your 'friend' removed we can do so. It is no problem."

"No, no, please don't do that," Helena asked. "It's just..." She glanced worried over at Rafferty, who was determinedly staring at the window trying to master himself.

"I understand," Éliott said, though there was no way he did. Helena was grateful for his sentiment anyway. "I have been there, believe me. I will inform the chef and have them pack up the rest of the courses for you to enjoy at home."

"Thank you, and please, apologize to the chef for me," Helena said, feeling terrible but also knowing this was the correct thing to do.

"I will. Do not worry."

Chapter 22

HAD THE CHEESE COURSE AT HOME

Helena didn't want to risk taking the train home so she splurged on a taxi instead. The driver was friendly enough, but it was difficult to keep up the innocent chit chat with him while Rafferty huddled, turned away and radiating that wrongness that made the hairs on the back of her arms stand up on end. The only silver lining was it didn't seem to bother her as much anymore. Unfortunately, the driver kept glancing at Rafferty, and it made her keep talking.

"Is your boyfriend there going to be sick?" the driver finally asked when they hit the expressway.

"No, no, he's just... not used to this climate," Helena said, rubbing up and down on Rafferty's arms as if to warm him up.

"Ah, from the South, is he?" the driver asked with forced cheer, trying to figure out what was happening since there was no obvious reason for his discomfort. "I have cousins who live down in St. Louis…" He launched into another story about said cousins that Helena didn't listen to, would never remember, and only gave obligatory uh-huhs and ah-yeses when needed.

Finally, they pulled up in front of Helena's door, and even before the car had fully come to a stop, Rafferty opened it and dashed out.

"Sorry. Thank you. Sorry," was all Helena could say, waving the driver off, letting the app take care of the payment as she chased after her demon while trying to hold the takeout boxes.

This was not how she had hoped the night would go.

Rafferty had to wait for her to follow him up the stairs and open the door, but as soon as she had, he pushed through and beelined for her kitchen. As he went, his jacket and tie were thrown over the dining room table, and he hauled off the black shirt, tugging it over his head just in time before his horns made it impossible.

"Rafferty, what's wrong?" she called after, but he said nothing as he disappeared through the kitchen's swinging door so hard it rebounded off the wall. It swung back and forth a few times before settling, and in the last pass, she saw his bare back, gray and tall, with wings flexing back and forth rapidly like an angry, defeathered goose.

Sighing, she let him be, setting the takeout containers on the table next to his discarded coat. Kicking off the beautiful but uncomfortable shoes she had been wearing, she padded to her room and more sedately discarded her own clothes for her bathrobe. There was no sign or sound of Rafferty, so she dashed to her bathroom and started a very hot and welcome shower. She spent a long time standing under the water, letting it bead down on her. If only she could wash her feelings away as easily.

"I don't need to decide anything until tomorrow," she assured herself, trying to put Chris's strange actions out of her mind as best she could, but the echo of his words haunted her.

It wasn't until she came out of her bathroom, swathed in her lavender terrycloth bathrobe and hair up in a towel turban, that she could be distracted from those darker thoughts. Eerie noises came from the kitchen. Discordant sounds that made the hairs rise off the back of her neck and would have given a haunted house a run for its money.

"He's a demon. What did I think he was going to do when he's upset?" she told herself and went into her bedroom to pull on some comfy pajamas. As much as she knew she needed to go take care of the takeout boxes, like put them in the fridge or something, she just felt exhausted and confused from the night. She couldn't even make herself go brush her teeth, so instead, she climbed into bed.

But she couldn't sleep. Her mind kept going over and over again what happened with Chris, buzzing like a hive of bees. While she tried to readjust her pillows to be more comfortable, a gentle knock came at the door.

"Yes?" she called, really loathing to get up out of the warmth of her bed.

There was a pause, then the door clicked open.

"I brought you the cheese course," Rafferty said, softly like an apology through the crack.

"Oh, okay. Come in," she invited, sitting back up in her bed a bit more.

He pushed the door open, and she saw him carrying a tray. It looked like he had taken one of her cookie sheets and covered it with one of her nicer dishcloths. On one of her new plates was arranged four cheeses, as well as tiny slices of bread spread into an arc on one side. There were also three smaller dishes that she usually used for snacks: one filled with some sort of jam, the other had pear slices in it, and the third had several very tiny pickles. In one corner stood a half glass of white wine.

"What is this?" she asked as she stared at a tray with amazement.

"Like I said, the cheese course," Rafferty replied, setting the tray before her on the bed where her legs were not so it would stay stable. Even though he was careful, the wine threatened to slosh anyway.

"But there is more than cheese here?" she said, rescuing the full glass of white wine before it tipped all over her bed. She took a heady sip and set it on her night table.

"The other flavors enhance the cheeses," he explained and stepped back from her bed, taking a stance beside her with his hands folded in front like a proper waiter. The only problem was he wasn't dressed like a proper waiter at all.

He was back in his human form. Otherwise, she wasn't quite sure what to think as he was only wearing the black dress pants and his black button up shirt, but he hadn't redone the buttons. His feet were bare. It was ... quite a picture.

"You sure you're not an incubus?" she quipped, feeling her cheeks blush.

He furrowed his eyebrows. "What?"

"Are you trying to seduce me or something?" she asked. "You look like you're getting ready for a romance novel cover photo shoot."

He looked down at himself as if he hadn't realized it and then shifted on his feet, looking unsure. "I... I don't have any other clothes. I wouldn't even be wearing this... but I don't know. I guess it didn't feel right to come in without a shirt on at all." His fingers went to the buttons and did up a couple to pull the shirt closed. That was when she noticed he had torn a couple of them off in his rush.

"What about your cooking clothes?" she asked, cocking her head and making herself focus on his face.

"They don't really exist," he said. "They're just created with the body as needed."

Helena took a quick breath in. "Oh no! So you don't have any other clothes unless you conjure them?"

"Yes," he said. "They're gone now. Basically vanished when I took them off."

She realized that had to be true since while the shop clerk had brought them a bag for his other clothes, she had no memory of putting them in the bag, and they certainly hadn't taken them with when they left the clothing store. She hadn't even noticed.

"Should I go take these off?" he asked.

"No! No, it's fine. You look good," then she noticed the twinkling in his eyes. "Oh shut up, you bastard, and sit down." She indicated the other end of her bed opposite the tray. "You're going to join me, right?"

"If you wish," he said and did as he was bid, taking a spot on the other side.

"Okay, cheese course. So what do I do first?" she asked, adjusting the blankets around her legs and focusing all her attention onto the tray.

Rafferty picked up a little card on the side and held it out to her. "They included this in the box."

"The Four Corners of France," she read from the top. Beneath it were listed four cheeses:

Northwest—Camembert de Normandie—a creamy cheese like Brie

Southwest—Roquefort de Midi-Pyrenees—a pungent, semi-soft blue cheese

Southeast—Picodon de Rhone—A goat's milk cheese that is dry and spicy, but smooth in the center

Northeast—Gruyere de Comte—cow's milk cheese, mild and slightly sweet

"The jam goes well with the blue cheese," Rafferty said while she read. He was already wielding a butter knife through it. As he cut, a strong smell wafted into Helena's nose. "It's like Swiss cheese and blue cheese had a baby," she said, noting the Swiss cheese-like holes.

"It's blue cheese, made properly." He held out his prepared offering, the cheese spread on one of the thin slices of bread with a bit of the jam tucked underneath in a similar way to how she had done it with the brie and jam.

Instead of taking it from him, she ducked forward and bit it from his fingers. The second her lips touched his skin, there was an explosion of tangy taste in her mouth, soothed by the calm sweet of the jam. "It's fig," she said around her full mouth.

"Yes," he said, pressing his fingers together a moment to rub them.

"Sorry. Did I bite you?" she asked, noting his gesture.

He cleared his throat. "No, I'm fine. I'm just glad I didn't accidentally steal the memory from you before you got to taste it," he muttered and moved to prepare another one.

"Actually, I've noticed—" she tried to say, but her mouth was too full.

"Do you like it?" Rafferty continued while she chewed.

She nodded. Before he could offer her another one, she used her free hand to redirect it toward his mouth. He barely got it open in time before the redirect upset the morsel, and her fingers continued to follow until they pressed against his lips. She giggled at her trick, but then went still as she felt the sensation moving from his lips into her fingers. Echoes of the tangy cheese and figgy sweet danced through her taste buds along with the electric sensation of his ... kiss.

Chapter 23

WITH WINE PAIRINGS

"I.. sorry," she said, trying to remove her fingers and sure enough, there was a small kissing smack as she pulled them away.

He didn't seem to mind. Instead, he closed his eyes as he chewed, but then his eyebrows started to furrow. Blindly, he recaptured her fingers. Only then did his face smooth out and a warm hum leave his throat.

Helena mentally kicked herself for letting go before he had finished chewing, robbing him of his taste. She also realized he wasn't trying to seduce her and probably didn't have those kinds of feelings at all. Without realizing it, at some point, she had stopped thinking of him as a demon. He was just a person to her, but in truth, he wasn't. He was an alien creature that was pretending to be human, whatever he might have been once.

But she was the one who was human. She was the one getting ideas.

"Okay, what's next?" she asked, refocusing on the plate.

"Take a sip of your wine first," he insisted, gesturing to it.

"Oh!" Helena followed the instructions. "Hmm, that's nice."

"Riesling with the Roquefort."

"Oh so there is a wine pairing with each cheese?"

"Of course," he said as if it was obvious. He dug in his pockets and pulled out four little bottles like one would see during a plane flight. "Champagne with the camembert. Pinot Noir with the comte. Riesling with the Roquefort." He gestured toward her mouth where she had already consumed it.

"And the ... Picodon?" she asked, referencing the card just to be sure.

"They sent a Meursault," he said, reading the label of one of the tiny bottle.

"Not what you'd choose?" she asked, reading his tone.

"No, no, it's fine. I've just never tasted it before," he said and twisted the cap off the neck like he was wringing out a chicken. He took a long sniff from the bottle, then gave a non-committal grunt.

"Take a sip," she offered, setting her hand to his arm.

Instead, he extended the bottle to her. "You gotta taste it first, or there is no memory to pull." A brief flash went through her mind of telling him to drink some first, then kissing him, sharing the wine between them.

She cleared her throat abruptly, then took the wine and sipped it from the bottle. He quickly sliced some of the right cheese off for her. "That's got a—" and then he popped the cheese into her mouth before she could finish speaking.

"Oh, oh that's nice," she said as soon as she swallowed after a lingering chew. Then he brushed his thumb over the corner of her lips, wiping away some crumbs.

"You should have a pickle or a pear to cleanse your palette," he suggested as if nothing had happened, lifting up both dishes from the tray for her to choose from.

"Uh, I guess pear," she said, selecting one of the slices to suck on. "My gosh, this is fun. It's like a game."

"That is why the cheese is a whole course all on its own," her demon explained. "French dining is an art."

"Just ask a French man," she teased.

"I told you, I'm not French anymore. I'm not anything."

"You're my guide through this world, so it's not nothing," she reminded him. "Next cheese, please!" She thrust a finger into the air.

While he prepared the next cracker, Helena watched him. "Would you ever want to go back to France?" she asked.

"I have. Many times," he answered neutrally.

"Really?"

"It used to be the only place I would be summoned," he said. "Then as the world expanded and people traveled beyond their borders and intermixed, the places I would be called to did as well."

"Until you landed here. In the back of my grandma's cookbook," she said. "How ... did you end up in the back of my grandmother's cookbook?"

Rafferty looked up through his eyelashes at her.

"Oh you're not going to tell me?" she accused, recognizing his stoic block tactic.

"I don't exactly know *how* she got the summoning spell for me. But the fact that I now know she was your grandma makes a lot more sense."

"Wait, wait..." Helena said, some things finally occurred to her that she hadn't realized at first. "My grandma only passed a month ago... Did you..." She swallowed, fortifying herself. "Did you have anything to do with that?"

Rafferty straightened, his face a mask again, his eyes distant.

"Rafferty, answer me," she ordered.

"It doesn't matter what I say. If you think *that,* then you aren't going to believe me no matter what I say," he said simply.

"Why would you say that?"

"Because I'm a demon."

Helena huffed a breath. "You know that is getting to be your go-to excuse for everything."

She waited, pressuring him with her eyes to answer her question, and he resisted for quite a while. To dodge her, he kept preparing the cheese morsels, adding different flavors to the different cheeses, but eventually he ran out of bits to put together.

"I didn't know she was dead until you just told me," he said softly. "If she did make a deal that failed and was taken, it wasn't by me. But I don't actually know and, considering who we're talking about, I doubt it."

"So you did know her?"

"We had made a deal once or twice, yes," he said, but he sounded like he was dodging.

Helena wrinkled her nose at that. "Then it is possible to make a deal and not get dragged into hell?"

"Yes, it is," he said, "Otherwise nobody would take the risk."

She thought about that. "I suppose it's like how casinos let a person win big money occasionally to let the others think it's possible."

Rafferty neither confirmed nor denied it, but Helena was pretty confident she was right. "So what did she want from you?"

More of the silent treatment as he picked up one of his prepared tastes and held it out to her.

She regarded it, then raised an eyebrow at him.

"I can't tell you," he said.

"Why?"

"Because that answer would cost you something if I got it for you," he said.

"But—" And again, when her mouth was open, he pushed one of the prepared cheeses into it, stopping her words. He did the same. The taste was mild and slightly sweet. He tapped the Gruyere de Comte part of the card since both their mouths were full. It was nice, but Helena indicated the pinot noir bottle lying on her bedspread. He cracked it and passed it to her while she made sure to touch his knee. Yet he grunted and shook his head, then replaced her hand on a bare section of his chest.

She went still as she touched his skin, feeling his ribs expand with his breath underneath. He breathed? It wasn't until he started snapping beside her face that she realized he had been motioning for her to hurry up and take a drink from the wine bottle.

Skin, she thought. *I must need to be in contact with his skin for the trick to work.* The Pinot and Gruyere together seemed to sweeten both, and finally she had to swallow no matter how much she wanted the taste to last.

"That one was nice," she said aloud, her hand still on his chest, which was much warmer than his hands tended to be. "Why..." then she stopped.

He opened his eyes to look at her. "You ask a lot of questions."

"Well, you're very interesting, and you don't volunteer too much about yourself. So I have no choice but to ask."

"Hmmm," he grunted and plucked a pickle from the dish to hold out to her lips. She wrapped those lips around the small tube, sucking the briny juices into her mouth.

Again she caught herself. *What am I doing? Cut that out,* she chided herself before she bit into the little pickle. She winced at the sharp taste.

"Hmm, does not mix well with the pinot," she commented as she leaned back.

He laughed. "Take a sip of your Riesling. It is light enough that it should help."

She leaned back to grab up the wineglass, and the stretch naturally pulled her hand off of his chest.

There. Safe, she thought. *Sleeping with him would be a bad idea.* She was already sharing the memory of food with him, but to share anything else... well she wasn't about to make a blood sacrifice and the idea of exchanging her body in any way seemed repugnant. *Except, aren't I doing that anyway, by letting him use my tastebuds?* That was an interesting question.

"Okay, then here's a question for you," she said, leaning back in her bed against the headboard with her wine wavering in one hand. "Have you taken other 'payment'

than memories? Or do demons only have their special-
ized 'foods'?"

"That's two questions," he pointed out, catching her
wine to take his own sip to clear his mouth, his hand cupping over her fingers so she didn't completely let it go.

"And you can't answer them because it might cost you?"
she needled.

He studied her face a moment, then stood up.

"If we're going to get into this, then I'm going to get
the dessert course."

She laughed. "Why?"

"Because what I'm going to tell you is going to leave a
bad taste in your mouth."

Chapter 24

FINALLY DESSERT

"**S**o this is like the seven deadly sins?" Helena asked as she took a sip from the small cup of coffee Rafferty had made with the dessert.

"I'm sorry about the inferiority of the brew," he said, indicating her cup. "You don't have a French press, so I had to make do with your coffeemaker."

"Why would I be upset about the coffee if I'm the one who owns the coffeemaker?"

"Well, then it's me I'm apologizing to," he said, taking his own sip and grimacing at the taste.

They were sitting at her dining room table now, enjoying the coffee he made while going over the desserts that had been provided for them. And of course the conversation drifted back to the nature of demons.

"It's not by any means the only way to categorize all of us. It's just a really handy guide to thinking about it."

"Alright, I think I remember this. There is Anger, Gluttony, Lust," she said, ticking off her fingers.

"Good," he nodded.

"Wrath." She stopped furrowing her brows. "No, that's the same as Anger."

"You are correct."

"Slooooth," she said slowly, though she didn't mean it to be funny.

He chuckled anyway, clearly enjoying himself.

"Greed," she added. Then she ticked off her fingers again because she forgot how many she had figured out. "Lust, Greed, Gluttony, Anger/Wrath, Sloth... Okay two more." She wracked her brain, but it just didn't come to her.

"Ugh, okay, I give up. What are the last two?"

He raised his eyebrows at her, teasing that he wasn't going to tell her. "Eeeeee-nnnn-vvvveeee—"

"Envy!" she shouted, which led her to "and Pride. I win!"

He grinned at her. "I'm not surprised you struggled with those last two. You have nothing much to do with envy, do you?" Rafferty said.

Helena shrugged. "I guess not, but Wrath? Oh yeah, been there."

"Really?"

"You should have met me in high school. Or actually it's better that you didn't."

"Better for you that *we* didn't."

That sobered the conversation.

"Like I said, will leave a bad taste in your mouth," Rafferty said, and he wielded a fork on one of the three desserts waiting on the plate between them to try. "Which do you want first: the mini hazelnut dacquoise, raspberry macaron, or mini chocolate ganache cake?"

"Yes, please," she said as a non-answer, smiling. There were in fact two of everything as the restaurant had sent home enough for her and her guest.

He gave her a faux-annoyed look and picked the chocolate ganache. Stabbing the mini dessert with his fork, he lifted the whole thing as one large bite and held it out to her. She opened her mouth and let him feed it to her before she quickly did the same, stabbing the other mini ganache. Her feeding was a bit more awkward, however, since her little cake decided to try to split in half, but it just made them both giggle as he had to chomp at the air to keep from losing it.

"Wow, that is rich," she said around her mouthful as they both savored. "We don't need wine. We need milk."

But as she got up to go get it, Rafferty stood quicker. "I'll go get it," he said and disappeared through the swinging door before she could even object.

"Well, okay," she said to herself and sat back down.

Lacking anything else to do while she waited and not really willing to get up and go find her mobile phone to mess with, she looked down at the plate with the other two desserts. All the offerings were mini versions, again because the chef was trying to showcase what he could do. She was really curious about the mini Hazelnut Dacquoise which was a little meringue layered with chocolate buttercream, the layers on display inside an equally little shot glass. The other delight was a Raspberry Macaron. The chef had stenciled the restaurant's logo on the top of each Macaron, probably with an air sprayer of food coloring, giving them a regal look. Wedged in between each of the dark pink cookies was a lighter pink Chantilly cream.

She couldn't wait to try them and soon enough, Rafferty returned with the palate cleansing milk.

"Okay, so if I were to take a guess," she said after a hearty swallow, "you would be a demon of Gluttony? Because of all the food?"

"Again, this is a hard and fast guideline, not really an official designation, but yes, I do tend to get people whose greatest desires tend to be around consuming more. But I do also get Prideful ones like you nearly as often."

"Prideful?" Helena asked, surprised. "How am I prideful?"

"Well, you just couldn't let yourself be embarrassed in front of your guests that you ruined the meal," he said simply.

"I..." But Helena stopped at that thought, turning it over. "Okay, I can see how that is prideful, but I didn't summon you on purpose because of it. It was an accident. And then once you were there, I didn't know what to do about... well, you. I mean, if I hadn't summoned you, yeah it would have been embarrassing, but I would have sucked it up and ordered Chinese or something. Though I'm sure that wouldn't have impressed Scarlet so much."

"And you wouldn't be winning at life right now," he pointed out.

"And that is the reason you, sir, are even here, being rewarded for helping me out, even though I didn't *need* it." She bowed her head at him. "I am very grateful for your assistance."

He shifted uncomfortably in his seat. "You're welcome," he muttered, then picked up a macaron and popped it into his mouth to cover his discomfort.

"Wait, wait," she said and snatched up hers to join him. "Oh, these are happy cookies."

"All macarons are happy cookies," he agreed.

"Alright then, so you usually get either the gluttonous or the prideful."

"I've seen them all," he stated, followed by a half-shrug.

Helena wrinkled her nose. "Lust?" she asked, ignoring her burning cheeks. "With food?"

"You act like you've never heard of such a thing?" With one finger, he slid one of the shot glasses over the plate toward her slowly to the sound of glass rubbing on glass. She looked from the dessert to him, wondering if what she thought he was implying was what he was implying or was she just reading into his human-like gestures again.

"Last one," she declared and picked up the dessert spoon that she didn't even know she had until Rafferty pulled them out from where they had been buried in her silverware drawer.

"Try to get all the layers onto your spoon at once if you can," he advised, and they scooped together.

"After this, I'm going to need to work out for a week," but before she could take a bite, he took his spoon and slid it down the side of her face, spreading the creamy dessert there.

"Hey!" she squealed at the sudden cold. Her hand reacted to slap to her cheek, but Rafferty caught it before she could. "What are you—" Then his tongue slipped up the side of her face, lapping up the cream. She went still, her eyes going wide as he removed the sugary damage he had done in one long, sensual swipe. Then he leaned back, smirking.

This time she moved to touch her cheek and he let go. "You... you should have asked for permission to do that," she said softly.

His smirk dropped away, his eyes showing concern and maybe a little confusion.

"I showed you what a Lust summoner would want with food..." He sat back then. She could see his walls coming back up, but she didn't care.

"I didn't ask you to demonstrate."

They stared at each other for a very pregnant moment. Then abruptly, he stood up and backed away from the table. "I made a mistake. I apologize." He bowed to her.

Helena picked up her napkin to wipe at her cheek, unable to meet his eyes.

"I will leave you," he said.

"No, Rafferty. Please wait," she said, belatedly, standing up to stop him with a hand on his arm. He did, turning back to her but keeping his gaze over her head.

She took a breath, but it was hard. "It's not ... that I didn't like it." She still couldn't look up at him. "You just didn't ask me is all."

"It would not be unreasonable for you to be disgusted by me," he stated. He still wouldn't look at her, just kept his gaze up over her head, staring into the middle distance, the formality his shield.

"I'm not disgusted by you," she said and took his hand so he could feel her touching him. "You're just a person."

He flinched under her touch, and she pressed her warmth into his coldness.

"I..." he started. They both seemed mesmerized by where their hands connected. "I didn't give you permission to touch me," he said, the ghost of a quip.

"Do you want me to stop?" she asked, matching his softness.

"I..." He cleared his throat. "You don't need my permission to do anything. I am your demon, summoned to your will. You can do whatever you like with and to my body, make me perform any act, any degradation."

"Is that..." She stopped. She knew human nature had a capacity for a great many terrible things. A few of them she could only imagine, but even imagining them was terrible. "That is what has happened to you."

"Better to endure those things in reality than the alternative," he said with the sort of strength that came because someone had suffered much.

"I'm so sorry, Raffie," she said and lifted his hand up to hold against her cheek.

"Don't. Don't pity me. I deserve this."

She shook her head. "No, nobody deserves this."

Chapter 25

LUNCH WITH CINDY

"**I** just don't know what to think about him, you know?" Helena asked as she held onto her glass of water. The cool condensation on the surface made the texture glass slick. It was very sunny for a winter day, though there was no snow on the ground to let anyone know it was winter other than the time of year. She had left Rafferty at her place so she could run to the office for a weekend meeting that came up at the last minute, which she could not have imagined doing before her promotion.

Luckily, Cindy was just getting off from work herself, so they were meeting for lunch.

After the ... events of last night, she thought she and Rafferty needed a little space from each other.

"If I'm honest, Chris is more your friend than mine," Cindy said, taking a long drag from her own glass.

"Yeah, but you know him enough. Do you think I'm misreading the situation?" Helena asked, hoping her friend could see how since she really couldn't.

"Here—just let me repeat it back to you to make sure I understand. You were out on a dinner date at Tower Top restaurant, and you saw Chris there ... with a woman ... and they were making out."

"Strictly, I only saw them kiss once," Helena declared. "But it wasn't a very chaste kiss. And by that I mean, it wasn't pornographic, but I wouldn't kiss my mother that way."

"Got it. Picture crystal clear," Cindy said as she brought her hands together in a prayer position that she pressed against her lips while she thought. "And then after that, he spotted you, came over and confronted you, and had to be chased off by the waiter."

"Yeah, before Rafferty and him came to blows, and I really thought it might happen there for a moment," Helena added.

Cindy nodded. "Mmm-hmmm, mmm-hmmm, okay. One question: Who is Rafferty?"

Helena felt the bottom drop out of her stomach. "Oh, right. Who is Rafferty," she repeated in a tone of voice that she recognized meant that anything she said after would immediately sound like a lie.

"He... is..." She sighed. There was no help for it. "You remember a few weeks ago I had that dinner party?"

"You mean that dinner party that changed the course of my life with its food and made me change my orientation to foodie? No, doesn't ring a bell. Continue," Cindy quipped.

"Well, you remember the guy I had over who helped me get the dinner together after I had bombed it initially?"

Cindy's eyebrows puckered. "The caterer? I thought his name was Lares."

At the sound of that name, Helena felt like she had been used as a clapper inside an enormous bell. "Lares?" she repeated. Even as she said the name, she realized it sounded familiar and at the same time felt like it was the first time she was hearing it. *He told me he ate his name so I couldn't summon him with it,* she remembered.

"Uh, yeah. Lares Rafferty, but he prefers to be called Rafferty," she said, adjusting the lie to fit the truth.

"Oh weird. That's very old world of him," Cindy said, wrinkling her nose.

"Well, when your name is Lares Rafferty, I can understand wanting to minimize the weird," Helena joked.

"I suppose that's fair," Cindy allowed, then leaned forward to rest her chin on her fingers joined like a little platform. "So tell me, you guys have been making sparks in the kitchen since?"

No power in the world could have stopped Helena from both blushing and smiling like an idiot. She was forced to hide her face while Cindy squealed.

"No, no, no! It's not like that," Helena tried to say, but it was useless and made her friend's hooting worse. "We're just friends!"

"The best relationships are with your friend! It's like you've not watched the literal show on the subject *Friends* or something!"

"Okay, Monica and Chandler aside, Rafferty and I, we're just enjoying each other's company right now. He's ... got a lot going on in his life right now and..."

"Do you like him?" Cindy asked, slapping her hand dramatically down on the table, which was thankfully clear of dishes except for their water glasses. "The court demands answers!"

"Dammit, Cindy, you're a doctor, not a lawyer." Helena laughed. "And I barely know him, okay?"

"You just took him out on a date to a very fancy and very romantic French restaurant."

"It was on the company dime," she defended.

"Just because you did it the smart way doesn't mean it wasn't romantic," Cindy countered. "What did you have to eat?"

"Quail, actually," Helena said, grinning. "It was very grown up." Then her face fell. "Which is why it is so disappointing that it had to end like that. I basically ran away after Chris got all up in my face about being there."

"What they should have done was ask Chris and his hussy to leave," Cindy sneered.

Helena sat up a little straighter. "You did not just do that."

"What?" Cindy asked.

"You just slut shamed a woman we don't even know because of the behavior and choices of a man we do," she said, completely serious.

Cindy's face froze a second as she took that in, and for a half-beat of her heart, Helena thought she was going to argue about it, but then she dropped her shoulders and nodded wearily.

"You are right. I did just do that, and I am ashamed. The programming runs deep," Cindy said formally.

Helena nodded. "For all we know, he could have lied to her about being single or just hasn't even told her yet, and as far as *she* knows, they are dating legitimately."

Cindy winced. "I'm sorry, Hel. I forgot about Shawna."

Needles pressed into Helena's throat, but she ignored them. "And we're not going to talk about Shawna. We're talking about Chris and what you think I should do with regard to what I saw and what I should or shouldn't tell Charlie. Because I know I would have liked to know when it had been me, but I…" She stopped and huffed. "But at the same time, I know there were several points I wouldn't have listened…" She stopped herself and corrected again. "I *didn't* listen, and I *own* that, but it also cost me several friends."

"Not all of them," Cindy said, reaching out to squeeze her hand.

Helena squeezed it back. "And I'm grateful for that every day of my life, Cin," she assured.

"And now I'm going to ask you…" Cindy warned. "Are these the reasons you aren't giving yourself a shot with Lares… Rafferty?" she added belatedly.

"No, sincerely." Helena shook her head. "He can't stay and so it would be a short fling anyway."

"And what's wrong with a short fling?" Cindy challenged.

"I have had plenty of them to know it's not what I want," Helena said.

Cindy's face became grave. "Hellie, I … had a patient die the other day."

That surprised Helena. "Cin, I'm—"

"He was a young guy like us," Cindy continued as if she didn't hear her. "He had just gotten married, like a month ago or something. He was fine last week and then he got bacterial meningitis. Killed him within hours. Even after we did everything we could to save him, we just couldn't. I was the one who talked to his widow."

She took a drink of water to clear her thickening voice. Helena squeezed Cindy's hand to let her know she was still there, still present.

She continued, "I can't honestly remember much of what we said, or even how this came up, but one of the things this woman said while we talked was ... she didn't regret marrying him, even though their time together was so short. That even if she had known this would happen, it was better than never having spent any of that time with him at all. Because then she would have lost that as well."

Cindy cleared her throat. "I think what I'm trying to say is, no matter how long or short your time with anybody is, it's never forever. You're going to have to let them go eventually, so that shouldn't stop you from being with them now."

They sat in silence with that for a long while until the waiter finally returned with their lunch plates.

"I'm sorry that happened to you, Cin," Helena said as she laid her napkin on her lap, feeling her words were totally inadequate and yet having nothing else to offer.

Cindy perked up and flashed a pained smile. "It's the job I chose. It has its good days and bad days, but if I wasn't there to do it, they would all be bad days."

"Okay, well that makes lunch on me," Helena said, trying to lift up the heavy mood as she made adjustments to her turkey BLT and French onion soup plate. It seemed perfect after all the rich food she'd had the night before. "And let me ask you this: how would you feel if a guy licked you?"

Cindy eyed her as she chewed around a full mouth of her Greek sandwich. "I guess I would need to know the context."

"It was something..." Helena hesitated. "Sorry, I don't know how I feel about it myself, but..." She sighed. Too late to back out now. "It happened last night. With Rafferty."

"Oh," Cindy said, her eyes twinkling now. "You were holding out on me. And now I need all the gory details. Spill it."

"We were trying to enjoy the desserts from the restaurant at home, and we had this layered thing with chocolate and cream, and we were about to eat, and we were talking about ... food and sexy play, and then he sort of slapped some of his dessert, you know, on my cheek and then licked it off."

Cindy's eyebrows kept rising as Helena spoke. "Oh. Wow. Okay, that's a lot to break down."

"Like I said, I just don't know how to feel about it. I think he was teasing me because you know we were talking about it and being silly, but it sort of threw me off because I was suddenly uncomfortable, but I know that wasn't what he intended, and now it all feels funny, and I don't know... I don't know... I just don't know."

Before Cindy could answer, Helena's eyes landed on the last person she wanted to see, just before he walked up to the table.

"Hi Yosef," Helena said, forcing her smile.

"Cityside catering called. They want an appointment today," he stated, holding out the message to her.

"Did ... you come to find me?" she asked, taking it.

"No, I just happened to see you," he said, acknowledging Cindy. "You better get going if you want to make it." Then he was gone.

Cindy's beeper went off. "And just like that, there's lunch. Well good luck with that. I'll call later and we can finish talking." Then she too was gone.

That left Helena no choice but to run too.

Chapter 26

IT'S NOT
OPERA CAKE

"Thank you for coming with me to this," Helena said to Rafferty as they walked up the sidewalk to the restaurant where the tasting was being held. It looked like it was part bakery, part catering service, with a window full of different kinds of cakes lined up as examples.

Rafferty grunted an acknowledgement, his hair dancing in the air as he squinted in the sun.

It occurred to Helena that she should get him some sunglasses. As well as some other clothes. They had made do with the clothes she had bought him yesterday. She had washed his shirt in her laundry, reattached most of the buttons, and he had ironed it himself once she showed him how the electric one worked. Apparently, the process of ironing hadn't changed much in the last few hundred years, and the only difference was hers heated up with electricity, not from being set on the hot oven or hearth.

For his pants, she did a quick spot clean since they were supposed to be dry clean only. Since he had only worn them a few hours, she figured they were squeaking by until after she could run him to Target or Kohls or something and get him more clothes. It was what credit cards were for anyway.

For now, they both had to settle with him looking like a semi-casual black shadow with his jacket and no tie. She dressed in a long wool skirt and cream blouse bundled under her winter coat. He didn't seem to mind the cold though.

"A little background information: I haven't had the best interaction with these people so far, and now I wish I had canceled the tasting, but I figured, let's just get it done, and if it's a complete bomb, we can go get something else afterward, okay?"

Rafferty grunted, and she grabbed the door to open for both of them.

The inside of the place smelled of baking goods, but with something else sour underneath, though putting her finger on that smell proved impossible. It did nothing to change her impression of the business. There was a long L-shaped counter that filled the space with glass in front to display a bunch of other baked goods, everything from cookies to pastries to more cakes like those in the window. An annoyed looking woman stood behind the counter helping another customer, her frizzy hair barely contained inside a hairnet.

Helena and Rafferty waited.

Then Rafferty made a non-committal grunt in his throat. Glancing up at him, he stood there with his arms crossed, staring down at the display case with a grumpy look on his face. She leaned in, grabbing his upper arm to pull him down a bit toward her so she could whisper more or less in his ear.

"What is it?" she asked.

"Those aren't opera cakes," he growled.

She glanced at the case, noting the small sign amongst a bunch of vertical-layered cakes that read "Opera Cakes" in flowery handwriting.

"What are they?" she asked.

"I have no idea, but those aren't it," he stated.

She grinned quietly and said no more as it was their turn to step up to the counter.

"How can I help you?" the woman said, not to Helena who had been the one to step up and try to engage with her. She directed her question poignantly to Rafferty over her shoulder as if Helena wasn't there.

He blinked, as surprised as Helena felt, and raised a hand to indicate the woman should talk to the human in front of her.

The woman's lips thinned with annoyance, and then she directed her harsh gaze to Helena. "How can I help *you*?" she repeated.

Helena put on a friendly face. "Hi, my name is Helena Rhodes from Scarlet Promotions. I'm here for the tasting on behalf of the Winter Rose Ball."

"Right," the other woman said and turned to go back through a pair of industrial swinging doors.

Helena stood there, stunned and unsure of what to do with no instructions. She glanced back at Rafferty, who seemed extremely bored, his arms recrossed as he moved back and forth a few steps.

"Okay, I guess we'll wait here," she said, wondering again what the consequences would be if she just left.

Ugh, I can't do that to Scarlet's reputation, she thought with an internal sigh.

To her relief, the woman came back a few minutes later.

"Come on," she said curtly and led them back into a large industrial-level kitchen, where people were moving about making huge trays of baked goods. The unpleasant woman led them to a table that looked out of place, set in a corner with a pair of gold-covered chairs with pristine white seats. The table was set with a nice dining set of white plates with gold edging. A water glass and wine glass waited with a carafe of clear water next to a basket of covered bread rolls in the middle. Flanking them were two small dishes, each with little scooped mounds of butter. The butters were odd though: one seemed to have little flecks of something golden in them and the other was more of a pink color. The final touch on the table was a beautiful bouquet of white and purple orchids.

"Feel free to take all the pictures you want," the curt woman said, indicating the table. "The Executive Chef will be with you soon."

"Oh, yes. Thank you," Helena said. The woman did not appreciate the thanks. Just walked off before Helena had finished speaking to head back up toward the front. "Okay, well the layout looks really nice. Pros and cons so far," she said softly to Rafferty.

For his part, Rafferty moved up to the closest chair and pulled it out for her to sit.

"Thank you, sir," she said to him, nodding her head, and sat down at the table with a view of the kitchen. Then she slid out her phone and did as she had been instructed, taking pictures of the layout.

Once Rafferty sat in the other chair, they both regarded the clanking chaos around them.

"Not the same sort of view as our other date," she noted.

He grunted, watching attentively as a pair of men watched a giant mixing arm turn and beat some sort of dough in a kettle large enough for Baba Yaga to boil a couple of children in.

"I wonder what they're making," she asked.

He partially stood up to look over the vast counters at someone with several baking sheets laid out beside him. He grunted. "That's the thing," he muttered. "He's making that fake Opera Cake over there."

"You want to go over and check it out?" Helena asked, but Rafferty shook his head. "Why not?"

"I do not have permission to enter the kitchen," he said and left it at that.

They sat together companionably, waiting for someone to arrive to give them more information about what was about to happen. Helena wished she could bring herself to talk to him about what happened last night. They had parted ways shortly after the licking moment, her going to her bedroom and him cleaning up the dishes. She just didn't know how she really felt about it and wished Cindy had helped her solve it.

Now sitting there with Rafferty, she thought, *Or I could just be a big girl and solve it myself.* But she still had no idea what to do or say.

But she knew she did have one really big, awkward question to ask.

Rafferty, do you find me attractive? she thought. Only that was not how she wanted to phrase it at all. *Why did you lick me last night? What does it mean? Were you trying to seduce me, or were you just trying to prove a point? What would happen if I slept with a demon? Would I be cursed? He said it was one of the things I could exchange for service from him, but is that all it is to him, or could he have relations on his own time too?*

None of these were questions she felt like she could ask in the middle of a room full of strangers, even if none of those people were paying any attention to them. The fact that there was a big ass crucifix on the wall framed by pictures of saints didn't help things either.

Rafferty himself had given her no further clues since yesterday. He had made her breakfast again that morning and then accepted graciously that she needed to run into work and then had been just as gracious when she returned to take him to the tasting for dinner. She didn't know what he was doing with himself while she was gone. Her place hadn't been overwhelmed by another feast for a thousand, but she figured he was at least getting a lot of good rest...

She furrowed her eyebrows as something occurred to her. "Rafferty ... where are you sleeping at night?"

Chapter 27

IT WASN'T
EVEN GOOD

Rafferty looked at her side eyed. "I..." Then he grunted a sigh. "I am in the kitchen," he said.

"You're sleeping in the kitchen?!" she said, surprised.

"Not exactly in the way you are thinking," he said cryptically.

"I guess I'm picturing you laying on the tiled floor," she said.

"What else is in the kitchen?" Rafferty asked. "On your tiled floor?"

It took a second, then she remembered, though for some reason it was difficult. *The circle,* she thought but didn't dare say out loud.

"Right," was all she did dare, and they both nodded in their mutual understanding.

But she still had more questions. "So why are you resting in there?"

"It is decreasing the imposition of having me in your house," he said.

"Okay, I can't tell how you mean that."

"Shh," he hissed just as an older man approached their table.

The older man was dressed like everyone else in the room, in white chef's clothes with a small toque over his head that fit close to his head. Yet despite his lack of an ostentatious toque, he wore a pin over his chest that read "Executive Chef." He had his knobby hands clasped in front of his body as he approached the table and smiled a grin that lacked enough teeth.

"Welcome, welcome," he said warmly. "You are Scarlet Kovacs, I presume?" he said in a thick Polish accent that almost was unintelligible.

"Oh, no, I am Helena Rhodes. I am representing Scarlet's firm for this tasting for the Winter Rose Ball," Helena said, standing up to take his hands. To her surprise, he stood a foot shorter than her, but she wasn't quite sure if that was because he was so short or because of how badly he was bent over. At her declaration, the Executive Chef's face fell.

"You are not Scarlet?" he asked, sounding hurt.

Helena felt awful at his distress. "I represent Scarlet," she said, desperate to clarify. "I am her deputy for organizing the Winter Rose Ball. Scarlet couldn't come today."

It was a kind of truth.

The Executive Chef took his hands back from her a little too sharply, still looking like a hurt child. "I do not understand. What is this woman saying to me?" he demanded, looking around at the nearby workers who frankly hadn't been paying attention and so had no idea what was going on.

Helena tried not to be offended. "I'm sorry for the confusion," she said and gestured for Rafferty to stand up. "If you would like, we can go?"

Please let us leave, please let us leave, please let us leave, she thought over and over.

The Executive Chef, who still hadn't introduced himself by his name, crossed and uncrossed his arms in a petulant huff. "No, you will stay. I already cooked." Then he seemed to think of something, and he pointed his finger to the ceiling to shake it at her. "You will tell Scarlet how good it is and she will come," he declared as if by doing so it made it true.

Helena had half a thought to argue about it but decided against it. This man clearly wasn't used to being countermanded at all.

She turned back to Rafferty, who stood at his seat waiting for her to make a decision.

She shrugged. "We might as well stay and have dinner," she said.

He grunted and nodded, then stepped over to pull out her seat again while the Executive Chef walked off muttering.

"Well, this is definitely not going well," she whispered.

Rafferty grunted a nod. All the grunting was getting annoying.

"Okay, why aren't you talking to me?" she asked.

He flinched and she realized that he was deliberately doing that and hadn't expected to be called out on it. To her surprise, knowing that hurt a little bit.

"You've been giving me grunts and minimal answers all day. The most interesting thing you've said so far has been about the Opera Cake, and now you're stonewalling me. Why are you playing games with me?"

He didn't answer that, only looked away.

Realizing that wasn't the right answer to the situation, Helena resettled in her seat and decided to start trying out the different butters until she thought of what the next right move might be.

Then Rafferty said, "I thought you were going to send me back."

Hand paused on the breadbasket, Helena looked up at him. "What?"

"After last night, I have been waiting for you to send me back."

"I'm not going to send you back," she assured.

"Why?" he demanded.

Helena huffed and then stabbed at one of the pink scoops to smear across the crackly roll she opened. "I don't have to answer why," she said when she couldn't come up with a good why in words. At least not one that involved diving into some dark places in her own history in order to explain.

Rafferty shook his head. "I do not understand you."

"What's not to understand?" She took a bite of the pink smeared roll and creamy strawberries burst over her tongue. "Oh my gosh," she said looking down at it as she chewed. "Oh damn that's heavenly."

She held some out to him to bite, which he did after only a half second's hesitation. Laying her hand on his, the strawberry flavor bumped up to eleven, as well as the

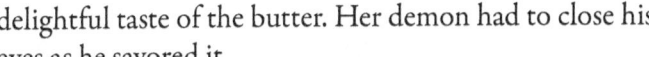

delightful taste of the butter. Her demon had to close his eyes as he savored it.

"You haven't eaten all day, have you?" she asked. They hadn't shared tastes at her breakfast. He had just served her and gone back into the kitchen, which she had been grateful for at the time. And then she had lunch out...

"No," he admitted softly.

"I'm sorry," she said.

"I'm sorry, too. For last night. I got greedy and wanted too much," he said and Helena's heart started beating double time at the implication.

"What did you want, exactly?" she finally asked, daring him to meet her eyes and be honest.

"There isn't a word to sum up what I want—what I have no right to have. You give me so much freely: your time, your companionship, the tastes, God, the tastes." He touched his lips as if his tongue was an organ he had only just discovered. "And you don't want anything in exchange for it."

"Yeah, but what more did *you* want?" she asked, willing him to say it, the thing she was afraid of giving voice to.

He drew himself up as if fortifying himself for her rejection. "I wanted to feel your touch," he confessed.

It wasn't quite right. It wasn't exactly what she wanted to hear, but it was so close. So very close to the right thing, the thing she couldn't define but had absolute faith that she would when she heard it. It wasn't something as simple as saying "I love you"; it was something more true.

"You mean, you did want ... *that*, last night." She waggled her eyebrows as if making a joke, but it felt so very wrong in comparison to the soft, gentle words he was saying. Yet he blushed all the same.

"I have no right."

"Damn right, you don't," Helena confirmed softly, then caressed her hand over his larger one, up the bareness of his wrist to brush back the hairs of his forearm. "But you could have privileges."

He stared at her for a long moment, unbelieving, his gaze so intense, the black stars in his eyes smoldered and burst. She should have been intimidated by their unearthliness, but now, she just knew they were his eyes.

And if anyone else saw them doing that, they would be in trouble. Quickly, Helena covered his eyes with her hand, glancing around to see if anyone else there had noticed. No one seemed alarmed or panicked.

"I think we need to stop flirting now, or we are both going to be in big trouble. And we need to get you some sunglasses," she whispered.

The long fingers on his hand lifted to touch the back of hers as if he were only just realizing what had happened. "Agreed. Speak of something else."

Helena's mind raced for a new topic, but the only things going on in her life at the moment outside of Rafferty was Yosef driving her crazy and what to do about Chris—

"Oh damn," Helena cursed, suddenly remembering. "I forgot to get some advice from Cindy about Chris and Charlie."

Rafferty pulled down her hand to look at her, and to her relief, his eyes had returned to a more human-like black or what people thought of as dark, dark brown.

"What about them?" he asked, sitting back as another person dressed like everyone else in the room approached and set two salads before them, along with two dishes of some sort of dressing.

Blowing out a breath, Helena looked down at what was frankly a disappointing salad, iceberg lettuce broken up rather than shredded with bits of carrot sprinkled over it and two radishes halved each. That was about it. "I just need to decide if I should tell Charlie or not about Chris's alleged infidelity. It seems if I do either, I'm screwed."

"Yes, you are," he said simply.

"Oh. Well, I'm glad we sorted that out," Helena said dryly. Served her right for asking a demon.

"Did he bring us the meal for the horse?" Rafferty asked, poking at his salad.

"I don't know, but if you don't want to taste it, I'd understand," she said, using what little detective skills she had to determine what kind of dressing was in the dishes before them. She decided to go with the one that looked like a vinaigrette and ladled it over her portion of iceberg.

"No, I will taste it," he said, choosing the same dressing.

As soon as they took a bite, Rafferty let go of her hand and took the fork out of her mouth, then slid the plate away from her. "Do not eat that. The dressing is rancid," he reported. Helena was already grabbing her napkin to deposit what food remained in her mouth.

"I didn't think we upset him that badly by not being Scarlet," she coughed.

"If your boss had been here, she would have been poisoned already," Rafferty said direly.

Chapter 28

THEN IT GOT WORSE

The following courses did not improve. Whatever course plan the "Executive Chef" was following was not modeled off of anything Helena recognized. They were able to finish some of the simple salad with the other dressing, which proved to be a basic ranch, eating enough of a dent to make Helena not feel guilty about sending the plates back. The rancid salads were followed by a soup that was basically broth. Its only sin was it hadn't been impressive, but its virtue was it helped wipe out the remaining taste of the bad salads.

Now she stared in horror at the main course.

"I don't think I can eat that," she said.

"Penne pasta, fried chicken breasts with a layer of cheese," Rafferty reported, diagnosing the dish with a detached, clinical eye.

"It looks like a cat vomited it up," she said. Holding her knife and fork before her on the table like weapons of war, she prayed that someone would come and intervene, whisk the plates away and present her with something that actually looked like food.

But Rafferty cut into his chicken fried penne pasta and even dabbed it into the marinara sauce in preparation for them eating it. She had no choice but to do the same.

It tasted like metal.

"Oh God, this is awful," she huffed under her breath as she tried to chew the lukewarm meat in mouth.

"Hmm-mmm," Rafferty agreed, still chewing his food with the normal amount of gusto.

"I don't suppose you could do the reverse thing where you can just make it taste like ash to me. Because honestly that would be an improvement right now."

He shook his head to that request while continuing to chew, his eyes staring off in the middle distance, like he was trying to figure something out. Helena had no idea what there was to figure out. It was the blandest damn marinara she had ever tasted, and there was no way any of this was fresh. It all had to have come from a can. And the chicken had obviously been frozen.

Dropping her silverware onto her plate, she picked up her napkin and pressed it to her mouth. "I think I'm going to be sick."

"Hmm," Rafferty said, unperturbed as he cut another piece with the side of his fork while keeping a hand on the back of hers so he could still taste it.

Helena let him and reached for a glass of water to wash out her remaining discomfort. The whole meal, no one had come to give them any wine for their empty wine glasses and frankly, she hoped they never did. It made it easier to not think well of any of them.

Unfortunately, the young man who brought them all the courses returned, empty-handed.

"Chef asked me to inquire about what you think of your meal?" he asked in a bored-tone, but the way he was blinking made her think he might be more exhausted than bored.

"It's terrible," Rafferty declared with no preamble or hint of regret.

Helena almost choked.

The kitchen worker's eyebrows rose up in his first real expression of the meeting.

Rafferty took that as permission to elaborate. "It's undercooked and made with pre-prepared ingredients. There are no seasonings to even speak of, and I would even question the food safeness of any of this. I'm advising my client here to not finish her meal as I am genuinely concerned for food poisoning."

He stood up then and offered his hand to help Helena up out of her chair.

The worker grew alarmed, raising his own hands as if to stop them. "But wait—there is a dessert," he said.

"Is it that Opera Cake over there?" Rafferty asked, gesturing at the worker who had stopped mid-icing along with the rest of the workers around the room to stare at the drama happening.

"Uh, yeah... I think so," the worker said, at a loss.

"Then we'll take that to-go, and I can let you know my thoughts," Rafferty declared, then looked to Helena. "We can wait a few moments with your permission?"

Helena wasn't sure if his intention was to empower her in this moment or throw her under the bus, but she nodded as her mind raced to save the situation. Though it would help if she knew whether she needed to save it for or from. "Yes, of course."

"Uh, okay," the worker said, more deflated than when he had come over initially. Helena knew he had to be bracing, and she was certain the Executive Chef was going to rage. She expected it would be in Polish as well.

Sure enough, after a few minutes of their standing there, waiting for the dessert to come back, an enraged voice echoed through the strangely quiet kitchen. Every worker had stopped and held their breath as a string of incomprehensible words followed by some fantastic metallic crashes came from behind a closed pair of double doors. Standing up, Helena could see that the pair of doors had a plate next to them that read "The Executive Kitchen."

"This is a nightmare," Helena murmured.

The double doors slammed open, making a horrible, sharp noise as they hit either side of the entryway, revealing the Executive Chef as he marched through to point an accusing finger at Helena.

Another litany of angry Polish words slapped her in the face, but she had no idea what he was specifically saying.

The woman from the front rushed past, her haggard, tired face now alarmed and fearful. Helena felt terrible as she realized that this woman was probably his daughter and the extent of their history was on full display for everyone present as she tried to stand in front of him, speaking urgently and soothingly at her irate father.

The old man never looked at her but kept his fiercely angry eyes on Helena the whole time. She was pretty sure if he felt like tearing her throat out with his own teeth, he would. Finally, pushing past his daughter, knocking her back into one of the kitchen workers, he charged straight for the source of his ire.

Startled, Helena tried to back away when Rafferty stepped between them.

"Oh, you think I'm intimidated by you!" the Executive Chef shouted, completely unimpressed. "I will kick your ass right here!" He made some rude gestures and slapped his chest as if daring Rafferty to hit him. Then he spit at Helena over Rafferty's shoulder.

Quicker than a human should have moved, Rafferty blocked the spittle with a sharply raised hand.

It was all the signal the Executive Chef needed, however, taking the gesture as an attack and swung his own fist at Rafferty's head. This the demon did not block or duck, but took full on the cheek, throwing his whole body to one side and half bent over. The older man then stepped up and seemed to be attempting to slam his knee repeatedly into Rafferty's stomach but did not have the height or the weight to be very effective with it. By then, several of the kitchen workers fell on their boss to pull him off and away from the actually more dangerous man.

Helena, for her part, dived for Rafferty, grabbing the back of his jacket in a mindless, animal instinct to pull him away from the fight and out of reach of the Executive Chef's attacks.

The grown daughter had come forward by then, standing between the two men, but shouting at Rafferty that she was going to call the police and report them for attacking her father.

"What!? He attacked him!" Helena tried to defend, but the woman seemed to think she could win her argument by shouting louder and more incoherently, getting right up into Helena's face as if she too was ready to throw down on her.

"I'm fine," Rafferty said, sticking his arm between the two women.

The daughter glared up at him in challenge, only for her eyes to widen rounder than saucers. Instantly she muttered something and crossed herself, backing up quickly and Helena knew what she had seen and who it would implicate.

She grabbed Rafferty's shoulder and turned him away, now terrified. "We need to go now!" she ordered and he came willingly. Sure enough, his eyes were smoldering with unholy starfire.

Ironically, the worker who had been serving them stood near the exit, holding a paper take out box as he stared with his own wide eyes at the whole situation.

Helena moved to rush past, but Rafferty plucked the box out of his hands, startling the man.

"Thank you," Rafferty said, slapping the man on the arm in a friendly way and followed Helena straight out of the kitchen, the shop, and back to the safety of the city streets.

"Holy shit. I can't believe that just happened," Helena said, shaking from the whole encounter.

"Are you alright?" Rafferty asked, following beside her, clutching their contraband in his hands.

"No, I am not alright!" she declared in no uncertain terms. Her whole self was shaking so badly, and she wanted to scream and run and fight and rage...

"It's okay. I'm here." She found herself pushed into a nearby alley, out of the sight and sound of the main road, which wasn't that busy actually with only a few cars rolling by and a couple of people walking dogs at that time of early evening. It was dim in the alley and there was a doorway sunken into one of the buildings that made a walled-in alcove that no one could see from the street. The door was boarded up, so no one was coming out of the building either.

Wings were around her then. A dark, leathery wall encompassed her while arms did the same, holding her close against a strong, sturdy body. Naturally, she tucked her face into the crook where the neck and the shoulder met, and she gripped a waist that didn't flinch with how tightly she squeezed. She even felt a tail wrap around her bare ankles, and she didn't care how weird that was. She wanted all of it, to be held by Rafferty's whole self.

"Oh God, I was so scared," Helena said.

"I'm here. I wouldn't have let him hurt you," the chest she clung to rumbled.

"Oh God, your face!" she said, leaning up to try to look at it, but the arms squeezed tighter to try to keep her from moving away.

"Please don't. Don't look at me like this. Just let me hold you, please."

She realized then that he was shaking too.

"It's okay. It's okay, Raffie," she soothed, drawing more strength from soothing than being soothed. She laid her head on his chest and sank into the spicy aroma of his natural self. He still wore the black shirt, the cloth the only thing between her cheek and his heartbeat.

She had no idea how long they stayed that way, but after her own heartbeat had calmed and the shaking for both of them had subsided, she asked, "Do you want to go get Thai food?"

Chapter 29

SO WE WENT FOR THAI

"**S**ee? I told you these were much better noodles than what that Executive Chef made!" Helena crowed delightedly as she spooled some crinkly glass noodles into her mouth.

"Yes, but that was never going to be much of a stretch," Rafferty argued before he tucked the same thing into his own mouth.

They were sitting on a pair of stools, like at the outdoor eatery kitchens in Asia, at one of Helena's favorite places on Little Thai street. The street itself wasn't actually officially called "Little Thai" street, but all the locals called it that, probably for marketing reasons, and every sort of Thai food could be found on that street so it fit. There was even an Asian grocery store at the end of the street that catered not only to the restaurants but to patrons who wanted to try to capture those flavors at home. Or could at least try.

To Helena, this felt more like a date than their meal at the Tower Top Restaurant. They had a perfect pair of seats, right in front of the outdoor heater that was going at full blast against the winter night. While perched on their stools with big ceramic bowls before them, their feet were crossed together at the ankles, so they could touch and eat with both of their hands at the same time. It felt like she was playing footsie with him, and to anyone else not them, that was exactly what it looked like, but she also didn't care. She was enjoying herself too freaking much.

The food itself was her favorite. Glass noodles, made from bean sprouts, with shitake mushrooms, slivers of carrot, bamboo shoots, green onions, and little slices of green bell pepper, tossed with shrimp. Mildly spicy.

Rafferty scooped some floppy mushrooms into his mouth, fumbling with his chopsticks. "Dammit," he muttered when he lost one, managing to catch it with his bowl.

"It's not so easy, is it?" Helena teased, delicately plucking one of his mushrooms to feed it to him from her own chopsticks. He ate, even as he shot her a black, annoyed look that she just couldn't take seriously anymore. He had returned once more to a normal-looking guy, and she had never felt safer than when she was with him.

Carefully, she helped him reclaim his chopsticks and guided his fingers to hold them properly again. "I can't believe in all your years of cooking, you never once needed to make Asian cuisine."

"It just never came up," he admitted, his eyes wandering over to the cooks behind the bar itself, stirring, sautéing, and flipping their woks full of colorful vegetables and different meats.

One of the cooks came up, his eyes smiling as big as his mouth, to set a small plate of fried dumplings between them with a soy dipping sauce.

"You want to learn how to make all this, don't you?"

"I am not worthy," he said absent-mindedly, and Helena slapped his knee with an open palm, making him jump.

"Hey, stop that," she chided gently. "It doesn't matter if you're worthy or not. It's about living and you're currently alive, so live now while you can."

He eyed her but didn't argue as he slid another mouthful of noodles into his mouth, more or less with the chopsticks. With his face slightly turned like that, she could see the bruise forming around his left eye. It was clearly red and swollen. She wanted to touch it but knew that it would only cause him more pain.

"We should get some ice on your eye," she noted, hovering her hand over it.

"I'll be okay. I've had far, far worse," he said. "When I rest tonight, it will vanish."

"And that is far, far from the point," she replied. "I can't believe you just took the punch like that." She scraped at her own bowl, capturing a shrimp in her chopsticks that had been hiding inside a small lump of noodles. "Also, thank you, by the way, for protecting me. *That* was something you didn't have to do."

"Yes, I did," he said softly.

Catching the note of confession, she shook her head, pressing on the idea. "No, no, you didn't. You could have let me get hurt. You *chose* to protect me. Therefore, thank you."

"If something happens to you, I lose my link to this 'city,' and I have to go home. So it is in my self-interest to keep you as safe as possible," he said.

Narrowing her eyes at him, she huffed, perturbed that he had maneuvered out of her argument. She had to think fast. "It would also be in your self-interest to let me believe that you saved me out of the goodness of your heart."

"Yeah well," he shrugged, "I suck at my job."

"And you like me."

"And I like you."

They met eyes then, both acknowledging what they had just admitted.

Helena grinned, finally hearing what she wanted to hear.

"And maybe you *love* me?" Helena asked, teasingly, pushing for more.

He looked down then and back at his bowl. "If I did, it would be the worst thing in the world for you."

And they were back to that old saw. "How so?" she asked.

"You're not letting this go, are you?"

She shook her head. "Oh absolutely not."

He sighed, then attempted to use his chopsticks to pick up one of the dumplings to feed her with as a way to shut her up. "Because loving someone like me can only end in heartache and tragedy. And you don't deserve that."

"You have no idea what I deserve," Helena said darkly, catching the dumpling in her mouth before he lost control of it. They needed to get better at feeding each other.

"There is nothing you don't deserve," Rafferty stated as if it were just a fact, not giving compliments. "You are a truly good, decent, honest, caring person, who for some unfathomable reason is messing with things she shouldn't, all out of a sense of honest compassion that doesn't exist in this world. Do you really understand you are such a unique thing in all of creation? Even the good people, some really *good* people, are tempted by the kind of power you have at your fingertips. For the right reasons, for the right intentions, they will call us to serve, and it will inevitably go horribly, horribly wrong in the end because most of us are actually effective at our jobs."

"So my continued survival is also dependent on you being really incompetent at yours. The fact that you haven't been working and manipulating things to get me to make the wrong decisions and fall for that temptation of abuse you keep expecting?"

He growled and murmured something she couldn't make out but got the gist of.

But she was winning, and she was not going to let this go. "Maybe ... the state of this current relationship has more to do with both of us and our choices than one of us being nearly saint-like in virtue?"

Grumble, grumble, grumble.

"And I'm not talking about me."

"What? Why would you..." He scoffed, clearly frustrated. "What do you have to be so down on yourself about? What could you have possibly done that would force you to see yourself as anything other than the pillar of annoying virtue that you actually are!"

"I've killed somebody."

She wanted to be flippant about it, but it still hurt to admit that non-secret out loud. The sensation of needles piercing her throat made it hard to swallow the mouthful she stuffed in after her declaration. She expected Rafferty to laugh at what she said, or dismiss it, say she was exaggerating, but he didn't. He sat there looking at her hard, and that was actually worse because she hadn't been prepared for it.

He believed her.

"You must feel so betrayed," she said out loud, naming the thing she feared most in that moment. "But it's true. I caused someone to die. So there you go. I'm not the pillar of virtue you think I am."

"Tell me," he said, his voice rumbling low. A thrum of wrongness crested off of him, rolling through the food eatery. Everyone there seemed to feel it and reacted to it like a wind had blown through, even though the air was still.

"I think it is going to snow," the young cook who had brought them their dumplings said, looking unsettled as he leaned forward to glance up at the dark starless sky. "We are going to pull everything in and shut the doors." He gestured to the pair of doors on the building they occupied that could be pulled in and turning the open air of the eatery into a closed contained building, especially on a winter night like this.

"It's okay. We're about done," Helena said, having completely lost what was left of her appetite. "Can we have a to-go tray?"

The cook nodded and returned with a pressed wax-lined takeout bowl that she dumped hers and his leftovers into.

"Thank you, again," she said to the cooks who all waved at her with smiles as they closed in the shop.

Rafferty followed, his eyes never leaving her, boring into her, as she refused to look at him.

Chapter 30

TOLD HIM THE TRUTH

"Her name was Shawna," Helena said from the seat of her couch. Pooka, skittish since her houseguest arrived, finally made an appearance, sitting on her lap and letting Helena pet her, all while keeping warning eyes on Rafferty across the room. "We were in high school together. And it's exactly what you think. She wasn't one of the popular kids and I was. So we bullied her."

Rafferty stood leaning against her front door, his eyes burning stars. His arms were crossed over his chest, and he had one foot pressed into the door while the other braced to keep him upright. Despite his otherwise human appearance, his tail was visible, and it would twitch every few seconds, agitatedly, the way her cat's was right that minute.

Focusing on his tail helped her get through what she needed to say.

"It's been a long time since I told this story, so you'll have to forgive me—"

"How did you kill her?" he asked, sharply.

She looked up to meet his eyes, but he didn't even blink as he stared her down. "It's not going to be as simple as I took a gun and blew her head off. It's not as direct as that, but it is the same thing as if I had. I've already been over this with many, many therapists and—"

"You caused her death."

"I posted the thing that pushed her over the edge and made her take her life, yes. I knowingly did something that I knew was causing someone else so much pain that they would end their life over it. I literally told her she was worthless and she should kill herself and she did. They found her phone lying next to her with my text on the screen."

The needles in her throat sank deeper, but she let them. She wanted to feel their pain.

"You publicly shamed her?" Rafferty asked, a lilt of his French accent slipping into his speech.

"Yes, I did." She wouldn't diminish or look away from her sin. "The worst of it was, I wasn't charged. The police refused to charge me. All the adults around us would tell me to my face that it wasn't my fault, that it was nobody's fault but her own for her death. That it wasn't just me, that it wasn't my responsibility solely. Any and all of the things. My parents sent me to therapy. Lots of therapy. I wasn't able to touch a cellphone until I finally went to college a year later than I should have. And each day it is one step at a time, and I only sometimes think of Shawna, but I carry her with me everywhere. My own personal ghost. Though I guess she's not even that," Helena said as a realization came to her, looking at her demon with his starbursting eyes. "You would have seen her or something, right? If I was being truly haunted by her and she was attached to me somehow?"

He shook his head. "There is no one around you like that," he said.

"Dammit," Helena said, lowering her head. "I actually find that disappointing. I used to talk to her all the time until the therapist said that wasn't really healthy and suggested I try to let her go."

She chuckled dryly. "You said a while ago that I am always looking to 'do the right thing, to find the right answer,' and you are totally right. I am absolutely trying to do that because I don't think I know how to live with myself any other way. Which also means I understand what you mean when you say you deserve it, everything that has happened to you and that you are unworthy. I actually honest to God understand what you are freaking talking about, what that feels like. And I don't even know what you've done that was so bad as to warrant being dragged into hell. But I get why you feel that way. I do. This is a horrible feeling to have to live with."

Tears were flooding her eyes and there was nothing she could do to stop them. They weren't for her; they weren't self-pity. They just were. Her body could do nothing else and she just let it happen, as she had so many times before in her life. She closed her eyes and let them take her under again.

"Helena," Rafferty said.

She could barely hear him, but she tried to respond. "Yes?"

"Can I hold you?"

It broke her. It broke her so deeply. She hiccupped a sob and held her hands out. Pooka made a run for it. Then the demon was there, sliding his arms around her, like he did in the alley. The wings rushed about to clasp at her. The man she had come to know knelt down before her on the couch and tucked her against them as they both drowned in the grief.

Yet, she didn't really cry. She couldn't. It hurt too much and yet the only way through it was to feel it. So she breathed and she ached and she held on.

"I abandoned my family."

Rafferty's voice broke through.

"I abandoned my family to work in the kitchens of the King. My mother was unwell and my sister was too young to work. My father had already abandoned us, and when the demon found me and offered me the chance to escape the misery of that life, me and only me, I took it. A man has to make his own chances and not let anything tie him down. I told myself that I could send my wages home and take care of my mother and sister, but I never did, and I never thought about them again after that. I just left and worked in the kitchens of the palace. Everything I touched turned out delicious. I was a rising star in a cut-throat world. I destroyed my rivals to win the favor and approval of the King's chef. And I kept pulling more and more on the demon's power. Better food, better ingredients. I vanquished my rivals, being able to find the things I needed even if they tried to sabotage me in the kitchen until it got to the point that the chef saw me as *his* rival. Then our relationship soured and I asked for something I shouldn't. I asked for the chef's life. The demon gave me the poison I killed him with. Fed his body to the pigs. But then the pigs were butchered before they too could die of the poison and that poison spread to half the castle. They all said it was the plague, but I knew what I had done. I said nothing. So many other people died because of it because of the fear of the plague, healthy people were left to die with the sick or just outright killed. And I was so sure what I had done would be discovered, so I gave everything I had to the demon to protect myself. I tried to invoke a miracle, to bring back everyone that had died because of me, to erase my mistake. And when I had given away too much, and my tab to him was too high, he took my life instead and dragged me to hell. Only there did I truly understand everything. I found out my mother had died of her illness and my little sister had starved to death. I had never even thought about them after I left. I just told everyone I was an orphan. I learned that if I had done what I had thought I would, sent my wages back, my mother would have recovered and my sister would have grown up."

His story stopped, and Helena lifted her head to look into the face before her. His horns swept back from his still gaunt face, but maybe it was less so then when he first came. His gray skin and star burning eyes were still unearthly, but she could see the man she had gotten to know inside the bone structure and planes of that face. He still wore the black shirt and pants since they were real, but she had no idea how his wings were coming through the back of the clothing without tearing. A small question in which the answer didn't matter at that moment. His tail wrapped around her ankle.

"So you see, Helena, you are still a better person than I am. You figured all that out while you were still alive and you chose to *live* with it. I couldn't bear it. I chose to die for it, to try to make what I had done untrue."

"Could you have brought all those lives back with demon magic?" Helena asked.

Rafferty shook his head. "No. It's not possible like that. Even with demon magic, you can pretty much only save one person—maybe—if the request is made in the moment of death, and often it's an exchange for another life."

She nodded. "It makes sense."

Leaning back, she slid from his arms until they clasped hands in her lap. "So there really is no way to bring you back to life?"

He shook his head. "No, there isn't. I don't even have my original body to try. And there are so many souls worthier than I. Like you."

She wiped away at her face. "I am so sorry," she said, attempting to break the tension. "I'm ruining your vacation again." Pushing her way to her feet, she stepped out of the circle of his wings. "I just want to go to the kitchen for a moment."

"No, Helena don't—" Rafferty said, standing up as well.

"I'll just be a moment. I'm just going to get some water."

"I'll get it for you," he said, surging forward to head her off to her kitchen door.

"No, I would really rather get it myself—"

"I said I'll get it!" he shouted, his whole frame now obviously blocking the door to her kitchen.

Staring at him, she lowered her hand from where she had intended to push the door inward. "Rafferty. Why are you keeping me out of my kitchen?"

Chapter 31

HORRIBLE DISCOVERIES

Rafferty didn't answer her. He stared straight ahead, his wings flared out over her door, arms behind his back, his feet splayed as if he were preparing to take a hit. Force wasn't getting through him. Words either.

Instead, she laid her hand on his chest, feeling the material of the black shirt he wore heave beneath it.

"Rafferty, just tell me."

He looked at her then, his eyes dropping to take in her face, painted in shame. "I can make you sleep," he said. "Just like I did before. I can make you forget about the kitchen again if you want."

"What?" She took a step back. She didn't want that. "What do you mean by again?"

His face was pained as he closed his eyes. "Of course, you wouldn't remember."

"Rafferty," she said, warning in her voice. "Let me see what is happening in my kitchen."

It was a command.

He obeyed it, standing to the side.

Laying her hand on the door, Helena could feel a strange heat from the other side of the door. For a brief moment, she thought her kitchen was on fire on the other side, but if that had been the case... the fire alarms would have gone off.

She looked over at the one attached to the wall beside the door, her fire alarm and monoxide detector in one. It was off. She could see that someone had pulled it off the wall, then set it slightly at an angle so it still hung there, but no longer connected to the base.

"Oh God," she whispered and then fortified herself to push her kitchen door inward slowly.

The smell that hit her was awful. She had no idea how she hadn't been smelling it in the rest of the house, but it was like cat sick and burning tires mixed with decaying body and a hint of pumpkin spice. Grasping at the top of her shirt, she pulled it up over her nose and it only helped a little.

Daring to open the door enough to actually see, she swore the room had its own light. Even though her kitchen came with windows, they were blacked out, caked with some sort of grease-like substance, both over the sink and covering her back door. The remnants of her kitchen remained, like the stove and the countertops, the dishwasher and the refrigerator, but all of her smaller appliances were gone, smothered under a sickly growth that branched around the room from no obvious source. In the center of the room, still burning into the tile, was the summoning circle. It had changed from when she last saw it. It had cut itself deep into the grooves of her floor, at least six inches below the surface. Smoke billowed from it, like someone had just snuffed out a candle, dancing on its own breeze in wicked curls and strangling shapes.

Blackness, different from what was on the windows, stained the rest of the tile. In places it flaked like drying blood on stone. Bits of detritus were everywhere, like the rotten foliage from a swamp or dark, sinister forest, but if she looked too long at what she thought was a twig, she knew such a thing could never have grown on a real tree. In fact, the longer she stared at it, the more it looked like bone.

She thought she would go in, but she couldn't make herself. It was all too horrible.

"How... how could this happen in a few days? I thought you said we had longer?"

"I made a mistake in my calculation," he said. "I didn't take into account how much demonic magic it would burn to keep me in reality in this body twenty-four hours a day every day. In a few days, we burned through what is normally two weeks' worth of energy."

"Two weeks!" Helena's eyes couldn't have been wider.

"You asked me where I was sleeping... when you're not here, I have gone back in to lower the strain on the circle." Rafferty stepped into the kitchen, unbothered by the decay and rot around him.

"You've been going back into hell?" she asked, horrified by the implications.

He tapped the circle with a toe. "To the threshold, not completely back in, but enough. Now..." Turning back to her, he folded his wings behind him, the black clothing ruffling about him in the stirring of the unearthly air over the circle. "I must return completely," he said with finality.

"Rafferty," Helena said. She wanted to say no, but how could she? What was happening was terrible and dangerous.

He shifted back to his human visage. "Don't worry. I've controlled the cost. You've given me enough good memories to cover it easily. And I'm sorry."

"Please don't be sorry—" Helena started to say, but he held up a hand to stop her.

"Wait. You don't know what I'm apologizing for yet," he said and crossed the space back to her. As soon as he was close, he brushed a hair out of her face gently, roving his eyes over her like he was trying to memorize every inch of it. "I'll never give up this memory," he said softly and cupped her face. "Never."

She held his hand to her face, pressing it in. She couldn't believe this was happening, that she was losing him, but they needed to do this. "What is it you're sorry for?"

He sighed and leaned forward, to press his forehead against hers, closing their eyes. "I've been eating your memories," he whispered.

"I know. That was the deal—"

"No, the bad ones. This isn't the first time you've discovered the circle, and I've eaten those memories so we could continue on, but now that it's over... I can't leave without you knowing that you're missing pieces of your life."

"But ... weren't they bad memories?" she asked.

He nodded against her forehead.

"And they don't ... taste good?"

He nodded again.

"But you ate them anyway?"

"So you wouldn't have to suffer," he whispered, the truth forcing its way out of him.

"I love you too," she whispered and wrapped her arms around his neck, tucking her face into his shoulder and squeezing hard.

"No, that's... that's not why I told you," he said, trying to push her away, but not having the heart or will to do it.

"Then why are you telling me?"

"You're... I thought it would help..." he struggled.

"You wanted me to hate you, so I would feel violated? To make it easier to let you go."

"Dammit." He gave in as soon as the truth was voiced. Dropping his head to her shoulder, he nodded against the crook of her arms. "How do you always know?"

"Because you wouldn't do something to me without my permission."

"I could have."

"No, you couldn't."

He growled low. "Your faith in me... I can't believe it."

"That's okay. I don't need you to for it to be real." She hated this. She hated it was ending this way, but...

"Couldn't I summon you again? Not all the time, but again ... sometime?" she asked, practically begged.

"You could," he agreed. "I can't stop you, even though I want to."

He hugged her back, squeezing for all he was worth, his body pressing into hers. Then he pushed away harshly like she was hot to the touch and burning him. It caused him to stumble. She moved to help him again, but he kept his arm locked to hold her back. "Don't come in here until I am gone. It could make you sick. I'll try to take as much of the damage with me as I can. Do you remember the recipe I gave to clean this all up?"

She nodded, her throat becoming too thick to talk.

"Good," he said. "The grooves will remain, unfortunately, until the circle is completely purged, which takes a year. You'll have to put down a rug ... or something."

"I'll figure it out," she assured him.

Reluctantly, he let her go, stepping back toward the summoning circle. Like a man preparing for his execution, he unbuttoned his clothes, taking them off. Helena thought about looking away, but she couldn't. He folded the shirt and pants she had bought him, laying them to the side of the circle while still wearing the boxer briefs. He stood one last time, not looking in her direction and stepped into the center of the circle. As soon as he passed the invisible wall, he shifted back to the demon with the horns that swept back and his triangle tipped tail that whipped behind him, conveying his anxiety.

As he moved, Helena noted his bare feet and realized something that made her giggle.

He paused and looked back, clearly perplexed by her inappropriate levity. "What?" he asked.

"Your feet," she said, gesturing. "You have horns and a tail, but human feet instead of hooves."

Looking down at his own feet, he lifted one up as if he had never noticed that before. "Maybe I'm not wholly demon then," he said with a sad smile.

And then in a flash he was gone.

Chapter 32

IT WAS WORSE THAN A BREAKUP

It took Helena all night to clean up what remained of the infested kitchen. When Rafferty went back through the circle, the tendrils and growth went with him, as well as the majority of the eerie detritus. As well as her coffeemaker and toaster. Her crockpot had been half dissolved and the dishwasher made a funny noise now, but it still worked. The inside of the fridge was also fine. Everything was still coated with the gross, unnamable film. It took most of the night to clean up. Amazingly enough, Rafferty's cleaning concoction, when she sprayed it on and left it for a few minutes, wiped the mess away almost instantly. She did the counters and walls first, the surfaces of the remaining appliances and then her windows before finally mopping up the floor, throwing away a month's supply of paper towels, so it was lucky she bought those sorts of things in bulk at the local warehouse outlet.

The whole time she went through a bevy of emotions from outright heartbreak and melancholy to even laughing at some of their shared memories. If anyone had been watching her, they would have thought she had been driven mad.

This was worse than a breakup, she decided.

Finally, just when dawn started to crest, she finished enough for her to go to sleep. She knew she would need to do this level of cleaning again for a while, but at least the sick feeling it gave her was much, much less. Yet, as she dragged herself to her bed, she caught a glimpse of herself in the mirror.

"Crap, I got to shower," she told her reflection.

The water burned as it hit her skin, like she had been out in a snowdrift. Leaning against the wall, she pressed her hands into the tile as she let the water hit her from above. Hanging her head, her hair streamed a curtain around her face. She endured it and after a few minutes of slow breathing, it got easier. The water slipping down the drain was black and greasy brown, reminding her of oil. It took everything she had to hold on.

"Rafferty, I am so sorry," she whispered. She knew she couldn't imagine the pain he had to be suffering at that moment; hers was definitely nothing in comparison. But she hoped he could hear her, wherever he was, and that it gave him some comfort.

After washing her hair twice and simply standing in the water until it ran cold, Helena made her way back to her bedroom, moving freely without fear of anyone else seeing her natural state for the first time in ages.

Though would it have really been so bad to let him see me naked? She had seen him in such a vulnerable state.

Despite her newfound freedom, she felt cold all the way down to her bones and dressed herself in her warmest, fuzziest pajamas complete with socks. Then she buried herself under her comforter and only then did it occur to her that she needed to call in sick at work.

"Dammit, dammit, dammit," she muttered before she realized that her choice of words were the wrong ones. If Rafferty could still hear her from the depths of hell because of the circle, then she needed to only send him good, comforting words. "Bless it," she amended, then wondered if actually, because of his circumstances, that would just hurt him in reverse. Bless a demon, curse an angel?

It was too much logic for her brain at that moment, and she just forged on, navigating her phone to call her least favorite person.

"Hi, Yosef," she said when her nemesis answered. *Good,* she thought. *I sound as croaky as I feel.*

"Hi, what's up?" he asked, already sounding like he had run laps around the city before breakfast.

"Well, as you might be able to hear, I am sick as a dog this morning, so I think I should not come into the office," Helena said, adding a sniff to the end to emphasize her point.

"You're not coming in!" Yosef practically shouted into the phone. Helena didn't realize she had a low level headache until he did that, but he made it ring now. "We have less than a month until the Winter Rose Ball, and you haven't even picked a caterer yet!"

"I know, I know. I'll be working from home," she said. *After I get a few hours of sleep,* she thought.

"Oh, you're going to work from home," he said sarcastically.

"Well, I could come in, but I don't know what I have and..." Helena had to think fast. "And I'm concerned about giving it to the rest of the office. Especially with Scarlet and everything."

"Oh," Yosef said, his ire cooling quickly. "Yeah... yeah, that's a good point. Okay, okay." She could practically hear him physically reset himself. "I'm sorry. I'm sorry for my overreaction. What you're saying is sensible. Okay, how about... you make a list of the things you need from the office, and I'll have a messenger bring them to you?"

"Um okay, I'll do that, but I'm going to try to get some sleep here so let the messenger know that if I don't answer the doorbell right away, they should call my phone," she said, putting Yosef on speaker so she could look at the clock on it.

"How about I schedule to have them delivered at 1pm. Will that give you enough time to get some sleep?"

"Yes, actually that would be great," Helena said, relieved. "I just feel if I got a few more hours, I might be okay, you know."

"Don't push it," he said, though it sounded absent-mindedly distracted, like he was reading something. Probably hiring a courier via an app?

She waited until he came back.

"Okay, we'll get this sorted. Feel better," he said and then he was gone before she could say anything more. Which was fine.

She let her phone drop onto the bed beside her, then rolled over, not caring if she tossed it off the bed or not. Laying there, her thoughts still buzzing, she thought she would never fall asleep.

But she did.

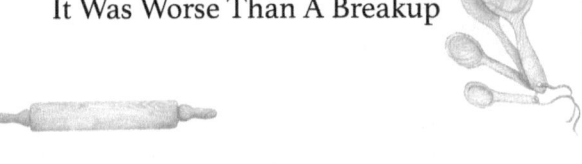

The next couple weeks went by in a blur for Helena.

Even though she spent a couple days at home, to cover for her "being sick" excuse, she worked just as hard as if she had been in the office. In some ways, she was more productive, having the extra 45 minutes she would have taken otherwise for her commute. There were so many things to plan, from seating to flowers to entertainment to etc. etc. And it all had to be done now or yesterday. But item by item, she got things sorted out and untangled, and she could start to see how this Winter Rose Ball was going to come together.

She would need to present everything to Scarlet soon for her final approval, which dragged her back into the office. Everything needed to be perfect, and if it meant she clocked in double the hours at the office, so be it.

"Get out," Yosef said near the end of the second week.

"What?" Helena exclaimed, lifting her head up from where she had buried it among the guest list seating arrangement plans. She had been moving and shuffling cards around for hours, trying to accommodate as many requests as she could when Yosef had made his strange pronouncement.

"You're going crazy. You've started talking to yourself," he said, plucking the cards from her hands. Helena felt her cheeks flush. She hadn't been talking to herself. She had been talking to Rafferty. But Yosef couldn't know that.

"When's the last time you ate? Or even went to the bathroom?" Yosef asked, gently pushing her back from her desk to look under it for her purse.

"Um. I don't know... I guess..."

He found it and pressed it at her. "Exactly, you need to get out of here for a bit. Go get something to eat and some fresh air," he said as he marched her over to the coat rack by the door.

"He's right, you know," Scarlet called from her own desk where she had been working on making personal phone calls to specific donors to guarantee that they RSVP'd. It was one of the few things she couldn't farm out. "This job is about pacing, my child."

"But I am almost finished. I just need to—" she tried to say, but Yosef started putting her coat on for her like she was a kindergartener.

"It'll still be here when you get back," he assured. "And besides, I need to give Scarlet her massage. So don't come back for an hour."

Any other protests were met with deaf ears, and in a trice, Helena found herself thrust out of the office with the door firmly shut behind her.

"Well... okay," she said to it, feeling almost hurt but realizing too that they were probably right.

She pulled up the phone app for a nearby Thai place that wasn't as good as the one on Little Thai street, but they also had a decent selection of Ramen Bowls in a sort of hybrid fusion thing that sounded appealing to her. It was winter after all, the best time for soup. "I wish you were here to try the Ramen. It's another Asian thing you would have loved."

"Oh, yes, that sounds delicious!" one of the other office workers said, who had also been waiting at the elevator door.

She hadn't noticed them, but she forced a smile. Okay, maybe she was talking out loud a little too much.

Chapter 33

RAN INTO CHRIS

"**O**kay, the broth is some sort of pork flavoring. The noodles are thin and springing, and they gave me plenty, so it's going to be filling. There are either chives or maybe these are green onions." Helena glanced down at the menu that the server had left and read through the list of ingredients under the bowl she had chosen. "Oh, okay, it looks like green onions. I've also got ginger and sesame seed oil... Yeah, I can taste the bite from the ginger. Oh, wait, this had chives *and* green onion in it. Red cabbage, yeah I see that, and chicken. Then on top I've got two soft boiled eggs that just sort of float in the broth." She took up her chopsticks and got a mess of noodles up to her mouth, slurping as was culturally appropriate. "You got to slurp too," she said around her full mouth. "It's a requirement." She giggled at the thought of what Rafferty's face would look like as he watched her eat.

"It's warm and the egg is creamy," she said when she swallowed and prepared another bite. "With that little bit of spice, it really wakes you up all the way to your toes…"

She trailed off in her description as she locked eyes with someone down the counter.

To her shock, Chris stood there, staring daggers at her, while the woman she had seen him with at the fancy restaurant stood beside him, receiving a plastic bag with takeout food in it.

Guilt pierced through her as she had completely forgotten what she had witnessed and the fact that she hadn't made up her mind whether to tell Charlie or not. Self-accusations of what a bad friend she was coupled with assurances that not interfering in her friend's lives was a good thing warred within her while she met Chris's eyes.

"Oh crap," she breathed out. "It's Chris."

The woman Chris was with tugged on his sleeve, ready to go. He turned to her and leaned in a moment, saying something in her ear. She glanced over toward Helena, then smiled at him and gestured outside. Helena couldn't hear what they were saying over the hubbub of the restaurant, but to her alarm, Chris started walking down the counter toward her.

"Oh crap, crap, crap," she whispered and turned to face her bowl. She did not want to deal with another public confrontation, especially considering how much stress she was under, but with each moment, it became clearer and clearer she would have no choice.

"Hey, Helena," Chris's voice said, coming from right next to her.

"Hey, Chris," she said neutrally. She looked up at him but didn't want to meet his gaze so returned it to her soup.

She heard him sigh next to her. "Look, about the other night," he said, and she braced. "I just wanted to say I'm sorry about over-reacting like that. I... I obviously panicked."

"Yeah," she said, focusing on maintaining neutrality.

"And I wanted to say thank you for not saying anything to Charlie. I really appreciate that," he said.

She couldn't stand it; she couldn't keep the words from coming out of her mouth. "You should be the one to tell Charlie," she snapped, feeling hot behind her ears.

"Yeah, I know. I know you're right," Chris said, surprising her by not fighting it. He sat down slumped on the stool next to her, backward so he braced his feet out into the aisle behind them. "I'm really sorry about you getting stuck in the middle of this, Hel, but it's all just really confusing right now, you know?"

His demeanor cooled her fire. "Who is she?" she asked.

"Co-worker. She's really nice. You'd like her," he said. "I don't know what to tell you. It just sort of happened and I don't know why. I mean ever since college I've only been *into* Charlie, but lately ... I don't know. It's like ever since your dinner party, something just snapped inside me."

"Since my dinner party?" Helena asked, another surprise.

He nodded. "I don't know. Something happened that night. Something that had been building for a while, and I just looked at Charlie and... *it* wasn't there anymore."

"What wasn't there anymore?" she said, her stomach feeling like lead.

"I don't know," he repeated.

"You don't seem to know a lot," she pointed out, a little irritated. "You haven't talked about this at all with Charlie?"

"If I can't understand it, how can I explain it? It's what I've been trying to figure out." Chris looked toward where the woman waited for him outside the front window. "And you know what he thinks about people who say they are bi."

Helena pursed her lips. She liked Charlie a lot, but he was the kind of person that once he made up his mind about something it was extremely hard to change it. Bisexuality and gender fluidity was always a subject non-grata with him.

"Still, he's your husband, Chris. You took a vow," she pointed out.

"You don't think I know that?" Chris snapped, shooting her a sharp look. "I'm going to talk to him. I am. Just give me some more time, okay? I need to come to him with answers."

Helena pursed her lips, debating. "I'll wait another week," she decided, "but if you don't tell him, then I will have to. I can't keep something like this from my friends forever."

Chris's expression darkened to a level of hate she had never seen before on his face. She felt herself pull away but resisted any urge to run.

"You do that, and I will destroy you," he growled in no uncertain terms. "I will tell him about what you did to Shawna. I've never told him in all these years." He stood up, using his higher position to loom over her threateningly. "I'll tell every one of your dirty secrets to everyone you work with, and we'll see how long you still have a job. You will keep your mouth shut. Do we understand each other?"

All she could do was nod as she struggled to hold the whimper in.

With a sniff, her friend... her former friend straight-ened up. Then nodded once as if that solved everything and turned to leave. She watched to make sure he had gone. As he exited the door, he turned, leaving the woman he had come with confused and trailing behind him.

"Are you okay?" an older man asked, leaning from the other side of her a few seats down.

"Yeah, yeah, I'm fine," she said airily, though she could feel the tears beading in her eyes. "Just having a rough day is all." She forced a smile to reassure him and he accepted it.

"That guy's an asshole," the old man proclaimed.

She laughed and nodded. "Yeah, he's being one today."

"If he had tried anything, I was going to kick his ass," the old man assured.

"Well thank you, but I'm glad it didn't come to that," she said and then went back to try to finish her ramen, but she didn't have the same appetite she'd had before. "I'm alright, Raffie," she whispered under her breath, so he wouldn't worry. "But I miss you."

She made herself finish her soup anyway because she still had a long day ahead of her. There was still a lot of time before she was supposed to return to the office, but the walk she planned to take through the downtown park was just too unpleasant as the cold winter wind whipped through. There was a dusting of snow on the ground this time, but the air was so frozen that it just made her feel like a walking icicle. With fifteen minutes left before the minimum allowable time for her to return, she gave up and decided she'd rather endure Yosef's censure than another minute out "in nature."

When she got back to the shared office, it was pretty much empty in the main room. It looked like everyone else had also gone out for lunches, and she kicked herself for not thinking to ask anyone if she could join them. Then she would at least have been safe from that unsettling encounter with Chris.

Deciding not to dwell on her mistakes, she went to Scarlet's office, then stopped, remembering that Yosef had said he would be giving Scarlet a massage. It wasn't the first time she had been kicked out for that reason. Scarlet needed them regularly to help with her circulation and to improve her quality of life. Helena figured they probably weren't finished yet but decided she could try to just sneak in quickly and grab her computer so she could get a few other things done while they finished up.

That's when a short, sharp cry of pain startled her just as she reached for the door handle. "Oh God, oh God," cried Scarlet's voice and then there was a bang sound from the other side of the door. Imagining Scarlet having fallen and broken something, Helena quickly seized the handle only to find it locked. Of course it would be locked!

"Dammit, dammit, Scarlet! Are you alright?" she called through the door as she scrambled to get her copy of her keys out of the coat pocket.

There was no response as she shoved the right key into the lock and wrangled the door open. Something was blocking the door, and she caught sight of Scarlet's wheelchair, lying on its side, probably the source of the crash.

"Scarlet!" she shouted as she burst into the room, only to stare at Yosef's bare ass facing her and Scarlet's legs splayed on either side of him.

Her outburst startled them both.

"The Hell!" Yosef shouted as he bucked back and twisted and by then Helena was already covering her face. "Get the fuck out!" he shouted as he struggled to pull up his pants.

She had to uncover her face with one hand so she could grab at the handle of the door to shut it. All the while as she struggled, Scarlet was cawing laughter at the top of her lungs.

"Get out!"

Chapter 34

NEEDED A HUG

"Get out!"

And Helena did. With the speed of lightning, she was out of the building, hailing a taxi, and didn't stop until she was back in her house. As soon as the door closed behind her, she went straight for her kitchen. She cast aside the kitchen carpet she had bought to cover the summoning circle and dropped to her knees next to it, laying her hands on the still warm lines.

"Lares... I summon you," she said.

Heat made her flinch back as the circle burst back into life. A figure appeared, kneeling in the center, his wings framing him. Slowly, he lifted his head and looked at her with his beautiful starburst eyes. He stood up to his full height, regarding her all the while.

"What do you command, mistress?" Rafferty said in a low, rumbling voice.

Tears filled up Helena's eyes. "I need a hug," she cried.

He held perfectly still for a moment as if trying to understand. Then he took one step forward and bent at the waist to wrap his arms about her.

"So do I," he said.

She had brought Rafferty to her room, and they laid together on her bed. Curled side by side facing each other. He had shifted into his human form, except for his tail, which he used to stroke her leg up and down affectionately.

When he had reappeared, he had been wearing the leather apron just like the first time. She didn't ask what happened to the underwear he left with. There were several more in the pack. Now he was dressed in some more clothes she had bought him, a pair of jeans and a gray sweatshirt, in the hope that he would need them when he returned one day. His other fancier clothes she had dry cleaned and waiting for him, hung up properly in her closet.

"How long can you stay?" Helena asked.

"You should send me back in the morning," he said, his finger playing with the end of her hair, twirling around the tip like a ring before letting it fall so he could do it again.

She wanted to say she would send him back never, but they already knew the price for that. She had scrubbed her kitchen every day since he left, and it was only now starting to smell and feel right. And she had just undone all of that work, but she didn't care. She snuggled into her prize's chest, holding him close and breathing in his unique smell.

"I'm glad you're here now."

"I'm sorry I wasn't there earlier," he rumbled.

"So you *can* hear me?" she said, relieved for the confirmation.

"Yes, it is both a pleasure and a torture," he said and kissed the top of her head.

"Oh, I'm sor—" she tried to say, but he pressed his fingers to her mouth.

"No sorries," he said affectionately.

She nodded her muted head, and he let her mouth go to brush his fingers through her hair once more.

"Man, I wish I could scrub the image from my mind," she muttered.

"Of Chris?" he asked.

"No, of Yosef's harvest moon!" she declared and rubbed her face against Rafferty's chest, as if that could wipe it away. "I am such an idiot."

"To be fair, when I heard you hear the thump, I had the same thought," he said. "I also had the passing thought that it was what it was, but also that she could have been in real trouble."

"Now I'm the one in real trouble," Helena declared, needing to sit up so she could express properly with her hands. "You know we would make all kinds of jokes about that in the office, but it's something else entirely to have it irrevocably confirmed! And she's more than twice his age! Like four times his age!"

"So?" Rafferty asked, and Helena looked down at the hypocrisy for that statement lying next to her.

"I suppose you're going to say that you and I are no different?" she said dryly.

His eyebrows popped up. "Oh. I guess I hadn't thought of that. No, I was going to say... when I worked for the King, I'd see that kind of thing all the time."

"Really?"

"There wasn't a lot of privacy for any social class, if you know what I mean."

"I guess I never thought about it much, but to be fair, I don't think too much about what life was like for 1600 France."

"Honestly, I'm surprised they stopped mid coitus."

"Wow."

Rafferty shrugged and turned onto his back so he could put a hand under his head.

"But I guess, how is it not different between the age gap of you and me? I mean, you're hundreds of years old."

"No, I'm not," he said. "I died, remember?"

"Yeah, but you still exist," she countered.

"Aging only happens in this reality. My existence elsewhere, there is no measure of time, which is why it's thought of as eternity. Time *is* but it doesn't progress. Only being here is there a linear change, and I'm here for such small slips of time at most. But elsewhere, we all still *exist*."

Helena struggled to take all that in. "So you're saying we... all of us... we've all always existed?" she asked.

"As far as I understand it, yes," he said.

Her mind blew at that bit of confirmed information. "So... from that perspective, you and I are about the same age?"

Rafferty shrugged. "You could think of it that way. If you need to."

"How old were you when you died?"

"Nineteen or twenty, about. I'm not exactly sure."

That surprised her even more. "So if we're measuring by time spent in this existence, I'm twenty-six, so you..."

"Would still be younger than you, yes, if we add all of the little slips of time of my being in this reality together," he agreed.

Helena flopped back onto the bed. "And the hits keep coming. That's just amazing."

Rafferty turned again to lie on his side facing her, this time his hand propping up his head so he had a downward view. "Helena, may I kiss you?"

"Oh!" she said, sideswiped by the request. "I..."

Her hesitation was the wrong answer, and he pulled back from his slight lean forward. "My apologies for asking. But you said I should ask. But I shouldn't have—"

"No, no, don't pull away," she said, reaching for his face. "You just caught me by surprise. It's been a roller coaster kind of day for that."

And she moved in to press her lips to his, closing her eyes. First he froze, then his hand came around and cupped the back of her head gently. His lips were firm under hers, like he didn't know what to do with them, but she massaged gently, showing him what she wanted him to do. When he had relaxed enough, she slipped her tongue just within the edge of his mouth. He groaned in his throat and broke the kiss. He didn't pull away far though, setting his forehead against hers as he gasped for breath.

"God, you are merciless," he whispered.

"What? What's wrong? Didn't you like it?" she asked, worried.

"I loved it," he whispered and pressed his lips to hers again, returning it more boldly this time. Somewhere on the edge of Helena's awareness, as they kissed over and over again, she was conscious of the flutter of leathery wings behind him, but it wasn't until his tail curled around the leg she had thrown over him like a snake that she became aware he had shifted.

She made a surprised *mew* sound in her throat, and his eyes flew open. A second later, he shifted back to simply a man.

"Dammit," he cursed and rolled over to sit up, his back facing her.

"It's alright," she tried to say, but the damage had already been done.

"I'm sorry. I couldn't... I couldn't hold it," he said, disgusted with himself.

"It's alright," she insisted. It didn't seem to do any good.

Abruptly, he stood and went toward her door. "I need to cook something."

Helena exhaled in a huff of defeat and dropped her pleading hand to the bed. "Dammit," she muttered and then clambered up to go after him.

Going into her kitchen wasn't great. The whole place had a fresh batch of that weird burning tire/pumpkin spice smell to it, but to her surprise, Rafferty tossed the carpet she had purchased back over the smoking lines of the circle. She watched as she expected it to catch fire, but it didn't. It even seemed to curb the smoking. Rafferty certainly didn't seem worried, and he walked back and forth over it like it was any other rug.

Helena hovered near the door. "What are you going to make?"

"I don't know yet," he said as he stared into her refrigerator, taking stock of what was in there before shutting it and going for the cupboards. After a while, he turned back to her, then cocked his head at her hovering by the door. "You can come in. It's safe," he said.

"Oh, okay," she said, crossing the threshold and letting the swinging door shut behind her. "So, I won't get sucked down into hell or anything?"

"No, you'll be fine. You're going to have to clean again, but the way is shut," he said, "How do you feel about a pot pie?"

"Uh, that sounds surprisingly normal for you," she quipped.

"Don't worry. The way I make it, it'll be life changing," he said and started pulling ingredients to assemble on the counter.

"I'm never worried when you're around," she lied, but it was one she wanted to believe.

Chapter 35

THEN SCARLET CONFESSED

The leftovers were just as good the next day. Rafferty had decorated the crust with leaves and vines, making it almost too pretty to eat. Almost. Somehow bringing the container with her to work made her feel more reassured as she marched toward what could very easily be her last day at Scarlet Promotions.

The tension in the main office could have been cut with a knife. Even the water wall wasn't running that morning, a guy in blue coveralls cranking on the pipes through a hidden panel at the side. Helena could hear everyone whispering, which immediately ceased the second she came around the wall.

Oh, crap. It's worse than I realized, she thought.

Before she could make up her mind about whether she wanted to try to engage with everyone or not, Yosef appeared beside her. He looked less than his usual put together self, but his face was as stoically neutral as ever.

"Scarlet would like to speak to you," he said softly.

Helena nodded. What else could she do? The second she turned her back, the office started to whisper again.

At least packing up my desk will be quick, Helena thought.

It was almost a relief to step into Scarlet's office until Yosef made to take her coat and her lunch box, being the courteous assistant again like he could be before her promotion.

She didn't know what kind of sign to take that as, so she just focused on Scarlet.

But the boss wasn't there.

"Where…" Helena started to ask, but Yosef was already indicating the side conference room connected to their office by a side door that had been made double wide to accommodate Scarlet's wheelchair comfortably.

Bracing herself again, Helena headed through the door.

Scarlet sat in her wheelchair on the window side of the room, gazing out over her beloved city. She didn't turn when Helena shut the door.

"Come sit, Helena," she said instead, indicating an already pulled out chair waiting for her.

The trepidatious younger woman complied as expected, though she sat on the edge of the chair, prepared to pop up the second she was fired to book it out of there.

Yet, once she was seated, she noticed that Scarlet was smiling wickedly at her.

"So the only real question is whether you want to stay or not?" Scarlet asked.

"Ma'am, I can assure you—" Helena started, but Scarlet held up her hand.

"If you choose to go, I will of course compensate you with a generous severance and glowing recommendations as well as annulling your non-compete agreement. And honestly, I would have given you the glowing recommendations to you anyway, even without you catching me in a compromising situation with my personal assistant."

She said the last just as Yosef appeared at her elbow to present her with a steaming cup of tea. If his ears could have burned redder, Helena was sure Yosef's hair would have caught fire. Scarlet only smiled serenely.

"If you choose to stay, nothing will change, though I will ask that you not speak of what you saw to anyone, even though everyone out there already has some ideas that might more or less be true. I just ask that you not confirm or deny anything. Frankly, it'll add to your mystery and that can pay dividends when I appoint you to succeed me in the company."

Helena did not know what to think. All she could do was sit there and blink while Scarlet waited for her to process it.

She even absentmindedly took her cup of tea from Yosef before she could put two thoughts together. *Don't ask her if she's firing you, don't even bring it up, don't ask if she's not firing you...*

"So you're not firing me?" she asked despite herself.

Scarlet's smile widened. "No, dear. That would be illegal."

"Oh." Giving herself another moment to think, Helena took a long sip from her tea. "I guess I would like to stay and just continue on as things were. Maybe with a code word for when you two are going to be ... preoccupied."

Scarlet snorted. "We did say I was getting a massage."

Helena snorted into her tea. "Well, yes, but also you *do* actually get massages."

Her boss shook her head bemusedly as she continued to stare out the window, the gray world of the city reflecting in the blueness of her eyes. "It must seem so crazy that a woman of my age would be caught in such a position with someone like him."

"Why?" Helena genuinely asked.

Scarlet looked down at her hands holding the teacup, as if she were just waiting for the liquid to evaporate so she could read the tea leaves. Of which there was none because this was a well-made cup of tea. "I know what you're going to say."

"*I* don't even know what I'm going to say, so tell me."

"That why should I worry about what anyone thinks of me. Men my age do this sort of thing all the time."

Helena had to nod at that. "You're right. That is one of the things I would say. Though if I'm being fully honest, I went through the depth and breadth of emotions yesterday, but I know that had more to do with me and my own hangups."

That elicited another chuckle. "Do you know how incredibly annoying it is for someone as young as you to be so wise?"

Helena smiled. "One of my therapists said I'm an old soul." Then she hesitated before adding. "I know what it's like to hold secrets that you know are difficult for other people to understand."

Now Scarlet looked at her, not speaking, again simply waiting, as if to say, *You know one of my secrets. What is yours? It's only fair.*

Letting out a long breath at the risk she was about to take, Helena steeled herself for whatever reaction she received. "In high school, I bullied a girl so badly she committed suicide."

Scarlet's eyebrows shot up, as surprised as Helena had been learning her secret.

Helena smiled, sadly serene. "I've carried that with me for years. And I will for the rest of my life."

Scarlet let out a long breath, "I am sorry for making you reveal something like that. For making you relive it. I did not have the right and I should have known better."

"Actually, you didn't. I have another reason I needed to tell you."

Now Scarlet's eyebrows furrowed.

The younger woman sighed. "I have a friend... though I don't know if I can really call him a friend anymore, who I recently have caught being unfaithful, and he's threatened to reveal my secrets here at work in retribution if I say anything to his spouse."

"Ah, I see." Scarlet nodded as if she were all too familiar with that sort of threat.

"I was already torn about having not told his husband, who is also my friend, but now I'm so deeply hurt by him, by his actions... That's really the worst part. He was my friend. For years." The familiar lump rose up in Helena's throat, and she took a deep drink of her tea to try to swallow it down. "I still care about him."

Drinking her own tea, Scarlet returned to her contemplation of the world outside.

"If I can say one thing about what I have learned in my life it is this, and it's not even mine originally, but the older I've become, the more true it's proved to be. We, every being in existence, is a collection of good things and bad things. They are independent of each other and cannot be balanced against each other, though we as humans try. The good things do not always soften the bad, and the reverse is also true—the bad things do not invalidate the good things or make them unimportant."

Then she reached out her wrinkled, yet still strong hand to rest on Helena's younger one. "What made Chris your friend is still there and always will be, even as it's time to let him go because his darkness is taking him away. As for what he could do to your work, there is nothing he can do that I cannot undo." She squeezed reassuringly.

A clatter came from behind them, and both women turned to see Yosef hovering outside the door. He disappeared the second they noticed him.

"Oh my dear child. It's so unfair to my dear Yosef," Scarlet said, shaking her head after where he had been. "I didn't believe it at first, but he is truly in love with me, and I will leave him sooner than later."

Helena smiled warmly. "So, how did it happen? What's your love story?"

"You know if I'm honest, I should really be thanking you," Scarlet said, finishing her tea.

"Oh? Did I do something inadvertently?" Helena asked.

"It was after your dinner party," Scarlet said. "I don't know. There was something about that night that just pushed past the last bit of resistance for both of us had and it just … happened."

The older woman was blushing now while Helena's face went pale.

Chapter 36

JUST KNEW SOMETHING WAS WRONG

"**C**ome on, Cin. Pick up," Helena muttered as her phone kept ringing for the third time. She glanced at the clock. Having already called the hospital, she knew that her friend wasn't working that day and had in fact taken the next week off suddenly with no explanation. All Helena could think was that something had happened to her, something involving the demon magic she accidentally fed to her friends.

"Dammit, Rafferty, what did we do?" she asked softly, but he couldn't answer her. She hadn't officially summoned him yet to confront him, and she knew she really wouldn't until she got home. And honestly, she had no concrete reasons to worry about Cindy. The most likely answer for her not answering her phone was she was sleeping. But still Helena couldn't shake her anxiety. She just needed her friend to pick up the phone and assure her that everything was okay, and she was just being paranoid.

Finally, she hung up the phone without leaving a message and checked her texts one more time. She had filled her screen with her blue colored bubbles, checking in on her friend, "Please call me as soon as you get this" messages.

Still, she made herself wait until the end of the day before deciding she would just head over to Cindy's apartment and knock on the door obnoxiously until she answered.

Turning down the hall felt like she had entered a world of disquiet. Cindy lived in a fairly silent building, full of carpet and literal policies to keep all noises below a certain level. Helena knew several doctors who also lived there, attracted to that very aspect. Usually, Helena felt tranquil, but maybe it was just the anxiety in her heart; she just couldn't shake that something was really very wrong.

Cindy's door was a nondescript dark brown, set in a sleepy blue-gray wall. Brass sconces lit up each doorway with a nice yellow light that was meant to mimic old-world gaslight and add to the ambience. The only thing on the outside that indicated to her that this was Cindy's place were the numbers beside the door, right above the doorbell, where Cindy had attached a gag cover of a man with googly eyes reacting to his bell button nose being pushed.

"Hey Cin?" she called through the door as she pressed the doorbell. Inside she heard the responding low-toned chime. After a count of twenty and nothing, she hit it again, then knocked. "Hey Cindy!" she called, daring to pitch her voice up over the allowable decibel.

She knew she had her set of Cindy's emergency keys, and she was prepared to use them if she didn't get an answer soon.

Still nothing.

That's when Helena stepped up to the door to set her ear against it to see if she heard anything. Her foot squelched on the carpet closest to the door. Surprised, she stepped back and squatted to feel. It was soaked.

"Oh God," Helena said. Whatever was wrong, it was very, very wrong.

With shaking urgency, Helena dug out her keys and flipped them through her fingers for the right one. Jamming two wrong ones before she got the right one, Helena kept calling Cindy's name with a growing alarm.

Down the hall, someone opened their door and hushed her, then slammed it before she could respond or ask for help. Finally the door opened.

Immediately, Helena stumbled into a pool of water. While the entryway was carpeted, just to her right opened into the tiled kitchen. Water stood there on the floor, but the sink tap wasn't on; it wasn't coming from there.

"Cindy!" Helena shouted, bolting into the apartment, past the kitchen to her larger main room which was also empty.

She turned then to look into Cindy's bedroom and office, both with doors open, the frames facing at a slight angle inward on the opposite sides of the start of the hall. And both were empty.

"Cindy, answer me please!" Helena called, but there was only one place left in the apartment she could be, and Helena moved toward it now. Double skipping down the short hallway, she reached to push open the bathroom door at the end. Her feet slapped the standing water, deeper as she came closer.

She pushed the closed door open.

"Cindy!" Helena shouted as she saw her friend lying in an overfull bathtub. Cindy's arms hung on either side of the freestanding tub, her head lolled to one side. Her eyes were closed.

Helena slid through the wet, the opening now allowing the pooling water on the floor to crest out the door. Heedless of how soaked she was becoming, Helena's knees hit the ground beside the tub as she grabbed at her friend's face, mere inches from the surface of the water.

"Cindy! Wake up!" she shouted as her fingers moved to find her pulse in her neck. Holding her breath, she held still, struggling to feel for her friend's heart over the sound of her own rapidly beating.

Thump.

Tha-thump.

Tha-thump.

Faint, but it was there. So weak, so hard to feel.

"Cindy, please open your eyes!" Helena shouted, but Cindy didn't respond at all. "Oh God!"

Helena scrambled in her pockets for her mobile phone, but her hands were shaking so much it dropped into the water. "NO!"

Grabbing it up the screen on her phone remained on, but the wet on it wouldn't let her fingers unlock it. She pressed at the buttons on the sides to try to trigger the emergency summon five times, all while snaking her arm around her friend's head to help keep it up. Somehow it worked, and the phone made the call.

"911, what is your emergency?"

"I need help. My friend—" And then the phone died.

"No! No, no, no! Cindy! Please, open your eyes!" Helena's voice cracked as her terror started to take over.

Desperate, she threw her arms under Cindy's, trying to lift her out of the tub, but she couldn't get the leverage she needed. She was too heavy and the balance Cindy's body had maintained on the tub edge was undone. She slipped under the still running water.

"Help me! Somebody help me!" Helena screamed as she desperately plunged into the tub, grabbing at her friend's naked flesh to pull her back up to the surface. "Rafferty—"

She stopped. That wasn't his name.

"Lares! Help me!"

The tiled floor erupted with steam as the summon circle burned its way through the water. Helena screeched but didn't stop as she pulled Cindy's head from the water as visions of grotesque creatures clawed from the walls with whispers and cries of pain.

"Oh, just shut up!" she said to them.

Strong arms came past her, reaching underneath the doctor to lift her limp body from the water. Sheets of wet cascaded off her body as she rose while Helena continued to protect her head, trying to keep it from whipping back. Out of the corner of her eye, she saw her demon shift to his human self, pulling back the eerie thrum of his presence behind his human facade. Otherwise he was as naked as he had always been when first summoned.

"Turn off the water. I've got her," he said.

Immediately, Helena set Cindy's head against his shoulder, then darted forward to do just that.

"What's wrong with her?" Helena asked, then slipped only for his tail to catch her and steady her on her feet.

"She's dying," he said, his eyes roving over the form in his arms. "I can feel her life force bleeding away. She's ingested something she shouldn't have."

"Can you save her?" Helena begged coming to the other side of Cindy, touching her friend before darting to grab up one of her overly large bath towels from the nearby shelf to cover her. "I'll pay any price."

Rafferty's eyes widened with anger and fear. "Absolutely not. I won't do that."

"She's my friend. I can't let her die!" Helena cried, her face twisting into an ugly sob. "Cindy, please open your eyes."

"Hold on to me," Rafferty ordered, sharply.

She didn't question, only complied and wrapped her arms around his waist.

The circle beneath them burned into existence again. She hadn't noticed that it disappeared before, but now it ignited to burn away the water it touched in a rush of scalding steam. It stung for a moment, but then was gone as Helena became aware of a sensation of falling into an ocean...

Pain.

Fear.

Eternity.

...and then the sensation of sharp rising, like breaking through the surface.

Helena wanted to scream, but she couldn't. She could barely draw breath. Beneath her shocked feet, the summoning circle disappeared into the damp pavement. Yet the marks remained indicated in the snow cover that blanketed the alley. Above her, snow fell in large clomping flakes.

Beside her, Rafferty stood, still holding Cindy's tow-el-covered body, but he was human and dressed in a rougher version of his black clothes and knee-high black boots.

A siren chirped to her right and Helena snap-turned to see the entrance to an emergency room, an ambulance already parked in front with its lights spinning.

Despite his burden, Rafferty tried to kick the snow to cover the lines of the circle.

"Just go! Take her in! I got this!" Helena cried. Quickly, she erased the melted lines with her feet and rushed to follow.

A car came to a screeching halt as Rafferty marched across the street, his longer legs eating up the distance. He didn't even turn his head, his eyes locked on the entrance. Helena held up her hands to the driver who was shouting despite the obvious emergency and then continued to follow once he was clear.

Before they even reached the doors, two para-medics spotted them through the walls of glass and were rushing out.

"What happened?" one barked as the other doubled back to grab an abandoned gurney. Two nurses were already bolting from the reception desk to their sides as Rafferty dropped her onto the gurney.

"I don't know," Helena answered, coming around to grab Cindy's towel to keep her friend covered. "I found her in the bathtub like this. She's not responding. She's got a pulse. He thinks she took something she shouldn't," she said, trying to relay all the information she could think of.

"What's her name?" a woman in a long white coat asked as she pushed her way in, sticking stethoscope ends in her ears.

"Cindy. Dr. Cindy Hawthorn. She works at Mercy General," Helena reported.

The doctor's eyebrows shot up, but she nodded and focused on her patient. "Cindy, Cindy, can you hear me?" she asked, pressing the stethoscope into her friend's chest, jumping around. Then she straightened and looked straight down at Cindy's unconscious face. "Dr. Hawthorn, you're needed in the ER," she barked in an authoritative voice, slightly deeper than her normal.

Cindy jerked. For a brief moment, her eyes popped open, then dropped back again.

"Okay, she's in there. Let's go! I need a blood test immediately. Let's figure out what she's taken," the doctor barked and Helena was grabbed back out of the way of those who knew what to do. A heartbeat later, she realized it was Rafferty who had pulled her back, his arm across her chest.

She didn't know what else to do, so she turned and buried her face into her love's chest.

"Thank you. Thank you," she whispered.

Chapter 37

THEN CINDY'S CONFESSION

"What happened?" Helena asked. They were sitting in Cindy's hospital room a few hours later. Cindy was awake and calm, lying upright in a hospital bed, swaddled in blankets, a gown, and squishy socks on her feet. Helena sat by her bed, still holding one of the thin blankets a member of the hospital staff had given her wrapped around herself. She had been so focused on Cindy, she hadn't realized that her coat had been soaked through with water and chilled. Rafferty had been much the same, but he had set his offered blanket to the side, leaning back against the wall facing the end of Cindy's bed, his arms crossed.

"I'm sorry, Helena. I know what this probably has done to you," Cindy said instead of answering.

Helena just squeezed her friend's hand. "No, don't do that. I'm glad I found you in time."

"It was so stupid. What did I think... that it would solve anything? I know better," Cindy said, setting her head back, then bumping it once in frustration.

"Hey, don't do that. We just got you conscious again," Helena said, lightening her voice and smiling. "I just want to understand what happened? What led to this?"

"It wasn't one thing," Cindy said, shaking her head. "It was everything. I don't know. It's like ever since your dinner party... I mean it was before that for months. Just this low level scream underneath everything. You know. I could laugh and have fun, but underneath it all was just one long, eternal scream, and it just wouldn't go away. Then something snapped after your party, and I felt like I was breaking through... It's like I've always had this margin ... and the last month the margin just disappeared. I couldn't keep it together anymore."

Even though she tried not to, Helena stiffened. There it was again. *Ever since your dinner party...* Ever since she had brought a demon into her life.

She didn't dare look at Rafferty.

Cindy smiled, reaching with her other hand to lay over Helena's. "I'm going to be alright now. You should go. You need to go home and get some rest and dry clothes and eat something." She glanced over at Rafferty with a knowing smile. "Get your sexy chef to make you something really good. And don't worry about me."

Helena stood up and placed a kiss on her friend's forehead. "That's never going to happen," she said, referring to the last thing Cindy said. "But if you think you're alright, then I will run home. And I *will* be back in the morning."

"They've got me on a twenty-four hour watch, so I can't even leave until then," Cindy assured. "And I'm not going to. Believe me. Come back tomorrow, but after work, okay? I don't want you getting into trouble because of me."

"Are you sure?" Helena stressed, not really liking the plan, but not really having a good reason to argue against it.

"Yes, I'm sure," Cindy repeated. "I'm going to call my folks in the morning and talk to them. My supervisor has already been by. I think I'm going to be put on medical leave really soon following this, so I might not have a choice about going home to visit now."

Both women chuckled at that.

"Okay, well I will be by tomorrow, after work. And I'm bringing cookies."

They both laughed and Rafferty pushed away from the wall to retrieve Helena's coat from the hook on the door. It was still damp when she slipped it on. It would have to do. She had nothing else.

She waved her friend good-bye and they retreated from the hospital room, which felt like the wrong thing to do, but it never felt right to leave a hospital room.

It wasn't until they got to the lobby that Helena realized something. "How are we going to get home?" she asked. She had no idea where her purse was, but if she was to guess, it was still at Cindy's apartment. With no money and no bus pass, they were sort of stuck, and Rafferty didn't have a coat.

She looked at him now, his dampened hair, slicked back over his head, his rough spun button up shirt and pants with those strange boots. All things he hadn't had when they had initially ... jumped?

"How did we get here in the first place?" she asked, pitching her voice low so it didn't echo in the great expanse of the hospital main lobby, which rose three stories above their heads.

"I dragged you through hell," he said, his voice low and rumbling, like it was hard for him to admit it.

A shiver flitted through her. She could remember the feelings and sensations of moving through that ... existence, but even in trying to describe or remember it herself, words failed her and memories made no sense. She didn't actually see or hear anything, but she had impressions of incomprehensibleness, and that was the closest she could get to understanding what had happened.

"Well, I don't want to do that again," she said, attempting to make it sound like a joke and being wholly unable to.

He set a hand on her shoulder. "We won't. It could have killed you. I went quickly enough. I'll figure this out," he said, then reached into his pocket. To her surprise, he pulled out a money clip filled with bills. Urgently, she covered his hand holding the bills.

"What are you doing? Don't do that!" she hissed.

"We need to get you home safe."

"You're using demon magic, aren't you?" she said, her soft words clipped and angry.

His chin lifted, pulling away. "Yes," he whispered. "It's our only option."

"Rafferty—"

"You can't walk home in a wet coat in the middle of winter. You could die," he hissed.

She couldn't argue with that, as much as she wanted. Outside the world was snowing heavily. "Fine," she said, removing her hand to flip up the hood of her coat, tucking herself deeper inside.

Rafferty went and talked to the hospital valet near the front, and within minutes, a taxi pulled up. Neither of them said anything to each other as they got into the car's warm back and were silently driven home. This driver was more interested in his podcast than in talking and that suited Helena just fine.

They almost had another problem when they got to her house since there was a good chance her keys were still hanging in Cindy's door, but as they approached it, Rafferty reached it first. Holding her doorknob in his hand, he turned and turned until something snapped inside it and the door opened.

"Nice. Now you've broken my lock," Helena said, irritated, but he just held the door for her until she stormed inside.

Once in, she tore her coat off and threw it at her couch. "What did you do?" she finally yelled in the safety of her own home. "To all of my friends, what did you do? Why are they all going crazy?"

Rafferty shut the door firmly, still staring at her but leaving his hand there. In the silence, she heard something that sounded like a reverse click-snap sound coming from it. Then he turned it, pulled it open, then shut it again, the door clicking closed like normal before he twisted the end to set the lock.

"Oh great. Now how much is *that* going to cost me?" she demanded, gesturing at his blatant use of demon magic. "You're just racking up the bill now!"

She turned in a circle, but still he stood there silently.

"And you're not answering me—what the hell did you do to my friends?! Why did Cindy almost commit suicide!? Why is Chris cheating on Charlie? Why is any of this happening? They all say it had something to do with your food. What did you do? Answer me!"

"I granted them their heart's wish," he said, his voice barely audible.

"What? What did you say?" Helena pressed, crossing her arms as she leaned forward one ear.

"That's essentially what demon magic is. It grants your wish. It's the same magic no matter who it affects."

"I don't understand." Helena spun in a circle again, burning her rage energy, when what she really wanted to do was hit something. "How is Cindy killing herself her heart's wish?"

Rafferty sighed and closed his eyes. "That's not quite right. I'm not explaining it right."

"Then do better!"

"It's magic, okay," he said, finally raising his own voice. "It... it puts the cosmic thumb on the scale. Sometimes we can manufacture things in this world, but often people want nebulous hard to define things so sometimes you get nebulous results. I think she wanted her suffering to be over, and it resulted in that."

"So you *did* put something in the food?"

"I used demon magic to make some of the food, to make up the ingredients I needed because you had burned half of it to shit. And you and your friends ate what I made."

"But what does that mean? Any food you make for me... you've been feeding me demon magic?"

"No, no. I've been cooking with real food, and real food is real food. I already told you this. It doesn't matter what hands make it, but if I made the food out of demon magic, that is what gets the demon magic inside you. And yes, I did *that* the first night. And—" He stopped, but she wasn't going to let him.

"And—?"

"And yesterday when I made that pot pie," he admitted. "You didn't have Parisian carrots or English peas, so I made them out of some demon magic."

"I still don't understand. If you are using magic to make a thing, how is my consuming it causing all of this?"

He pressed his fingertips together, using them to point at her as he spoke. "Because the magic is formed by my intention for it. I intend the food to be delicious and whatever else I want it to be. So that night, I gave it the intention to push you through whatever barrier was holding you back."

Helena stood there stunned, finally getting it.

Chapter 38

CHOSE BODY THIS TIME

"**I** was trying to give good service as a demon," he said, throwing his arms out sharply as he paced in an erratic circle. "We don't really have to deal with the consequences of what we do. But whatever happened that night... my food pushed you through to the next level in your career, didn't it? You said or did something that got you noticed by your boss, and now you have everything you want." He gestured sharply at her, figuratively throwing the statement at her feet.

"It affected your friends differently. They all wanted different things, but something was holding them back and my magical meal pushed them through it. You're welcome!" he shouted. Then he fully turned to face the door like he meant to leave, but instead he stopped and stood there.

"We don't choose what we get to do in this world. You choose. You tell us what you want and we provide—for a price. But whatever it is, we don't get a *choice* in what it is. We can only do our best to... *I* could only do my best to mitigate the damage." His voice cracked, and with it, Helena's anger started to bleed away.

This wasn't his fault. It wasn't hers either. Cindy had been in trouble either way.

"I'm sorry," she said. "I haven't been fair to you—"

"No!" he shouted, slashing the air. "Don't do it. Don't pity me. I can't stand you *pitying* me. I'm a horrible person alright. I earned this! I just didn't... I just didn't want..."

"What?" she urged when he couldn't finish.

He lifted his head to look to the unresponsive heavens, his back still facing her. "I just didn't want to hurt you," he said, his voice thick.

She came up behind him, slipping her arms around his waist, pressing her cheek against his back.

"I'm sorry," she said.

"Don't—" he said and tried to pull away, but she wouldn't let him. Besides he had nowhere to go, as he was still facing the door. Instead, she came around to push him away and face him.

"Helena—" he pleaded, and then she silenced him with a kiss, pressing her lips to his while holding his face so he couldn't pull away.

She slipped her fingers through his hair when the kiss broke. "I'm sorry," she said. "I was upset. And I blamed you for things that weren't your fault when you were only trying to help me."

He nodded with tiny shakes of his head, his face still a wreck with his unshed tears. "It's just... when things go right, they're miracles. And they just don't go right so very often—"

She kissed him again, swallowing his words, making something go right for once in his existence. His hands hit her sides then, grasping her hips to pull her against him. Their kiss broke, and he buried his face in her half-dried hair, and she could feel him shudder in her arms as he held on.

After a long moment, she spoke. "In regard to the payment I owe you this time—"

"No, no," he said, straightening, sliding one of his hands against her cheek to hold her face as he gazed earnestly into her eyes. "You don't owe me anything—"

But then she set her fingertips against his lips.

"You said that demons can be paid with mind, body ... or soul?"

His eyes widened as he understood what she was offering him. "But I don't want you that way," he said, "Not like this."

"It's alright. *I* want this," she whispered back, rising up on her toes to kiss his cheek. "Let me give this to you. Please."

"But..." he said, still hesitating.

"What?" she said, stroking his cheek.

He captured her fingers and kissed the back of them. "If we do this, I can't maintain..." he indicated his own face, "this. I can't hold this image for you when I ... give myself over."

She smiled. "Rafferty, I've already seen you naked."

He scoffed. "Trust me. It's different when ... you're in the throes of passion. Nobody wants to see it."

"It's going to be fine," she said, meeting him dead in the eye. "I love you."

With those words, Rafferty gave in. There was nothing more for him to say.

This kiss was far more patient and toe-curling than the romantic pecks they had explored. With a growl, he grabbed her, lifting her to her toes, using her clothes for purchase. She wasn't going to be nearly that patient. Instead, she scrabbled down his chest, reaching for the buttons of his shirt.

"Just tear them," he said on the third button. "They'll disappear the second I take it off."

She giggled as she did so, the buttons snapping and vanishing as they separated their connection to Rafferty. "Okay, I've never done that before."

"There are going to be a lot of firsts tonight," he said and dived back toward her for another kiss.

She started to work on her own clothing, which was a sweater that went down to her thighs. It only had two buttons near the top that held it in an artful fold over her shoulders that she had to undo to get her head free. While she wrangled the wooden buttons through the tangle of soft acrylic threads of the sweater, she felt Rafferty's hands on her head, sweeping up the sides of the sweater's neck.

"No, don't. Mine doesn't disappear when you tear it," she said before she realized he wasn't going for the sweater, but actually pulling at the hair tie she had used to ponytail back her hair at the hospital. Sweeps of her red-gold hair, that in her mind desperately needed a brush, cascaded around her face. Rafferty patted it slowly, tracing his fingers carefully through her tresses so he wouldn't snag anything.

"You're beautiful," he breathed.

She grinned, then pulled the sweater up and off, letting it drop to the ground. "How about now?" she asked with a sultry smile.

Rafferty couldn't say anything, only watched as she reached behind herself and unsnapped her bra, letting it drop to join the sweater.

"How about now?"

He fell to his knees before her like a supplicant, and she laughed at the show of passion. His arms came around her waist as he buried his face into her stomach. She ran her hands over his hair, then down his back, peeling the shirt away from him. It came away easily without a ripping sound, even though it didn't need his arms to come through the sleeves to do so. He arched his back against her exploring hands as she ran her palms back up.

"There's something missing," she said as her hands lingered over the spots where his wings should be.

His head hung lowered before her, his hands holding onto her hips as she moved. Then it was strange. She could see him shift before her, his skin go gray, his horns appear curling back over his hair, and his wings forming under her hands. Yet it felt like they were always there. They didn't shift up like they were being displaced, the wings simply were there and had always been.

The wrongness feeling buzzed up her arms too, now that she saw him for what he was, but she also didn't care. It didn't hurt her. It was just a part of what he was. She didn't like it, though she would never admit it to him. She could tolerate it in favor of the other things about him she hungered for.

Carefully, slowly, she slid her fingers along the wrist-like bones of his wings. He groaned loudly. The wings rose and fell as he panted, and before she knew what was happening, he clawed at her leggings, pulling them down until she was entirely stripped in seconds. Before she realized what was happening, he dived for her, pressing his mouth into her nether region and dispelling all doubts about whether he knew what he was doing or not.

Gasping, she grabbed at his head this time, as shudders made it difficult to keep standing. Her world exploded in sensations, and though it had been a while, she never remembered anything feeling *this* good. His arms came about her, grabbing her backside to add some support while his wings crested around them both. It wasn't enough though as his work forced her to spread her legs more than she was ready to, and she lost her balance. His extra appendages prevented her from crashing completely to the ground. Instead, she was swept up into his arms, cradled against his chest.

"Where... where are we going?" she asked, her head swimming with the heady mixture of his intense touch and an inability to breathe against it.

"To the bed," he said, the tip of his tail coming up to caress her across the cheek as he navigated her down her slightly too narrow hall for the way he was carrying her *and* his wingspan. He shifted once more to his human form to accommodate the space while she cuddled her head into her shoulder, feeling perfectly safe and happy.

Chapter 39

LET'S GET IT ON

Landing on the bed took her breath away, and she started to laugh again. Rafferty looked down on her, lying beside her with his arms framing her body.

"Why are you laughing?" he asked, concern pinching his face.

She reached up to rub it away. "Lovemaking has lots of laughter in it," she said sweetly.

"Lovemaking," he repeated softly. "Then I'm not doing something wrong?"

"No, of course not. You're doing something very right," she assured him. Raising her head, she nuzzled it into the crook of his shoulder where it met his neck, kissing and nuzzling until she found the perfect spot. Again, her lover shuddered and cupped her in his arms like she was the only buoy in a raging sea.

"Helena, I don't want to hurt you," he whispered.

"Then don't," she said and slid her fingers down his stomach to open the button on his pants. Like with the shirt, when she went to try to slide them down from his body, she found the material simply gave, tearing silently away. He shifted above her, so that his bare skin pressed along hers, and she opened her legs to welcome him in. His mouth came down to engulf one of her breasts while one of his hands attempted to wrap around what couldn't fit and failed. This time she arched against him and let his obvious show of skill speak to her.

Again she giggled when he released it.

"You are surprising me," she said.

"Why?"

"One moment, you seem like you don't know what to do, then the next you do something like that, like an expert. It's a bit discordant." She slid her hands down his sides to cup the bones of his hips, encouraging him to slide forward as she kneaded her fingers into the flesh of his backside.

"I... I've had sex before," he stated with a note of defensiveness, "but... this... It's not like that at all."

"No, it's not. It's better," she assured, then gasped as the tip of him bumped her. He didn't go immediately in as she expected but slid himself along her, sharing the intimate touch. She loved it too and arched once more to exert more pressure as he slid back, eliciting just as much sensation. The tip of him bumped her pearl of pleasure, and they both reacted to the spike of lightning.

"I can stop," he offered. "I can still please you without..."

"Could you get me pregnant?"

That froze him like he had turned to stone, as if the idea hadn't occurred to him. "Uh... yes. The magic of this body is the same as the magic I would put into food," he admitted, already backing away. "It could force you to conceive if I intended it to—"

"Then would you wear a condom?" she asked, as if it were the most natural thing in the world to request of a demon.

"Uh... I..."

"Will a condom stop it?" she asked, sitting up more on her elbows.

"The magic can overcome any earthly barriers... but again only if I will it to," he confessed.

"So I'd have to trust you not to will it to?" She arched an eyebrow at him. "Can I trust you?"

"No, I'm a demon," he started to say, but she cupped his face to meet her eyes. His denials shifted to acquiescence. "Yes," he whispered. "Yes, you can trust me."

She smiled at him, then turned to her side drawer and removed a pack from within. It was a new box, and as she tore through the side and then individual wrapping, he leaned down to kiss her bare shoulder and places on her back that tickled and pleased at the same time.

When she turned back, he let her take control, waiting patiently as she slipped the condom over him, measuring his girth and length with her hands.

"There," she said softly, satisfied with his proportions. He made his own adjustment while she grabbed up a small bottle of lubricant, just to assure the next few moments would be entirely successful.

He kissed her again on the mouth, sweeping his tongue in. She needed no coaxing to meet it. Again, she slipped her hands around his hip bones and encouraged him forward. This time when his tip met her, she angled her hips so he slid where she wanted him to.

"Oh yes," she moaned as he slowly filled her, taking his time for their bodies to acclimate with each other.

"Helena," he groaned in return when he had reached his hilt. He held there as she squirmed beneath him, her own body clenching and unclenching around him in response. "You mercy, you grace."

"You torturer!" she gasped and laughed in the next breath.

Grinning, he pulled back again so he could press forward, slowly at first then building in speed as their breath kept pace. It felt wonderful. She locked her legs around him, holding him closer, as each stroke felt like a conversation inside, him discovering nuances and eliciting her responses. Her focus was so fixed on how it felt and what they were doing, that she didn't notice at first that as the pace increased, Rafferty kept physically shifting.

Like someone was playing with a switch, she saw him flip between the two selves as he struggled to hold the human illusion. His pace would slow as he started to lose control and increase when he got it back. Helena didn't say anything at first and focused only on how it felt, letting him try to work it out without her distracting him. But while the teasing was delightful, the more he struggled, the more the pace was thrown off.

"Raffie, let it go," she finally gasped out between breaths.

He shook his head, unable to say anything beyond a guttural grunt as he tried to do two all-consuming things at once.

"Raffie... Raffie, please," she begged as the tension inside kept building, screaming for release. She needed to cum so badly. "Raffie..."

"Hel—" was all he said as his wings spasmed into being behind him, creating an umbrella over them. She vaguely heard the sound of her lamp being knocked to the ground and the room became dimmer as the majority of the light was now cast under her bed. In the darkened room, she looped her arms around his neck, feeling the wrongness of his skin as he kept fluttering. She didn't care. She needed him. Now.

"Let go!" she shouted.

"Helena!" he ground out like plea, like a desperate prayer, finally doing what she asked, becoming the full demon he always was. She grabbed his horns for purchase as the feelings inside her crested, the wrongness stimulating in an unprecedented way. Her eyes screamed shut as she slammed back into the bed. She could feel him doing the same as they locked together. Energy coursed through her, igniting every nerve with mind-blowing pleasure.

If this was what people felt when enjoying the company of succubi and incubi, she got it. It was so much better than anything she had ever experienced.

Yet, she couldn't imagine what was so wrong or dark or evil about this. She had had empty sex before. It had been pleasurable, but this was something so much more. She knew she had said she loved him and she thought she had, but this was something else. This was something she couldn't put words to. Looking up at his twisted face, he shifted once again. He wasn't demonic, or human—he was... just Rafferty.

As the last tremors of their lovemaking shivered between them, he returned to himself and the world shifted back to her bedroom around them. And then he physically shifted off of her, pulling himself free.

She couldn't move or comment on any of it, but he rolled onto his side to fiddle with himself, probably removing the condom. Then he righted her lamp on the floor so it threw out twilight, enough to see but also dim enough that she could just go to sleep.

"Are you alright?" he asked, his voice warm when he turned back to her, holding back as if afraid that she may pull away now that the deed was done.

She turned herself to face him and reached, demanding him to come closer with a child-like sweetness. Kissing his chest just below his collarbone, she then nuzzled him with her nose as her answer, all the while smiling.

He pulled her close to him. "You are a miracle, Helena."

"Hmm, that is a much better compliment than 'Well, you've paid in full.'" She had meant it as a joke, but she felt him stiffen inside her arms and not in the good way. "I'm sorry. I shouldn't have said that."

"Why not? It's true," he said disparagingly as he stroked her hair.

"Oh I don't know. I feel like you've given to me as much as I've given to you."

"That's why this act is so easy for one of my kind to draw from. It's the natural way it works. You get pleasure, but we take from you, like the monsters we are."

"Shhh, that's enough. That's my boyfriend you're talking about, and I'll have to beat you up if you keep talking shit about him," she said sleepily.

"Boyfriend?" he whispered.

She wanted to say something back, to clarify or confirm what she had just said, but the deep, warm waters of sleep were pulling her under, and she didn't have the strength to resist them anymore.

Chapter 40

THEN CHARLIE CAME OVER

Lying in bed in the morning, Helena felt so darn snuggly and delicious she thought she might burst into cream-puff bubbles.

Despite her assurances that she accepted her lover as he was, Rafferty had shifted back to human.

"You know, I noticed something," Helena said, examining him now in the soft glow from her bedside lamp.

"Oh, yeah?" he asked, his eyes closed, one hand tucked behind his head, the other curled up on his stomach, totally at rest.

Helena rolled on to her stomach, propping her chin onto her palm. "When you look like your other self—"

He immediately made a disparaging face, which made her laugh.

"No, don't do that," she chided, smoothing the expression with a tender hand. "I'm just saying, when you look like your other self, you look less gaunt. You've thickened up. Put on some weight."

He pinched his eyebrows a little at that observation.

"Here, come on. You switch back and I'll get you a mirror," she said trying to bounce up but found it difficult as her legs got tied up in blankets. "Go ahead. Switch."

"No," he said, "I don't want to."

"Oh come on. Let me see your other face," she pressed, but he just jutted his chin and crossed his arms.

She sighed. "Well, why not?"

"I like this face," he said, peeking up at her. "It looks like yours."

Smiling, she leaned forward to giving him another one of the soft kisses she just couldn't get enough of.

"Are you hungry?" he whispered.

Wrinkling her nose, she took stock. "Yeah, I guess so. I was thinking I was going to reheat up that pot pie you made me and try to finish it off for breakfast."

He scoffed at that.

"Hey, don't do that. I liked that pot pie," she defended. It had been bright and happy and comforting both when served originally and when she had it cold for lunch yesterday.

"I'll make you something fresh," he said and pulled away the covers to get out of bed. The sight made her pause as she took in the line of his natural body while he moved to the top of her dresser where she kept his real clothes.

"Is that how you looked before? When you were alive?" she asked.

He paused and looked down at his body, then up again to the mirror over her dresser.

"I don't remember, actually," he said. "My sense of self was destroyed when I died, so possibly?"

He kept looking at his face though, turning it this way and that.

"When's the last time you looked at yourself?" she asked, knee-walking out of bed.

"When would I have needed to?" he countered, but she remembered he had seen his face in the mirrors at the clothing store. Still, she wondered why he was being defensive about it.

Slipping her hands around his waist, she enjoyed the feel of his solid form. She fervently wished she could keep him forever, that he didn't have to go back and there didn't have to be this terrible cost to even this innocent moment of intimacy between lovers. No amount of demon magic could grant her that wish, she knew.

"Come on. I'm hungry," she said and turned to pluck her terry bathrobe from where it hung from her closet door instead of getting dressed properly. "I think I'll take a quick shower—"

Just then the doorbell rang.

The two of them looked at each other in alarm. "Who could that—" she started to say, but then a possibility struck her. "Cindy! Last night. What she did... police would investigate." She pressed her fingers to her lips in concern. "But how do we explain how we teleported her to the hospital?"

Rafferty's eyebrows furrowed hard as they both thought. "I could always kill them?" he offered.

She smacked his arm. "No! You cannot always kill them!"

"Ow, I was kidding," he said, rubbing his arm, then pulled on his shirt to work the buttons. "Teach me for trying to make a joke," he grumbled.

"Okay well, I need to put more clothes on if it's the police. Could you go answer…?" Then her phone pinged. "Just go answer the door and keep them busy. Please," she said as she dove among the devastation of her bed to find her phone.

"As you command, my lady," he said, stepping out of the room, receiving a pillow at the back of her head as payment. He chuckled back at her.

Helena finally found her phone not in the bed but on the floor beside it, face down. It pinged again just as she got her fingers around the edge. The screen lit up to show the message notifications from Charlie.

"Helena, it's not the police," Rafferty called.

"Crap," she whispered, deciding she would respond to him after she dealt with the door, and took a shower… and procrastinated a while longer…

"Who is it?" she asked as she left her bedroom to pad down her hallway, still in her robe.

"Helena?" Charlie's voice called.

Oh crap, she thought, but there was nothing for it now. As she came into her main room, she spotted her friend standing by the door, his eyes red from crying. Please be about Cindy, please be about Cindy.

But the look he gave her told her it wasn't.

"Did you know?!" he demanded, pivoting from Rafferty, who prudently shut the door, to Helena.

"Charlie, you need to take a breath," she tried to say, but he wasn't going to have it.

"Did. You. KNOW!"

Helena stiffened her back. "No," she said.

Charlie stood there panting. He blinked as what she said registered. "No? You didn't know?"

"No, not 'no.' No, you are not going to come into my house and start screaming at me because you're angry at someone else," she stated in no uncertain terms.

Charlie's eyes flared again as he understood. He opened his mouth to scream again, but then the mature part of his brain, not dictated by emotion, forced him to hesitate. Then to take a breath. Then to deflate. His head dropped and Helena moved, opening her arms to her friend. Holding on, he buried his head in her shoulder.

"Oh God, Helena! What am I going to do?" he sobbed.

Over her friend's head, Rafferty indicated he was heading to her kitchen and Helena gave him a tiny nod, with a mouthed "Thank you." As he passed, Rafferty squeezed her shoulder reassuringly.

She stayed that way, rubbing Charlie's back and letting him cry until all that were left were shaky breaths. "Here, let's sit down and talk, and I will tell you what I know," she said, encouraging him toward the table.

"Thank you," Charlie said tearfully, sniffing hard. "I'm sorry about all this."

"This is not your fault, Char. And it's not mine either," she said.

He horked another sniff. "You're right. It's fucking Chris's," he agreed and dropped into a chair so he could plop his head onto the table's surface. "I wouldn't have cared as much if he told me or at least asked for my permission. I would have understood, you know. I mean, we've both done boys' weekend before, but this... this isn't the same."

"No, it's not the same, is it?" Helena agreed, dropping her tissue box in front of him before sitting down kitty corner from him at the end.

Rafferty reappeared, poking his head out of the kitchen. "Helena," he said softly, "where is your coffeemaker?"

"Oh, I'm sorry, Charlie. Can you wait a moment? I'll be right back," she said, patting his hand.

"Yeah, okay," Charlie said, clutching his third tissue already. Then before she disappeared he added. "No sugar in mine. I... I am supposed to be watching my intake." And he broke down crying again.

Helena decided to just leave him be for a moment. Getting him coffee would probably help more. In the kitchen, she beelined past Rafferty to go over to the cupboard above her stove. "When the circle cl—when you had to leave the 'city' real fast, my coffeemaker got destroyed, so I went out and got you this." She pulled out a glass carafe with a plunger in a lid out of the cupboard, the purchase tag still swinging from it, and presented it to him.

"Ta-da! French press!" she said grinning, wishing she could have given her gift under better circumstances but still eager for his reaction all the same.

Rafferty's eyes lit up. "Oh yes," he said, taking it to slide the lid off and look inside at the netted component at the end of the plunger. "Oh this is perfect. I will be able to make you a decent cup of coffee now!" Then his face shifted. "That is if you bought the whole beans and not the pre-ground stuff."

She laughed at his reaction and then reopened the cabinet to show him. "I even got French roast," she quipped.

Pleased her gift was received so well, Helena moved up to him to steal a kiss, which surprised him as much as the coffee press. "I love you," she whispered and then turned to go back to administer to her wounded friend.

Chapter 41

IMPROVED LAVENDER CREAMER

By the time she came back, Charlie had calmed down again, and they were able to talk. She told him everything she knew about what Chris had been up to, and she learned that Charlie had discovered what had happened when the woman, whose name was also Charley, short for Charlene, called looking for Chris. At that point, Rafferty brought them the coffee.

"He's literally replacing me with the female version of me! It's just sick!" Charlie bemoaned, not unjustly. Helena had a difficult time wrapping her head around it.

"I never actually asked her name," she said.

Charlie sniffed again and took a thoughtful sip of his cooling beverage. "The thing is, I don't think she had any idea about me either. I... I feel bad for her. Is it alright for me to feel bad for her?"

"Yes, but that makes Chris seem even worse," Helena said, shaking her head, holding her cup in her hands but forgetting to drink it, even though it was amazing coffee.

Then Rafferty appeared beside her and poured something into it.

"What did you do?" she asked as he turned to go back into the kitchen.

"I fixed it," he reported, which clarified nothing.

So she took a sip. Vanilla danced on her tongue, but after she swallowed, she realized he had added her lavender creamer. Or his version of her lavender creamer.

"Why didn't you tell me when you found out?" Charlie asked softly, shaking his head.

She swallowed. "At first, because I was in shock, and I wasn't sure if I would make things worse or better and I didn't want to act—"

"Until you had the right answer, yeah. That makes sense," Charlie said.

She took a breath, in for a penny, in for a dollar. "And then Chris said he would tell you himself, and for me to give him time, which I could understand, but then he threatened me."

"He threatened you?" Charlie asked, furrowing his eyebrows harder.

"To tell everyone in my life about some personal secrets that I have and he knows," she said.

Charlie's face popped open to big Os, both his eyes and his mouth. "Oh God damn," he said as he leaned forward to prop his arm on his table and cover his mouth with his fist. "No, he didn't."

"Yeah, he did," she confirmed.

"God, Helena, I'm so sorry," he said, setting his hand on her leg and squeezing his apology.

She covered his hand and smiled gently. "It's okay. I'm okay. I told my boss at work and she's aware, so if he tries anything, she's prepared."

"Oh crap," Charlie added, shaking his head. "You shouldn't have had to do that. He has no grounds to break your trust like that."

"It's alright. It's too late now, and I'm fine."

Charlie nodded and accepted that, then looked up as Rafferty came once more through the kitchen door. He set two plates of quiche down in front of each of them, and Helena's eyes popped out. "Rafferty, this is..."

"Breakfast," he said, "Bon appetit."

He moved to go back into the kitchen, but Charlie held up a hand to him. "I'm sorry. I came in here a hot mess, and I didn't even introduce myself to you. I'm Charlie, Helena's friend."

Rafferty took his hand and shook it.

"You two actually met," Helena admitted, her cheeks pinking up.

"Oh?" Charlie asked, looking quickly to her and then back to Rafferty, his eyebrows popping up as he realized it. "Oh, yes. You were the caterer that night. Oh man, your food is delicious. I swear to God, there had to be some magic in it because I had the biggest breakthrough on my golf game the next day. I had been plateauing for years, and after your dinner... It was a miracle."

"It affects different people in different ways," Rafferty said.

Charlie didn't know how to take that, and Helena almost choked on air, but her friend just rolled with it.

"Well it was delicious, and if you made this quiche, I'm guessing it's going to be the same."

"I'm glad you're going to enjoy it," Rafferty said and turned to go back into the kitchen.

"Oh," Charlie said to his back. "Aren't you joining us?" he tried to ask but Rafferty kept moving into the kitchen, so he redirected the question to Helena, "Isn't he joining us?"

"Raffie, are you joining us?" she called after.

There was a pause. "Do you want me to?"

"Yes, get in here and eat breakfast with my friend."

"Fine."

She glanced back at Charlie, who finally had a proud, smug grin on his face. "What?"

"Cindy owes me $20," he said.

"No, you did not bet on me hooking up with..." She indicated Rafferty, who picked that moment to come in with his plate and move to the seat at her right hand, opposite Charlie.

"What's not to like, Hel? Tall, dark, reasonably good-looking, and he can cook," Charlie said blatantly as he watched Rafferty take his seat.

"Yeah, but..." Helena tried to protest and then Rafferty held his hand out to her to take, and Charlie's smug smile grew even deeper.

Trapped, Helena smiled, sighed, and took her boyfriend's hand, cutting a slice of the quiche with her fork. The quiche was perfect, warm and savory, with bits of ham, finely diced green peppers, and cheese evenly mixed in. But she didn't notice any of it. Only Charlie's happy/sad smile as he took his first bite.

"How is it?" Rafferty asked. It was only then that a horrible thought came to Helena, and she shot him an alarmed look.

He looked back at her, pinching his brows together to ask, "What?"

She wiggled her fingers at the food, while making pointed eyes. *Did you put magic in the food?* she thought asked.

He pinched his fingers together a tiny amount.

Helena flared her eyes and nostrils at him. *What?*

It'll be fine, he gestured and indicated Charlie with a nod of his head, who had indeed tucked into his quiche, eating calmly even as tears rolled down his cheeks.

Pursing her lips together, Helena did not feel convinced in the slightest. She leaned in, tugging on Rafferty to do the same, so she could whisper in his ear. "What did you do?"

He returned the whisper, pulling her hair back to clear her ear. "I wished him peace. He'll be fine. The chances of something bad happening from that are incredibly low."

She had to accept that; Charlie was already halfway through his quiche and the explanation of why he should throw it up involved explaining her demon summoning exploits. That was clearly one revelation too many at the moment.

"Me and Chris were like that, in the beginning," Charlie said, noting the whispering. "I'm so happy for you, Helena."

"Don't talk like that... I mean, in the past tense, you don't know..." She struggled for the right way to say it. "Is it really over between you or do you think you'll try to work it out?"

"I don't know," Charlie said honestly. Then there was a chime song. He dug out his phone and held it up. Predictably, it said Chris across the top. He didn't answer it, just stared at it until the jingling went away. Then Helena's phone began to dance and jingle.

"Do you want me to answer it?" she asked.

"No," Charlie said, completely calm. "We're having breakfast right now."

So she muted the ring, and they kept eating silently while both their phones continued to blow up with missed calls.

"Have you talked to Cindy yet this morning?" Chris asked.

Helena glanced at her phone clock. "I was going to before you came over. She told me to go to work, but I don't see how I can. How did you hear about it?"

"She called me late last night before I got the call from the other Charley. We talked for a long time. So on top of everything else, I feel guilty about that too."

"Charlie," Helena said, leaning over to take his hand. "This is not our fault."

"But I was wondering. I noticed some things, but I ignored them, that she wasn't as alright as she wanted all of us to think. But I'm not like you, Helena. I'm not good at saying what needs to be said when it needs to be said. I just kept sitting around and waiting to see, you know. And this whole time she was a thin thread away from snapping."

"Maybe she needed to snap," Rafferty suddenly said.

"She needed to hurt herself?" Helena challenged.

Rafferty shook his head. "Maybe that was the problem. She didn't feel like she could. She didn't feel like she could be weak or let anybody down, so she just extended and extended and locked herself up so tight that she couldn't ever let go. That sort of thing will kill you or make you do stupid desperate things to guarantee that you don't fail. But what she really needed was to fail, so that it could be over, so she could let go, and now she's got a chance to actually heal."

Charlie nodded his head at that. "I've heard something like that before. That another way to look at depression is not as a bad thing, but your body telling you that you need to stop and rest. Depressed. Deep rest." He examined Rafferty a little closer and Helena grew worried about what he saw. "Probably a common thing in culinary school, right?"

"The place I trained was very brutal. A lot of people didn't make it," Rafferty agreed.

"Ha, I bet," Charlie said, cutting another bite from his quiche. "Well, you are a good guy, Rafferty, and you make a damn good quiche."

"I am not a good guy," Rafferty said, then nodded. "And I make an alright quiche. Could have used something more. Another spice. I don't know." He licked his teeth as he thought about it.

"And that is the sign of a true chef," Charlie pointed out. "Not like Chris. The freaking poser. He thinks everything he cooks is amazing."

"Yeah, I know," Helena said, flashing the demon, who was refusing to look at her and yet unable not to. "I don't know how I would have gotten through the last couple months without him."

Chapter 42

KIND OF DITCHED HER

"I wouldn't bother with that. It's not going to make a difference to the damage done," Cindy said while she moved through her apartment, walking clothes over to her suitcases sitting on the couch. Helena laid out the last of Cindy's towels to try to create a dry-ish path. Her bedroom had been completely flooded, and there was better light in the living room.

"Yes, I understand. Whatever adjustments you need to make to the arrangements is fine, as long as they fit the color scheme we dictated," Helena said into her phone, which she had pressed to her ear with her shoulder.

Cindy noted her on the call and mouthed, "Sorry."

Helena rolled her eyes, indicating her opinion of the caller. "What do you mean? Why would that change the price?" She listened for a moment. "That's outside of the agreed on budget."

She could hear the woman on the other end wheedling.

"Alright, if we approve that, we will have to take more money out of what is being raised at the Winter Rose Ball, and what is being raised right now is money for the children's hospital's new emergency room. Do you think a headline about how we couldn't purchase one more breathing machine because the flowers cost too much would be of benefit to your shop?" The florist sputtered a moment, but Helena didn't wait for her shtick to take too much of an effect. "I'm not supposed to tell you this, but I think I need to inform you that a feature is going out in a week about all of the different businesses contributing to this event..." She paused for a moment to let the woman have her reaction to that bit of news. "Well, yes. We thought it was the least we could do to all of those going above and beyond for this event. Unfortunately, we have no control over what the journalist writes, and we want to give them the best headline we can..." She listened a little longer. "Thank you. I appreciate it." At last she could hang up.

"Sorry, Cindy," she tried to say, but her friend waved it away.

"I'm sorry to be pulling you away from your job like this."

"Oh trust me," Helena said as she pressed a foot into the towels to make sure they soaked up the damp. "As soon as your dad gets here, I am abandoning you," she quipped, then sighed. "I'm loving my job, but it's also a lot of stress and work."

Then she glanced at her friend.

"Not that it compares," she added, only for her phone to ping again, forcing her to flip back and send off another quick message confirming that she was still coming to the afternoon meeting. Cindy stood in front of her suitcases ignoring it all, folding and distributing the remaining clothes from her dresser while she stared off into the dark abyss of her thoughts.

"I can't believe they are kicking you out because of what happened. This is not your fault," Helena said, then chided herself internally for not picking a cheerier topic to talk about.

"It's fine. I wanted out of the lease anyway. I hate this building," Cindy said, dealing out the last stack of clothes among the suitcases like they were large playing cards. "Are you sure you shouldn't be at work?"

Yes. No, Helena thought, but instead she pulled out her phone to check the time. "Should I order shawarmas?"

"Oooh, yes please," Cindy said as she went back for the clothes in her closet. "Oh hell, I should just throw all of this away and start over, you know."

"Giving away all your possessions is one of the signs—"

"I know, I know. I retract the statement," Cindy said. "Some doctor I turned out to be."

"Some friend I turned out to be," Helena countered, kicking herself. She just didn't seem to be able to say the right thing even though her friend needed her to.

"Hey," Cindy said, turning around to come back. She extended her arms and her tall friend wrapped them around Helena's head for a hug. "Thank you so much for coming and finding me. I wouldn't be here if it wasn't for you."

Helena rocked with her sister-friend, so relieved that she could do so. But while she did, her phone binged three times in quick succession. She ignored it but couldn't *not* feel the urgency with each ping.

"I didn't want this to happen, I swear," Cindy said.

"I know, I know," Helena assured, even as she snuck a peek at her phone. It was Yosef. *Call. Emergency. Now.*

They pulled apart, both wiping their noses, then laughing. "And thank God for your boyfriend. A damn angel," Cindy added.

"You have no idea," Helena said, truthfully, then texted to Yosef, *Two minutes.*

"Yeah, but you know what this means? I owe Charlie $20," Cindy said as she turned to get back to packing.

"Yeah, sorry about that," Helena said, flipping to Cindy's dad's text messages to find the link for his GPS location. He had sent it to her so she could estimate where he was. To her relief, he was fifteen minutes away. "Your dad's almost here," she announced.

"It'll all be worth it if you tell me the sex was good," Cindy said.

"With your dad?" Helena asked before catching on that Cindy hadn't pivoted the conversation with her.

"What? No, with your sexy chef." Cindy peeked out, cocking a teasing eyebrow. "Do you have fantasies about my dad?"

"Ha, ha, ha." Helena blushed, realizing there was no covering or being cool with that as her reaction.

Cindy stuck out her tongue, then turned back to her closet. "See, I told you it would work out with this guy if you just gave it a chance."

"Well, nothing has really changed," Helena admitted. "His circumstances are such that we can only be together sporadically before he has to go again."

Cindy threw her a confused look over her shoulder. "Why is that?"

"He has ... obligations elsewhere."

"Okay, that sounds mysterious," Cindy said as she pulled clothing off of her closet hangers. "Does he cook for the president or the pope or something?"

"At the risk of adding to the mystery, I really can't talk about it." Helena held her arms out for Cindy to lay hung clothes over.

"That's alright. I understand. So it's just casual?"

Helena pursed her lips, and Cindy's eyes went wide. "Oh."

"No, I don't know. He cares about me, that much I know is true, but with his life being what it is..."

"Have you told him you love him?"

Helena turned sharply to carry her burdens to the living room. "Yes, okay."

"Wait, has he said it back to you?" Cindy called, grabbing up her own armfuls to follow.

"What do you think?" Helena shot back, knowing she shouldn't be getting defensive but unable to help it.

"Oh God, did he say something cliche like 'I know'?"

"I doubt he's ever seen a movie, let alone *that* movie."

"Wow, he's really that hardcore?"

"About cooking, absolutely." Helena shed the clothes on the only spare space on the couch.

"Okay, then when do you get to see him again?"

"I don't know. Probably be a while, but you know what? That's okay. I've got the Winter Rose Ball literally in two weeks, and I need to focus on that, not get distracted." Helena shook out a garbage bag and drew it down one of the bundles of hanging clothes. "I've picked a caterer and made all the other big arrangements, but there are a hundred and one little details that have to be worked out. I

wouldn't be able to nurture a beginning relationship properly anyway."

"I'm sorry I'm not going with you," Cindy said, helping
by grabbing up the bottom of the bag to pull the strings
and tie it. Helena laid the packaged clothing on her dining
room table while Cindy went for the next bundle. "I know
I was supposed to be your plus one."

"It'll be fine. Chris and Charlie will be there," Helena
tried to assure, but hearing the statement out loud, clarified to her why that was not as reassuring as it would have
been a couple months ago.

"You still haven't told Charlie yet about Chris?"
Cindy asked.

"Actually, I have, but I didn't say anything because we
didn't want to burden you," Helena admitted.

Cindy froze at that declaration. "Oh. Well. How did
he take it?"

Before she could answer Helena's phone rang out. This
time it was Scarlet.

"I'm so sorry. It's my boss," Helena said, answering it
before Cindy could even nod. "I'm so sorry, Scarlet. I'll
be there soon—"

"My dear," Scarlet's voice said, cutting off any and all
other conversation with a tone that commanded kings to
bow. Helena's eyes went wide. "If you are not in my office
within the hour, do not bother coming back at all. Do you
understand me?"

"Y-yes, ma'am," Helena said, her feet already spurring
her toward Cindy's door. The phone hung up before she
even got there. "I have to go. I am so sorry. Your dad is
almost here, but I got..." But she couldn't finish that sentence as she jetted down the hall. Luckily, the elevator

binged open at just that moment, and Helena jumped on it, throwing a last glance at Cindy watching her leave from her door.

Helena tried to wave, but her friend didn't return it.

Chapter 43

ALMOST GOT FIRED

Helena rushed into Scarlet's office with a heavy heart. She had made it under the deadline, but she knew she was far from out of the woods yet.

No one noticed her return as everyone in the office was running around, focused on their own tasks. Which was fine because Helena beelined straight for Scarlet's door. Or she would have, but Yosef intercepted her.

"Stop," he ordered, grabbing her upper arms to encourage that idea as he stood between her and Scarlet.

"No, I have to get in there—" Helena tried to say, but he didn't let her pass.

"Take a breath," he commanded.

Automatically, Helena obeyed that command, having been trained to all her life by parents, therapists, and friends. As she took another one, Yosef helped her take off her coat and bag.

"You're here. You made it. Now center yourself," he continued to say in a soothing, practical tone.

After three more breaths, he let her go through the door.

Scarlet sat at her desk, reading something and making notes. The diorama of the Wrightwood Ballroom where the Winter Rose Ball was held sat next to her with its mini paper tables and chairs, showing the layout of the space. As Helena approached, her boss didn't look up but continued writing, leaving Helena to stand there. After a few more moments, Helena went to sit on one of the chairs in front of the desk.

"Don't sit down," Scarlet ordered, still not looking up. "Depending on how this goes, you may not be staying long."

The heart that Helena had calmed sped up again as she straightened and continued to wait until Scarlet was ready.

At last, Scarlet slid off her reading glasses and looked up at her. "First off, how is your friend?"

It was the last thing Helena thought she would say, and it took Helena too long to answer. "She's... she's not okay... but she is okay."

Scarlet nodded, indicating she understood that answer. "I am sorry that that happened. I am not going to pretend that this isn't a hard thing. And yet, it does not change the situation we now find ourselves in."

"But Scarlet—" Helena unwisely tried to say.

"No!" she barked. "You will not speak until I say you can, do you understand me? Another word and this conversation is over."

Helena shut her mouth and nodded, clasping her hands to keep them from shaking.

"Now I have been debating on how to *have* this conversation. I have never been terribly good at these things.

I could cite my history, the amount of work I put into building this place to nurture creative talent as my legacy. I could talk about the history of the Winter Rose Ball and what it means to not just me but this city. But honestly, I don't matter in this equation. This city and its unreasonable expectations don't matter. The children we're trying to help, they do matter, but this is not about that, is it?"

She waited and Helena realized it wasn't just rhetorical. "No, ma'am," she said.

"This is not even about the trust I put in you. Or about your frie—" Scarlet checked herself, clearing her throat.

"It's not that I do not have sympathy for the things that are happening in your life right now that you can't control. I have tried to give you some leeway up to this point, to let you find your own way through it."

The city matriarch set a hand on her desk, letting it hover a second before pressing it, pinning the thought down.

"I do understand," she insisted, "but that is also the thing. There are always going to be issues in this life we cannot control. Even if things at the Winter Rose Ball went entirely wrong, and it wasn't our fault, it would still be one very essential thing."

Scarlet held still, holding Helena's gaze. Helena didn't dare breathe.

"Responsibility. It would be our responsibility. Yours and mine."

Now Scarlet sat back, more confident in what she was saying.

"Despite everything that is going on in your or my life, it is our responsibility to bring this event together. And if you wish to claim that I am not as entirely dedicated to that vision as I am asking you to be, I will point out to you that I am likely to be dead within the next year."

Now Scarlet looked away as she fiddled with straightening things on her desk. "My doctors tell me I should be lying in a bed somewhere and doing everything I can to focus on myself and try to extend my life a little bit longer, but instead I am here, fighting through my pain and my exhaustion for an annual ball."

She lifted up a paper miniature of the ballroom's chandelier and hung it from the middle of the diorama.

"I wish it were as simple as it's just a party and who cares if the flowers are wrong or there aren't enough settings for those who were invited, but it isn't just that, is it? Any little thing that goes wrong could destroy the reputation of a business like ours. And without that reputation, we, Scarlet Promotions, are nothing."

Scarlet nailed Helena with her gaze, sharp and powerful regardless of her age or state of health.

"This isn't just about you and me. This isn't just about my legacy," Scarlet gestured toward the main room. "If the Winter Rose Ball fails, this is the end of this company. I don't have what it takes any more to build it back from a disaster like that. And everyone out there will lose their projects, their jobs, their commissions. Our clients will pull their business because the only reason we have their business is because of the Scarlet name. This place is already going to take a hit when I pass on, but if I can do anything to mitigate that from happening I will, but anything going terribly wrong at the Winter Rose Ball, and anything I could do to stop such a disaster would be inadequate."

"I care for all of you, but this is what it means to take on the crown, Helena. The people who rely on me? Who will one day rely on you and Yosef? Their lives will be irrevocably altered. If this company loses its reputation in such a public way, their ability to find other jobs in this or any adjacent industries is destroyed. They will be tainted by association."

Scarlet's eyes were haunted as if she could see it all happening before her, like an oracle confronting a terrible vision. Then she closed those eyes.

"I chose you to help me in my last year because I thought you could handle it. You seemed to me to be a person who not only cares about *what* she does but *who* she does it for. Your talent and creativity, your way with people, is a true skill that cannot be denied. I thought I could entrust you to be the guardian of this place when I'm gone." Her voice rose now with emotion, her own desperation bleeding through her collected exterior. "These people. *My* people. My *flowers*. Was I wrong?"

The question felt like a slap in the face. Helena's mouth was dry. Her gut screamed as it cramped and the needles in her throat pierced deep.

"No, ma'am," she said, tears beading in her eyes. "I'm so sorry to have given you that impression. I will work harder. I swear."

"Do you understand what is at stake here? What is being asked of you to do?"

"You're asking me to step up and be the leader this company needs to ensure its survival. I am responsible for that, and I haven't yet taken that responsibility as seriously as I should have. For that I cannot apologize enough. I can only learn from this and be better. I *will* take responsibility. All of it."

The words were like glass as she said them. Words she had said before in a different but just as dire context. Words that couldn't bring back an innocent girl, but maybe could save the livelihoods of everyone here.

Because if she left, then there would be no one who could do what she could do right now, it would be too late to hire someone so close to the ball and not hurt the company's reputation just the same.

Scarlet continued to search Helena's face, seeking out the answer that her words hadn't been able to convey. For a long, long moment, Helena was sure she wouldn't find it, and she scrambled to find something more to convey her sincerity. She knew she could do this. She knew she could be what Scarlet Promotions needed. This situation was nobody's fault but her own.

At last, Scarlet sighed. "Very well. We've spent enough time on this already. Let us get back to work." She leaned back and lifted up a written list on a pad of legal paper, sliding her glasses down so she could read it. "Where are we with the flower arrangements?"

Chapter 44

HAD A SERIES OF PROBLEMS ALL AT ONCE

"**I**just need to confirm that the food has been delivered this morning," Helena insisted to the kitchen contact over at the Wrightwood Ballroom. Talking through a hands-free headset, Helena's hands kept busy as she flipped through the table setting cards, checking against an official list where every name had been spell checked and honorificked correctly. "Alright, that's fine. I'll hold. Just hurry."

Half the day was already gone, and she was already wearing her gown for the night, not trusting that there would be time to change between final arrangements and the ball's start. The dress she wore was an inspiration of what Scarlet wore in the picture she had shown her all those months ago, a bright rose red that layered around her like petals. Scarlet had insisted on the dress herself as a show of continuity and a public show of her company exchanging hands. Yosef had already dressed as well, his matching cummerbund wrapped around his waist over his tuxedo pants and shirt. His jacket hung off the back of his chair, but in its lapel was a holiday rose, bright and festive. For Scarlet's part, she was going to wear a gown of pure white to match her whitened hair as the winter rose itself.

She could see it. They were so close to the finish line. Helena had never worked so hard in her life. Dedicating herself with a fervor she had never known previously, she had discovered an endurance she hadn't known she had.

Finishing the stack of cards and checking off the last name on the list, she slid them into a manila envelope and sealed it with the metal clip in the middle. "The guest list is checked," she called across the room to Yosef.

"Good, we need to go over soon," he said as he dialed his own phone and pressed it to his ear. "Yes, this is Yosef over at Scarlet Promotions returning your call…"

Helena shot a glance at Scarlet sitting at her own desk. There had been an unspoken tension between them now. Yosef kept assuring her that this was just Scarlet's focused demeanor, that she was like this every year before the Winter Rose Ball, but Helena had done two Winter Rose Balls under Scarlet since she started working for her, and it hadn't felt like this then. But she hadn't been a part of the leadership staff either, so she swallowed her apprehensions back and focused on what was next in front of her.

She would not let Scarlet down.

Finally, the ballroom contact came back to the phone. "Yes, the food was delivered," the woman reported.

"Alright good. The last thing I need is for the chef over at the Tower Top to call screaming at me again." She meant it as a joke, but she got awkward silence instead of chuckles on the other end.

"Um, I don't know about that, ma'am," the voice said politely.

Helena took a breath and held back her sigh. "I'll give him a call next. Thank you for confirming delivery. Bye."

She hung up.

Shaking her head, Helena tried to stack all her materials together. "I think I need to get over there. Nobody seems to know what they're doing."

"That's fine, child," Scarlet said as she pressed her fingers into her temples.

Helena paused as she noted it. "Scarlet, are you alright?" she asked.

Scarlet looked up at her blearily. She seemed for a moment like she didn't know where she was or who she was talking to, then she said. "Yes, yes. I'm just more tired than I want to be..."

Yosef looked up from his phone call and exchanged a worried glance with Helena.

Then Scarlet collapsed back into her wheelchair.

"Scarlet!" Helena shouted as she rushed from her desk to her boss's side. Yosef was there a second later.

"Pull the chair back!" he ordered while trying to dive for something under the desk.

"Scarlet, are you alright? Can you hear me?" Helena called to the older woman, whose lead lolled as her breathing became strained.

Yosef yanked out an oxygen tank from under the desk, his fingers desperately working through the tangle of tubes to get to the mask.

"Hold this to her face." He handed the mask off as he made adjustments to the tank's meter and turned on the air.

Almost instantly, Scarlet opened her eyes as she breathed.

"Slowly, slowly," Yosef said as she jerked. After a moment, Scarlet's eyes cleared of confusion, then she reached up and slipped the strap to hold the mask on over her head.

"Dammit, dammit, dammit," she cursed. "We don't have time for this."

"No," Yosef said in no uncertain terms as Scarlet reached for the brake on her wheelchair, as if she intended to roll away from her problems. "You're not going anywhere. I'm going to call Dr. Phelps."

"No, don't do that!" she insisted, reaching again for the oxygen tank in order to put it in its bag on her chair, but Yosef pulled it out of her way and handed it to Helena.

"Put your foot in front of the wheel and don't let her leave," he said, turning angrily to go back to his desk where he had tossed his phone in his panic.

"You can't hold me here!" she growled after him. "You're fired. You hear me!"

"Fine," he shouted back, unphased by her empty threat as he unlocked his phone and tapped quickly until it rang.

"Helena, we can't... It's tonight! There is still so much to do," Scarlet said, pleading with her other subordinate where shouting had failed with the first. Yosef's voice carried low and urgent as he talked to the doctor.

Scarlet's head lolled again for a second before she snapped it back up. "Dammit. This isn't how it's going to end. I won't allow it!"

"I'll take care of it," Helena assured her. "We're almost done. I can handle the last of the details. I'll go over right now and double check everything while you talk to the doctor and get checked out. It'll be fine. Then you can meet me over at the ballroom." Helena hoped she wasn't lying, but it seemed to placate Scarlet as she turned to watch Yosef, who was dragging out the massage table while he still spoke to the doctor.

"They'll take me away and put me in a bed, and I'll never get out again," Scarlet said fearfully. "I don't want to die on my back."

"You won't die on your back," Helena said. "They'll have to drag you off kicking and screaming."

Scarlet looked up at her. "Damn right they will." The thought seemed to calm her down, and she reached up to Helena's hand on her shoulder, giving it a squeeze. "Get going. I'll stay here and comply. Just don't let me down, my girl."

The pain in Helena's chest finally eased and she nodded. "I won't."

Yosef returned and took over guarding Scarlet as Helena moved back to her desk.

Finding her elegant kitten-heeled shoes, Helena bundled herself into her coat and adjusted her hair before gathering up everything she needed to take with her. She had someone in the office call her a cab to take her over to the venue and gave instructions to the rest of the office, three of whom were joining her on the crossing over. Before they left, Scarlet's doctor and nursing assistant arrived, beelining to her office with grave looks that spread tension to the rest of the room.

"Hey, everybody. Everything is fine," Helena said, commanding all eyes to her and hoping she was doing it the way Scarlet would have.

"Is Ms. Scarlet alright?" one of the office workers asked, glancing nervously toward her office.

"It's a big night tonight, and the doctor is insisting on checking her vitals before giving his approval for her to go over. It's just for insurance reasons," Helena lied. But her lie worked and the room all nodded, shoulders dropping as they accepted that reason. "Believe me, Scarlet is furious." That got her a few chuckles, everyone's belief at their boss's feistiness holding true. "Alright, so we got our jobs to do. We can't let Scarlet down. I'm heading over now, and Yosef is helping with the checkup so any further questions or emergencies, forward to *me* for now. Let's give Scarlet a chance to get her game face on and show her what we can do."

That rallied the troops nicely, and Helena actually felt confident as they headed on down the elevator and out to the waiting cab.

She could do this. It was all going to be alright.

The other three in the cab with her were chattering away when the first rush of calls came to her phone. To her surprise, it was an unknown number.

"Hello, is this Madame Helena?" a familiar voice asked on the other end.

"Yes, it is. Who is this?"

"It is Éliott from Tower Top Restaurant. I served you when you were here."

"Oh, yes, I remember you. Éliott, how are you?"

"Honestly, not good, madame. There is a problem that I need to discuss with you. About the dinner for tonight."

Fuck, Helena thought but didn't express. "Whatever it is, we can fix it. What is the problem?"

"The chef. He is gone."

Chapter 45

NOWHERE ELSE TO TURN

"What do you mean he's gone?" Helena asked as she stared down Éliott, despite his being a foot taller than her. The chef's cousin, who stood before her clearly wanting to be anywhere else in the world but exactly where he was, muttered in French a moment.

"I do not know exactly where, madame," he said, going green around the ears as he switched back to English. "But ... he left this morning."

"When is he coming back?" Helena demanded. This can't be happening. she thought, even though she knew it was.

All Éliott could do was shrug a shoulder.

She wanted to run her fingers through her hair in frustration, but it would have undone her French twist (ironic) and the little red crystal hairpins that held it all together.

"But I don't understand what happened?" she insisted.

"It sometimes happens with him," his cousin tried to explain. "Not for a long time, but he gets to the point where he can't... he can't take it no more and he..." He stuck a finger in his mouth and popped his cheek like a bottle cork. "And then he run away."

Helena wanted to scream, but it would do no good. "Okay, okay, so what has been finished? Where are things right now?" She glanced at the clock. It was already three hours before appetizers were supposed to be served. They were already sunk, but she chose to not give up yet.

"Nothing is cooked," Éliott admitted. "The food is here but no one to prepare it."

"But where is his staff?"

"They all quit. He..." Éliott struggled for a moment. "Burned their bridges." He shrugged as he knew he wasn't using the idiom right, but it got the idea across.

He looked back at the small crowd of people behind him, all dressed like him with matching rose embroidered shirts and festive aprons. "The wait staff are all here," he said, but that didn't really help things without food for them to serve. "We have the wine."

That too wasn't much help. This was a disaster.

"Okay, I just ... need a minute to think," she said. "I'll be... Is there somewhere private I can go to make a call?"

Éliott surged forward and went to open a nearby door for her. She nodded and went through. It was the loading dock where it connected to the kitchens. There were many twists and alcoves all over as well as cleaning staff and workers. But they only cast an incurious eye at the ballgowned woman and continued on with their own business. Desperate for somewhere to be, she plunged through the maze looking for somewhere secluded where she could make the call she needed to make.

At last she came across a room marked, "Hazard, do not enter," with worn caution tape crisscrossing it. She almost went by it, but a familiar wrong feeling skittered across her skin when she touched the door.

"No, it can't be," she said softly, then tried the handle, expecting it to be locked.

But it wasn't.

Slowly, she opened the door, which gave an ominous horror movie creak as it swung inward.

"Hey, ma'am," a voice interrupted thickly with an accent she couldn't place.

"Oh, sorry," she said, jumping back to face a mustached janitorial worker in coveralls.

"You can't go in there. It's off limits," he said ominously, pointing as if she hadn't seen the caution tape. "Bad things happen in there."

"What sort of bad things?" she asked.

He shrugged. "Don't know. It was a while ago. They just tell us to not go in there and leave it alone."

"Oh, okay," she said, holding up her cell phone clutched in her hands. "I was just looking for somewhere private to make a call."

"You can't make a call in there. You're better off going outside." He indicated the way she had come. "You take a left at the junction, that will take you outside," he said.

"Oh, okay, thank you," she said and turned to go the way he indicated.

Walking slowly, she could feel him watching her until she was just about to the corner where she was supposed to turn. Satisfied, the janitor went on with whatever he had been doing, assured that he had done his duty. As soon as he was gone, and she was confident no one else was around, she scurried back to the forbidden room.

She shut the heavy door behind her and was immediately plunged into absolute darkness. Wherever she was, the room was small; she could hear her own breath gasping. The wrong feeling had grown stronger.

"Okay, okay, okay," she whispered to herself as she fumbled with her phone until she got the flashlight feature to come on.

Sure enough, she was inside a small, concrete room. There was no real sign of what it could have been used for at one time, but the gray concrete of the floor sank in the middle toward a single, dinner plate-sized drain. Beside the door was an old yellow janitorial bucket on wheels with a mop sticking out of it, along with a rusted canister with "Purify!" written across it and a small bag of something white spilling out. With the toe of her shoe, Helena pushed the bag up to read it.

"Sidewalk Salt?" she read. Furrowing her eyebrows, she cast the light from her phone onto the concrete floor. At first she didn't see anything except the tiny shadows leaping up from the roughness of the surface. Then almost to the drain, she stopped and backed up. Faintly imprinted in the concrete was a small symbol. She didn't know what it meant, but she recognized it. Now that she knew what she was looking for, she backed up and let the light shine down on the rest of the floor.

"A summoning circle," she breathed. While it seemed like a crazy coincidence, she imagined that yes, a place like this where a lot of high stakes events took place, she could believe someone else would also be desperate enough to summon a demon for help. "Why the door is unlocked though beats the hell out of me. That definitely doesn't make me feel comfortable." But she really didn't have time to focus or debate that clear OSHA violation. It was working to her advantage now.

She moved to the edge of the circle and sucked a breath in to hold it a moment. Am I really going to do this? she thought, doubt making her hesitate. But she didn't have any other options, not even failure.

"Lares, I need you," she whispered.

Instantly, the faded summoning circle flashed to life, the lines of fire whipping over the concrete. In its center a kneeling creature with wings and horns flashed like a shadow, only to be replaced by a man in a blue chef's shirt and black pants with a cook's toque set on top of his head. Then the circle died, leaving the figure in the circle of her phone's flashlight.

Slowly, he raised his head. "What would you command, my mistress?" he asked.

She regarded her friend, her lover ... her demon before her. She knew what she was going to ask, but facing him now, it was like she had never seen him before.

"I just want..." she started, hesitating again. "I just want to know what can I do? How do I solve this?"

Rafferty stood up in one smooth motion, then braced his feet in a sort of parade rest, bringing his hands to clasp behind his back. "You ask me to cook for you," he said simply, his expression detached.

She furrowed her brows, then shook her head. "No, no I can't do that. I know that to ask for such a thing... I have an idea what it will cost."

"If you thought you had another option, you wouldn't have come to me," he said coldly.

"No, I'm sorry this was a mistake," she said, backing up to the door and turning away. What was going on? Why did she feel so unsettled facing someone she cared so much about? It had been a couple of weeks since she saw his face. She thought she should feel elated to see him again, but dread sat in her heart instead. She needed to get out of the room, where it was easier to think.

Suddenly, he was behind her, his hand pressing into the door before she could open it. The speed of the move startled her so much that she dropped her phone, plunging them back into darkness.

"Just ask me," he whispered into her ear, making her shiver, but also frightening her at the same time.

"Rafferty?"

"You didn't ask for Rafferty. You asked for Lares. Lares is here," he said. "And if you command it, I can cook for you."

His fingers came around her face in the near dark to grasp her chin and turn her to face him. His starburst eyes flashed in the darkness, glowing eerily. "Just ask me," he breathed.

This is how they do it, she thought, remembering everything he had told. They make you trust them and then when you are vulnerable and weak...

"You said you trust me," he said, cutting off her thoughts. "Do you trust me?"

He isn't a monster. He isn't a demon. He's my...

"Yes, I trust you," she breathed, wishing she was as sure about that as the first time she had said it.

"Then ask me."

She cupped his cheek and her demon went still, looking deep into those starburst eyes, she leaned forward. Closing her eyes, she kissed him. "Rafferty, will you help me?" she asked.

"As you wish, my mistress."

Chapter 46

DO IT FAST OR DO IT RIGHT

Rafferty backed away then, his face disappearing into the darkness, and Helena couldn't help feeling like she had made a terrible mistake.

"Thank you," she said lamely. "Um, what should we do now?"

"You need to take me to the kitchen and grant me the authority to cook in there," he said, again with that cold, impersonal tone.

"Oh. Right," she said and slid her hand around the door until she found the knob.

She was so ready to get out of that horrible room that she opened the door faster than was prudent. Plunging them back into the light, it blinded her for a moment.

"Helena? What are you doing in there?"

Jumping at the voice, she realized Yosef stood right in front of her. She tried to back up, but Rafferty came right up behind her, blocking her path.

Yosef looked from her to him and back to her. "They said you came back here to call for help... that we don't have a chef?"

"Yes, yes, I did. I called for help," she agreed, motioning to the demon behind her. "You remember Rafferty. He cooked at my dinner party a few months ago. He's come to help me."

"Oh," Yosef said, looking unconvinced. "What were you two doing back there?"

"Making out," Rafferty said, so completely deadpan that Yosef had no choice but to take it for the truth. Especially when he looked to Helena for confirmation and she blushed.

"Well, wouldn't you? If your boyfriend came to save the day," she said.

Yosef blinked rapidly, then shook his head. "Okay, fine. We don't have time for this. Let's just go." And he pivoted to head back toward the kitchens, leaving Helena and Rafferty to follow.

"How is Scarlet?" she asked, catching up with Yosef to walk beside him. Rafferty followed behind quietly.

"She should be in a hospital bed, but she convinced her doctor to let her make her speech tonight. *Then* she swears she'll go, but I doubt it." Yosef stopped and ran his hand through his hair, mussing it up. "Dammit."

"Hey, hey," Helena said, setting her hand to his back. "It's going to be okay. She's going to be alright." But Yosef shook her hand off.

"No, she's not," he said sharply. "Dammit. I was born in the wrong time..."

"You really do love her?" Helena said.

Yosef whirled on her. "What the hell does that mean?" he demanded but didn't give her a chance to clarify. "Of course I love her. You think because she's so much older than me that what? I'm just after her money or something?"

"I didn't mean—" Helena tried to say, putting her hands up in surrender, but Yosef kept coming until Rafferty's hand on his chest stopped him.

"We don't have time for this," Rafferty reminded him evenly.

Yosef took a step back and straightened. "I'm sorry. The stress is getting to me," he said lamely. "I will ... just take a minute to collect myself." He turned and walked off, much to Helena's relief.

"Let's get," Rafferty said, turning in that direction.

She wanted to thank him for intervening, but he didn't give her the opportunity to as he pushed into the kitchen.

The wait staff still stood there chatting with each other and waiting for someone to give them instructions.

"Everyone," Helena called, commanding the attention again. Gratifyingly, they all turned to her. "I am really sorry for all of the confusion but thank you all for sticking around."

"We are still getting paid, right?" one of the waiters asked from the middle of the crowd, with several of them "yeah"-ing in agreement.

"Yes, of course. Nothing else has changed," she assured. "Except this. I called in re-enforcements." She turned to Rafferty and gestured to him. "This is Rafferty. He is in charge of this kitchen. You will follow his directions."

That announcement seemed to relieve many of the staff.

"Prepare to serve the refreshments, check the wine, and sort yourselves out," Rafferty ordered, taking charge.

"What? Just him?" another server asked. "Where is the rest of his staff?"

"Nothing's been cooked yet," another added. "We have nothing but wine to serve."

"Hors d'oeuvres will go out on time," Rafferty barked. "You do your jobs, and I will do mine. Deal?"

There were nods and half-hearted "yes, chefs," but Helena couldn't blame them. Once the staff dispersed to prepare, she followed Rafferty to the large walk-in fridge.

"How are you going to do this? This meal... You should have been cooking all day in preparation and now..."

"You have a choice to make," Rafferty said, turning around inside the cold fridge, crossing his arms to face her. "The easiest thing would be to magic up the food. It would also be the cheapest."

"No!" Helena said, swiping her arms across herself in the universal arm gesture of "absolutely not." "What's the other option?"

"We bring in more hands," he said.

"You mean—"

"I'll take care of it," Rafferty said. "Go enjoy your reward."

He turned away and started opening boxes. Helena hesitated. "Raffie, are... are we alright?"

"Get the hell out of my kitchen. I got work to do," he barked. An invisible force pushed her away. She thought she was going to slam into the refrigerator door, but then it opened by itself and she stumbled out into the kitchen. A couple of the wait staff looked up, but she caught herself and cleared her throat while straightening her dress. They looked away uninterested, which was fine since she couldn't come up with a good cover.

"Please let nothing else go wrong tonight," she prayed.

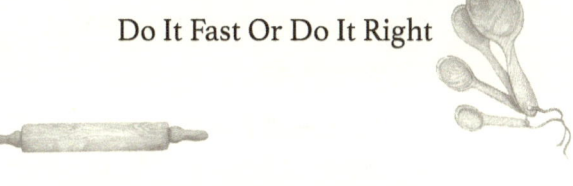

The ballroom was coming together beautifully. Despite the issues with the kitchen, everything else arrived on time with little to no resistance. The flowers were beautiful and even more extravagant than originally budgeted for, all the embellishments gratis. The article had done the trick it needed to. She was glad Scarlet's carrot stick trick had worked and that Helena had been able to pull off the "I'm not supposed to tell you this" little white lie. She had never been that good at lying, but Scarlet's explanation of "just helping people get out of their own way with whatever they are willing to accept" advice helped a lot.

The table settings, the chairs, the lights, the quartet in the corner tuning up: everything was almost ready. The room was winter festive splendor with evergreen trees clustered in the corners, festooned with icicles and white lights twinkling like stars. Enormous silver and gold bunting wrapped around the walls, and suspended with the chandelier, a thousand snowflake-shaped crystals spun slowly to create the magical winter wonderland.

Helena walked around the tables, setting each place card she had been checking earlier at the top of each plate before checking it off on her clipboard. At the front of the room, techs were going over all of the requirements for the microphones and lighting.

At last, the final card was set and she passed her clipboard with its diagram of what everything was supposed to look like to one of the other office workers to do a walkthrough double check.

"Madame," Éliott said, coming up to her and bowing a little at the waist. "Your presence is requested in the kitchen."

Bracing herself, Helena nodded and thanked Éliott. She didn't like this. She didn't like feeling afraid to go see Rafferty. As she wove her way through the tables toward the doors to the kitchen, which were hidden inside a fake little tunnel made to look like ice, she wished she had never called him for help.

That's ridiculous, she thought. *I should be allowed to call for help from my boyfriend.* But was he really her boyfriend? Yes, she had said the words, yet she couldn't remember him agreeing to it or even calling himself that. Had she presumed a level of relationship that wasn't really there?

I am a demon, was all he ever called himself.

Her faith in him truly shaken, she pushed her way into the kitchen.

The place was bustling with people. Cooks and assistants of all stripes were moving about the room preparing food of all colors and platings. She stopped in utter awe at the personnel. *Where did they all come from?*

"Excuse me," one of the wait staff said, trying to get past her with a tray covered with little dishes of pink and honey-yellow butters for the tables.

She stepped inside to get out of their way as two more of the wait staff exited with the same thing on their trays.

Drifting over to one of the cooking counters, where a young man was chopping up and preparing garnishes, she reached out to touch his sleeve. Wide black eyes shot back at her as he froze completely at the invasion. She retreated immediately, but it was like she had attracted the attention of an angry snake. He wouldn't look away. If anything, he started leaning toward her, his gaze hungrily locked on hers.

"Um... I'm looking for..." she said, as the blackness of the cook's eyes began to swirl like a whirlpool in inky water.

He's a demon!

She looked away to the rest of the room. All of the cooks that she could see had black eyes.

They were all demons.

Chapter 47

A KITCHEN FULL OF DEMONS

"She's not for you," Rafferty's voice said, his arm cutting in front of the swirling eyes and breaking the creature's focus. It blinked once, then narrowed its strange eyes angrily at the other demon.

"Fix your sight," Rafferty growled low.

"I see why you chose her, Lares. She's an old, old soul," the demon hissed, his eyes shifting to Rafferty. "Yes. Very nice. Does she taste delicious as you once did?"

Rafferty didn't react to the baiting. "Fix your eyes. You agreed to obey me in this."

The demon grinned smugly and looked back to Helena. "He is being very uncouth and rude, is he not, my dear? He isn't even introducing us. Oh well. I look forward to getting to know you better when he drags you down with the rest of us... as I did him."

Helena's heart beat faster, and she grabbed for Rafferty's hand. A vision of this creature tearing her throat

308

out crossed through her mind, and the demon's grin grew larger, as if he were the one who put it there.

The demon's eyes noted her hand clasping at Rafferty's. "Oh that's sweet. She thinks you're going to save her. Well, it's too late, tasty little old soul. The deal has already been struck, hasn't it?"

Rafferty pulled his hand out of her grasp and planted it on her bare shoulder instead, pushing her back and away roughly.

"Fix your eyes," he repeated to the demon, "or you forfeit our bargain."

The creature narrowed its whirlpool eyes, then blinked once before rapidly fluttering them. When he opened them again, his black eyes had shifted color to a light hazel. "That goes for all of you!" Rafferty barked to the room. "Keep your eyes on your tasks."

All of the demons turned to him for a few moments, like they were confused, but then a few got it, and eye colors began to shift across the room, hiding the last telltale sign of their unnaturalness.

Satisfied, Rafferty turned back to Helena, resetting his hand on her bare shoulder firmly to steer her away.

"My name is Vassago, by the way—" the chopping demon tried to add, but Rafferty whisked her away to his workstation, unable to even respond if she wanted to, which she didn't.

Once there, Rafferty gestured to a prepared plate sitting there. "Do you approve?" he asked.

Helena blinked at the plate, trying to parse what she was seeing. A prepared quail sat in the prominent position on the plate beside a fluffy mound of whipped potatoes with something melted on top. By the smell of it gruyere.

A second little mound of potatoes was smooshed next to it, and Helena realized it formed a tiny igloo on the plate. Next to that were little Parisian carrots all sliced up to their tops and pressed to make little fan-shapes, resting upright on a small pile of some sort of greens, like a little merry vegetable fire. Next to that were two little round mounds of herb butter with two tiny, tiny herb branches sticking out to make a snowman.

"It looks delicious," Helena said truthfully.

Rafferty growled in his throat. "I know it does, but is it an acceptable presentation for your event?"

Helena blinked at the plate, not really sure what she was supposed to be looking for, but she struggled for specific words. "It looks festive and on theme. Like a mini holiday dinner. Can I taste it?"

He handed her a fork. The first bite sent familiar happy shivers through her. "The meat is tender," she started to say, then grabbed his hand and offered him a bite.

But instead of accepting it, he snapped his hand out of her grip. "I don't need to taste it," he said as he took a step away from her.

"What? What do you mean?" she asked, truly confused.

He seized a glass of the wine and presented it to her. "This is the wine pairing. Do you approve?"

Helena set the fork down as her throat tightened with needles. She just couldn't eat anything anymore. If she did, she knew she would choke.

"Rafferty, what is going on here? Who are all these people? And why are you acting so differently?"

"You know what they are," he said, poignantly only answering one of her questions. Angrily, he set down the wineglass she wouldn't take. Picking up a knife, he slid a

Parisian carrot in front of himself and sliced the round vegetable in quick motions so that it formed the fan-shape when he pressed it down. He set that one against the first carrot fan to make a more layered "fire" look.

"Yes, but Rafferty..." She turned to throw her gaze across the room.

"You had two choices. If I couldn't create the food from demon magic, then we needed hands to make it. And even then I've had to take so many shortcuts, it's a wonder I have any fingers left." She glanced down at his intact fingers and decided he meant that metaphorically.

"But..." she said in a very small voice, glancing back at the demon prepping ingredients. He waved at her with his knife. "Even the one who ... deceived you and dragged you to ... there?"

"He knows how to cook," Rafferty said simply.

She took it all in. A kitchen full of demons, coming at his summons to help fulfill her wish. This all seemed so surreal.

"How much is this going to cost?" she asked softly.

It would have been better if his eyes had remained cold, but a wicked, bitter smirk crossed his face. He looked down on her with an aspect of triumph. "As Vassago said, it's a little late to ask that now," he said, nodding toward the chopping demon.

The needles in her throat stabbed deeper. If he had crushed her throat in his hand, it would have hurt less.

She took a step back from him, unable to keep the horror building. "I asked you for help..."

"And I gave it," he said, pleasantly, taking a step after her. "I am giving you everything you asked for. Aren't you *pleased*, mistress?"

She took another step back. "Rafferty—"

His hand snapped out to grab her wrist, arresting her retreat. "I told you," he said, in a low voice. "The temptation is always too great."

She wrested herself from his grip and he let her go.

"So I ask you again, mistress, does this meet with your approval?"

"Helena?" a voice cut in and they both turned to find Yosef standing beside Vassago, watching them. "Is everything alright?"

"I'll be right there," she said, looking back to Rafferty. "The meal is fine. I approve." Then she escaped, moving to pull Yosef away from Vassago who had started talking to him. The last thing she needed now was for Yosef to get wise to the hell she hath wrought.

"Is everything alright?" Yosef asked again as she pulled him out of the kitchen.

"Don't worry about it. It's handled," she said. "What's the update on Scarlet?"

Yosef glanced back at the kitchen. "Okay, if you say so. Um..." He pressed his fingers to his temples like a mentalist trying to perform a trick. "She's..." He shook his head. "She's not fine, but ... she's got that doctor wrapped around her finger, and she's convinced him to let her come for the speeches and dinner."

He had already told her that, but Helena didn't point it out. Yosef seemed to be barely holding it together. Instead, she reluctantly nodded. "Well if it's what she wants—"

"It doesn't matter what she *wants*! What she *needs* is to be in the hospital right now and instead she's killing herself ... for this," he hissed.

A few eyes turned toward his frantic gestures, and Helena grabbed his waving hand, aware of how it looked.

"Hey, hey, don't do that," she said, rubbing down the back of his hand in soothing strokes. "The last thing you need to do right now is panic because if we start panicking, they all will start panicking and thinking something is really wrong with Scarlet and that *will* be all anyone will talk about tonight. And then it will be all over the papers. That is the last thing we want, right?" She had to make him meet her eyes. "That would be the last thing *she* wants."

Helena felt him wanting to resist, but then he let out a breath and reset himself, flashing a reassuring smile at a pair of waiters setting out butters nearby. "You're right. You're right. There's nothing we can do now. And it's not like she's going to start listening to me now, anyway." He cleared his throat one more time. "Where are we with the valet situation?"

"Got it handled," one of the office people reported, popping up beside them. "Helena, we have one little snag..."

"That's fine. I'm coming," Helena said, swallowing back her feelings.

"This is going to really come together," the office worker said, excitedly looking around as the lights shifted down to bring out the splendor of the hanging lights above.

"Yes," Helena agreed. "But it's not over yet. What needs to be done next?"

Chapter 48

IT WAS AN UNMITIGATED SUCCESS

The ball opening was an unmitigated success. Once the guests arrived, the hors d'oeuvres went out exactly on time along with the wine pairings. She and Yosef gave opening remarks on behalf of Scarlet when the ball began and the initial elegant dancing commenced. Compliments showered on Helena and Yosef, who were overrun with socialites and politicians all wishing them well, but also wanting to see if they could get more information on Scarlet's state of being.

Helena followed Yosef's lead, saying that Scarlet intended to make an entrance and that everything was fine while paying compliments in return. More than one man asked her to dance, and she had to agree to do so with more of them than she would have liked, which was none. All the while she had to keep her smile in place and prayed it reached her eyes some of the time.

When it came time for the meal, Scarlet made her appearance. The applause was thunderous as she was wheeled in. It was as if a queen had entered her court. Yosef stepped forward, handsome and gallant to offer his arm to her, and she stood on her own two feet. Helena was already at the microphone. With a gesture from Scarlet, she crossed to meet them. Scarlet wrapped her arms around Helena in front of the world and kissed her cheek. A torch passing to the next generation could not have been clearer.

With her arms linked with Helena's and Yosef's, Scarlet went to the microphone.

"Thank you all. Thank you," she said with a few more platitudes as the audience calmed themselves down in anticipation for their matriarch's words.

"I am ... genuinely brought to tears," Scarlet said. "This place is beautiful. The venue... I don't think I have ever seen this room more magical, and as much as I wish I could take credit for what has been assembled here tonight, as many you know I have been fading as the years have finally caught up with me."

There were protests from the audience, but they were cheerfully waved down, and she continued.

"I cannot and will not take credit for this success, but I will take credit for my protégés whom I have nurtured and who have learned from me, and then blessed me with the greatest gift any teacher could hope for... they surpassed me."

The applause became as thunderous as it had been when Scarlet entered, but this time it was for Helena and Yosef. The waves of approval were overwhelming, and Helena didn't know what to do with herself. How could this moment of greatest triumph also contain the heaviest her heart had ever been? When she looked to Yosef, he and Scarlet were embracing, and she could see the same tears in his eyes that were in hers. Somehow, that slice of empathy fortified her. How else could life be but bittersweet?

We are a collection of good things and bad things. And they do not cancel each other out or make them unimportant.

When it was Helena's turn to embrace Scarlet, the older woman whispered in her ear, "You have a wonderful future ahead of you."

Helena nodded and smiled tearfully because she was expected to. While she truly felt it, she also knew it wasn't true.

Her life would end tonight.

The speech continued with Scarlet thanking the rest of the office, all of the cooking and serving staff, the politicians who graced the room with their presence, and all of the donors who came to support such a worthy and important cause.

Helena heard very little of it. She only looked out at the fairy lit dark, trying to take it all in and memorize every detail.

They'll strip everything from you, every memory that you hold precious. Everything you ever were, she thought with Rafferty's voice.

I don't want to forget, she thought in her own.

She didn't want to forget about any of it, this night, the last few weeks... her time with Rafferty.

It may have all been a lie... but how she felt for him hadn't been.

At last, the speeches were over. Yosef and she escorted Scarlet to their table. The courses flew by, Helena barely tasting any of it. They were all familiar to her. Rafferty was in every flourish, their memories in every bite.

At last, they came to the dessert.

"My gosh, what is this?" a woman at their table exclaimed as the slices of layered cake covered in white, sugared fluff were set before them. A sprig of cranberries framed the cake.

"Opera cake," a self-important man at the table declared in no uncertain terms.

Helena broke out laughing. She tried to cover it with her hands, but it was impossible as she realized what was before her. The whole table turned to her with surprised expressions.

"It's icebox cake," she finally managed to say as an explanation. "It's very similar to opera cake. It's just made with layers of cookie wafers instead of layers of cake." Rafferty had been determined to figure it out, and it looked like he had.

"Brilliant!" the original woman declared. The table agreed as each took their first bites and returned to their conversations.

After a few minutes, Scarlet sat back from the table. "Well, I do not know about you all, but I haven't eaten so much rich food in quite a while. Yosef, would you be a dear and escort me to the little lady's room?"

Yosef stood up quickly and helped Scarlet out of her chair, tucking her hand into the crook of his arm. They stayed that way for a moment too long and just as Helena realized that Scarlet might fall back into her seat again, she started moving forward.

"My gosh, she is a splendid lady," the know-it-all gentlemen, whom Helena thought was a city alderman or something like, commented.

"She looks like she is on death's door," another woman commented snottily, only to get nudged in the ribs. "What?" she asked, then followed a none-too discreet fork jab in Helena's direction. "What? What about her? I don't understand you, Harold," she said just as loudly and with a complete lack of self-awareness.

Yet, Helena couldn't even be offended. All she could think about was the cake. And about the demon who made it.

"If you will all excuse me, I need to check on something in the kitchen. I'll be back," she assured.

"You see what you did," the woman's husband chided as Helena moved quickly away.

It proved to be a challenge to get through the room with everyone stopping to congratulate her on a successful event. It took Éliott coming up to her and saying there was an urgency in the kitchen that required her attention to disengage her.

"Thank you," she whispered to him as she escaped down the fake ice tunnel.

Despite steeling herself for whatever she needed to say, it was still a shock to walk into the kitchen. The servers were still moving in and out with desserts and wine, but the preparation areas where the majority of the cooking happened were completely empty.

All the cooks and assistants were gone.

The stations were all cleaned up and spotless as if nobody had been there.

All but one.

At Rafferty's station, the final cakes were being prepped. Each slice of the layered icebox cake had been plated. He stood before them, tearing apart one of the flower arrangements. It looked like one of the dozen larger ones that had been by the entrance. With a paring knife, he pruned off the flowers to add the last embellishments to his dessert.

She approached his station slowly, not sure what she was going to say to him, instead watching as his fingers flew. He moved quickly, gathering the newly cut buds and setting each on the plate. He never adjusted the impromptu garnish once it was set; each flower seemed to find its perfect place instantly. A waitress approached the station to take the final tray just as he finished.

"Go, go, go," he barked, waving away the tray as he dropped the last flower in place. For a second, he turned back and forth, looking for the next thing to do, but that was it. He had finished. So his hands found his towel to wipe the remaining torn up leaves toward the garbage can by his hip.

Only then did his eyes drift up to her. "It is done," he said.

"Where is everyone?" she asked, looking again at the otherwise spotless kitchen.

"They've all returned back to where they are supposed to be," he said.

"But..."

"What?"

She licked her lips. "What about what they're ... owed?"

"I've already taken care of it," he said. "I bound them to me and paid their prices in order to keep them under control and everyone safe."

Warily, Helena stared at him. "Rafferty," she said softly, calling for his attention, but he still refused to give it. "What did you pay them with?"

Suddenly, Rafferty stumbled, collapsing backward.

Chapter 49

IT GOT
SERIOUS

Suddenly, Rafferty stumbled, collapsing backward.
The only reason he didn't land on the ground was
his hand slamming onto the counter behind him, keeping
him upright.

"Rafferty!" she cried and ran around the workstation
to get to his side.

"Is he alright?" one of the waitresses asked as she
fetched more wine.

"No, of course he's not alright," Éliott said, coming up
to chase the waitress back out to the floor. "The man just
pulled off a miracle. I'm surprised he is still standing at all.
Now get a move on. Table eighteen needs refreshing."

Helena nodded her thanks to Éliott, who had proved
as reliable a head waiter as his cousin had proved a failure
as a chef. He nodded back and gestured for the back. "Get
him out of here. Rest. I will handle what remains."

She nodded and took Rafferty's arm over her shoulders. Her demon moved alarmingly slowly, and she was just relieved that he let her help him. Together, they navigated out of the back into the dock area, which was far more deserted now that most of the business of the ball had been taken care of.

Only a security guard looked up from his paperback with a bored, disinterested expression on his face that became more acutely interested at the sight of them.

"Is he alright?" he called.

"Yes, we're fine. It's just been a big night," Helena called back.

"There's an alcove over that way with some chairs if you need to sit down," the guard offered.

"Thank you. We'll do that," she agreed, waving and smiling for all she was worth.

But they didn't make it far toward that alcove before Rafferty began to stutter. Helena noticed it as the thrumming wrongness flipping on and off like a toddler with a light switch. Glancing up, she saw his wings flit in and out of existence, along with his horns and gray skin as his face remained a contorted mask of pain no matter what form he was in.

"Oh, no, please Rafferty. Hold on just a little farther," Helena begged.

"Hey! What's going on there?" the security guard called after them.

Helen tried to compel their steps faster, but Rafferty bucked again, groaning in pain as his legs gave out underneath them. He fell onto his side, catching one of his wings beneath him. A sharp snap bent his wing wrong, and he howled in pain.

"Rafferty!" Helena shouted as she pulled on his arm to try to get him off his own wing, which instantly disappeared, only to reappear again as he rolled onto his hands and knees on the ground. The wing was clearly bent at a wrong angle.

"What the hell?!" the security guard exclaimed from too close.

She looked up to see him standing only a few feet away, staring wide-eyed down on the anathema beside her.

"Get... get the hell away from it!" the guard shouted, his hands shaking as he went for his enormous flashlight at his belt. Holding it in both hands, he hefted it like a billy club, then took a hop-skip step toward them.

"No, don't!" she tried to shout, but she couldn't get to her feet in time to step in front of him as the guard aimed for the demon's head.

Instead, Rafferty flexed his wings back mightily. They *womph*ed the guard, upsetting his already precarious balance to knock him back onto his butt. The flashlight fell from his hands and Helena scrambled to grab it. As she did that, Rafferty turned on his knees and seized the guard's head.

"Forget," he growled out.

"Rafferty! Don't!" Helena cried, throwing the flashlight away before pulling on his arms to force him to let go of the guard. "Don't hurt him, please!"

Rafferty yielded to her, releasing him weakly, but the guard just kept staring ahead blankly.

"What did you do?"

"I ate his memory of the last few minutes," Rafferty said, turning away so he could use the wall to regain his feet, shifting back to human as he did so. "He will be fine."

"Rafferty, what is happening to you?"

"The price needs to be paid," he said, leaning against the wall, his arms tucked against his sides. "Take me back to the circle."

"But ... it was my price to pay."

He shook his head. "No. I won't do it. I won't take your life."

Using the wall to help himself, he continued to walk down the hall toward the forbidden door. Helena stared at him as she realized what he was saying. "You ... never intended to make me pay for tonight."

"No, but you thought I was going to, didn't you!" he shot back. "The second things got hard, you turned to your demon."

Suddenly, his coldness made a different kind of sense. He wasn't tricking her. He was angry and disappointed in her.

"I reached out to *you,* not 'my demon.' I needed help. I didn't know what to do!" She stood up to go after him. "So I reached out to the person I trusted most, my... my boyfriend, if we even are in that relationship."

He groaned as he leaned against the wall. She came around to help hold him up at the shoulders. "You need to take from me whatever you need. My mind, body, or soul—whichever. I don't care!"

"No," he said, grabbing her shoulders to push her away. "You don't understand. What needed to be done tonight... it had a very high cost. This cost will kill you, maybe even wipe you from existence forever." He cupped his hand around her cheek. "I can't let that happen to the person I..."

Helena went still. "Did you know that when I asked this of you?" she pressed.

His eyes told her the truth.

"So everything you were saying to me, how cold you were being... it was because you were angry at me? I ... disappointed you by asking for it, right?"

"Everyone does in the end. Why would you be any different?" he said snidely, his contempt bare now.

It hurt, but not as much as losing him was going to hurt. "But why didn't you *tell* me what the price was?"

"You didn't ask until it was too late to change it!" he barked back. "You proved me right by not caring what the price was, just that you got what you wanted!"

"You have your own agency, dammit! You could have told me without making me ask twenty questions," she barked at him. She wanted to shake him, but instead she pushed in and hugged him tight. "No, you can't die. I won't let it happen."

He deflated a little bit, wrapping one of his arms around her. "I'm already dead, Helena," he whispered. "I've just been putting off the inevitable."

"It's not inevitable. We can figure this out. Please. Stop trying to be right and start working with me to figure out how to save you!"

"You... you want to save me?" he asked as if he were only just now hearing it.

"Yes! I love you! That's what I've been trying to tell you. I didn't want all of this in exchange for your life. If anything I wanted... I wanted your help, but mostly I wanted a hug!"

"Then why didn't you ask for that?"

"Because ... I don't always have the right answer right when I need it!"

Rafferty blinked at that, understanding finally. "Oh dammit. I screwed up." He leaned forward to set his weary head on her shoulder while she thought desperately.

"What if..." she said, idea starting to form. "If the price would kill one of us, what if ... we share it?"

"What?" he grunted groggily.

"You and I. If we combined what we have, would that be enough to right the imbalance without killing either of us?"

"I..." He shook his head. "I don't know... maybe?"

"Okay, well, it's all we got, so we got to try. Put your arm around me." He leaned his weight into her and immediately Helena regretted it. Now he was really giving in to her, and she just did not have the right shoes on for this. Still, they stumbled across the hall toward the forbidden door.

"But Helena, it will hurt. It will leave you devastated," Rafferty mumbled, shifting again to his demonic form.

"Yeah, well you can't heal if you're not alive, and at this point, I would say this situation is both our doing, so it makes sense we're going to have to fix it together." They were only a few feet from the door when another woman's voice screamed.

They both stopped, staring at the door.

"That came from in there," Helena said.

"Someone found the summoning circle," Rafferty said warily.

Together, they spurred forward, Rafferty reaching out his free hand to push the door open as she hauled them both through.

Within the darkened room, the summoning circle glowed, casting up a sickly, dim light. Helena stared at it.

She could feel its eerie gravity pulling at her, its hunger. The debt was large, and it needed to be satisfied.

Rafferty laughed dryly. "Huh, I racked up a bigger debt than I imagined." Then he cried out in pain.

"I should say so. Holy hell in a handbasket, that was quite the feat tonight." Within the depths of the dark, Vassago's voice sang out mockingly musical. "Come in and shut the door already."

"Helena! Get out of here! Go get help!" Scarlet cried from the opposite side of the circle. To Helena's shock, her boss and mentor stood on the other side, held there by Yosef. Madness had filled Yosef's eyes.

"That's right, Helena. You should turn around and just walk away," he warned.

"Oh, no need to worry. No need at all. You're not the only one selling your soul for a miracle. Look what the cat dragged in, as they say."

The wrong feeling returned, and Helena knew that Rafferty had shifted again without her even needing to look.

"Ah now there's a beautiful face, isn't it?" Vassago laughed as Scarlet and Yosef's eyes went wide. And she knew what they saw.

"Oh, Helena, not you too," Scarlet moaned.

"It's not what you think," Helena tried to say.

Vassago gestured at the door, and it slammed shut behind Helena and Rafferty, plunging them all into the unholy light that held them all enthralled.

Chapter 50

I JUST FELL FOR HIM

In the glow of the summoning circle, all was revealed. Vassago's true body was hideous. He stood taller than even Rafferty with two sets of horns fanning out of his head at odd angles. Below those horns, an emaciated lion-like face split open as he talked. Within were two rows of wicked-looking, shark-like teeth. His body had a reddish shininess to it, like he had been skinned alive. His feet ended with two enormous hooves that he clomped every few words as if he couldn't keep them still. Each foot made an irritating, crunching sound on the concrete beneath him. Behind him, his twin tails twitched and flicked as if each had a mind of its own. One seemed like a scorpion tail, flicking out over his shoulder as if at any moment it wanted nothing more than to sink into one of their bodies. The other was closer to Rafferty's tail, a triangle that had been split into two triangles and very violently by the look of it with a horrible jagged scar. The demon tail twitched wrongly and looked painful when it didn't, though nothing showed on Vassago's face.

Helena looked from Vassago to Yosef. "Listen to me—you can't trust him. Whatever you think you'll get out of this won't be worth it. I promise you."

Scarlet tried again to pull away, but Yosef tightened his arm on her waist.

"If you've done this, then it must work," he growled as he fought against Scarlet's thrashing. "Just stop it! I'm trying to save you."

"Yosef, you can't!" Helena said, realizing what was happening. "You can't save her life this way. The cost is too high—!"

"Don't listen to her. Of course it can be done. She just wants all that power for herself and her own demon, but it is not at all impossible to gain what you most desire," Vassago said, cutting her off.

"I just want to save her life," Yosef pleaded.

"Then stop dilly-dallying," Vassago said, gesturing toward the circle. "You said you were willing to do whatever it takes to get what you want."

"Yosef, no, don't!" Scarlet screamed, but her thrashing did no good as the younger, stronger man walked them both into the circle.

Immediately, the lines crackled and popped with purple electricity. Unearthly whispers filled the air, making the hairs on Helena's arms and neck rise. Then Vassago stepped into the circle with them. He bent forward at the waist, like he was offering them both a gallant, courtly bow when his tails snapped out. The forked devil's tail grabbed Yosef, pulling him toward the demon, heedless of how hard he fought while the scorpion tail stabbed Scarlet in the middle of her chest.

"No!" Helena shouted and tried to surge forward to intervene, but Rafferty wrapped his arms around her and held her back.

"Don't," was all he could say because what happened next went by too fast. The scorpion tail seemed to pump and throb as Scarlet dropped to her knees. Underneath Vassago's skin, lumps skittered up and down, like his whole form was shifting and changing as he violated the young man. Meanwhile, his mouth opened inches from Yosef's face. While he twisted and fought, the demon grasped the back of his head and forced him toward his mouth. The creature's tongue lolled out as he stuck Yosef's head into his maw. The stink of his breath made Helena gag, even from several feet away.

Then Rafferty covered her face with his hands, and all she could hear was the crunch as Vassago bit down.

She thought she was going to throw up at the sound. Then it was over as two bodies slumped to the ground.

"Ah yes, most satisfying. Oldish soul, not as old as the one you got there, but he had a nice tang to him," Vassago crowed gleefully. Helena could feel Rafferty shudder, and she pushed away his hand so she could see.

On the ground were two bodies, but their forms were covering the glow of the circle's light, making it even darker in the room than before. But when she looked back at the horrible demon still standing there, his whirlpool eyes were clear to see in the dark.

"You lied to them!" Helena cried.

"Shitty bargainers. Why give something away when you can just take it? Survival of the fittest; you know the platitudes. Might make right, that sort of thing. There is only so much finite power in the world, old soul, and I intend to have my share."

His eyes raked over Helena lustfully.

"You look like shit, Lares," Vassago noted with a sniff. "How about this? I'm flush with power right now. Give me your little pet there, and I'll give you enough to pay off the debt you incurred."

"No," Rafferty said, holding Helena tighter to him.

Vassago looked put out, his terrible face pouting like a child's. "You know I can just take her from you. You're so thin on power right now. Let's make a trade. Gimme your old soul, and I'll save your existence."

Helena felt Rafferty's arms tighten around her, his wings creating a protective cove. She knew, she trusted, that he would never do such a thing, but she also knew that what Vassago spoke was the truth; her lover wouldn't be able to fight in his condition.

Still the circle pulled and beckoned.

"Rafferty, I want to go home," she said, her eyes still glued to the glowing lines, whispering incessantly.

"What?" he breathed, his own focus still on the danger in the room.

Vassago scratched at the concrete, cracking it with each stamp. "Come on, Rafferty. Just take the deal and make this easier on us all."

Helena turned her face toward Rafferty, so she could whisper in his ear. "Take me through Hell. You did it before."

He growled his objection in his throat.

"We don't have any other options," she insisted.

"We won't make it," he said.

"But we could." She didn't wait for his approval. Turning, she grabbed him around the neck and threw all her weight back. He didn't expect it and even though he tried to flare his wings to stop their fall, it was too little too late. Instead, he wrapped his arms around her and held on.

Helena could feel the pulling in of the circle draw them down, past the point they should have hit the concrete. She was mildly aware of the other bodies being pulled down with them, but she could do nothing for them, and they fell away as they sank under the surface of a vast cosmic ocean.

Pain. Hot burning pain.

Helena wants to scream.

Her body burns away, pulled into the vastness around her. There is nothing between her and it. She feels it all, her fear, her anger, her sadness. It burns. She reaches for Rafferty... she reaches, but she has nothing to reach with. She is only... she is...

It's alright, *she thinks.*

She can still think.

Let it burn.

She relaxes and allows her pain to come in.

It burns.

It eases.

She cries.

She allows.

It goes and she is left empty.

She feels love.

Her friend's faces, her memories. She enjoys them and lets them drift into the abyss.

She lets herself be what she always was.

She feels the call, the pull of oblivion. She gives in to it. There is no point in fighting. I'll pay the debt. *She repeats Rafferty's words.*

She gives it all she has. Take it. It is what you are owed. *She gives all she is freely.*

It returns it all and more.

Energy, pure and strong fills her. The power that had always been within herself and even more joins it.

She is becoming. She is aware. She understands and she knows that understanding will fade when she returns to the other reality.

But that is alright. That is how it's supposed to be.

Eternity is always where she has been, even if she doesn't remember. Even when she's there.

Her love for herself, her love for the infinite, it is all the same.

She finds him, at last. He is contained within himself, clutching against the pain. He resists it, holding himself there.

She reaches for him, to pull him out of his dark bubble, but he can't let go. She does touch him and feels what he feels, his pain, his sorrow, his regret. His belief that he has lost love forever and that Helena is dead.

Helena?

She remembers. She is Helena.

I'm here, *she tries to say, but he can't step out of the darkness. He's trapped, even though the Eternity around him calls to pull him out, he resists. Afraid to fall apart and let go.*

There are so many black bubbles. She watches as some try to eat each other, taking what little they have from each other. Unaware of the feast just outside of themselves. It's too scary. Too unknown. She can't reach any of them.

But she can pull him away. Back to the place where he could change. The spark within him is her way in.

He loves her. His being sings it out. The spark of it he holds in his center. He is trying to protect it from the darkness all around him, eating him tiny bites at a time. Tormenting him.

Rafferty, take me home, *she says.*

He opens, just a small crack. She reaches through and takes his hand. They have hands now and the idea makes her laugh. They have bodies, created for them from the same stuff. He twists it, believing it is what he is, what he cannot hide. She has to accept that is where he is, but he does not have to be if only he could see it.

It is time to rise.

Time to go home.

Time to...

Wake up.

Epilogue

MAYBE IT'LL BE OKAY?

"This is sad," Agent Archon said, shaking her head as she peered into the crime scene.

The summoning circle inside had ceased smoking, but the smell lingered in the air and would for a long time.

Her fellow officer, Agent Sophia, approached, an annoyed look on her face. "So far no explanation as to why this room wasn't still locked. They have documentation of performing the cleansing ritual up until September and that's it."

"That's a citation at best. Few thousands of dollars and they'll go back to forgetting," Agent Archon dismissed.

"What do you think happened here?" Agent Sophia asked, looking inward. Flashes sharpened the horror of the scene as the techs kept up with their work: documenting.

"Someone summoned a demon," Agent Archon said.

"Well, yes, that much is clear."

"But that is all we know. They could have just been victims. They could have been the summoners... Have we made any progress on finding the other assistant..." Agent Archon glanced down at the notes. "Helena Rhodes. Do we know if she's safe?"

"No one here has seen her. The guard is getting checked out, but he seems to have suffered from the demon attacking him. He doesn't remember anything. And of course the minute the summoning happened, all the cameras back here fried. I've sent a unit to her house to confirm if she's there or not, and we have a call out to all the hospitals. I do have a report that she was last seen helping the chef for the event." She glanced at her notes. "He seemed sick."

Agent Acheron tapped her teeth. "Hmm, that sounds promising. High stress jobs are prone to demon summoning."

"Cooking is high stress?"

Agent Acheron looked over the rim of her glasses at her partner. "Sophia, you need to get out more."

The blip of the ambulance made both agents glance over as they took away the survivor. "First stop is the hospital though, where I'm sure a lawyer will be present to make sure we don't get anything," she said dryly. "Come on. It's going to be a long night."

"You were right, honey lips. I will admit it. You saw something that I didn't, and I will own it," the being calling herself Honey said.

"While I thank you for the acknowledgement, I do question it," the being called Éliott said. "If we had intervened when you said to, an innocent person would be alive right now. And the anathema would not have been created."

"We can't interfere in their choices. No more than a demon under their control can ignore a direct command," she reminded him, then laid a hand over his, patting it. "But this is not entirely a tragedy, and that is thanks to you. You should have more faith in your judgment. She pulled the demon out of hell."

"But he is still a demon. Sort of."

"One step at a time. There was something to be redeemed within him."

"But I do not understand what has happened?" Éliott insisted, fluttering his wings in a show of agitation. One of his gray feathers dislodged and drifted down to sit between the crest of the ram-like horns circling the sides of his head.

Honey lowered the newspaper she was reading to look at the other angel sitting before her. "Well, what do you think happened?" she asked as she leaned forward and caught his feather off his head, holding it up to study its beautiful patterns.

"I do not know. That's why I'm asking you."

She fluttered her own pure white wings behind herself. It felt so good to stretch them out. "Well, to be frank I've only ever seen this happen a couple times myself, but every so often when a very old soul, one who has lived many lives and figured out many things, they sort of, take a leap and become one of us."

Éliott thought about that, mulling it over. "Is that how we came into being?"

"I'm not sure. I don't have any memory of being a mortal before. There are some questions I don't know if I

337

can ever answer, but that is what she did. And now we'll have to deal with that."

Éliott nodded, looking down at the headline and sub headline of her paper. *Socialite sacrifices assistant in demon ritual for youth and beauty. Federal agency for demonic security and prevention (DSP) investigating.*

He shook his head. "It didn't have to happen that way."

"But it did, crab cake," Honey said, folding up the paper. "They make their choices and we can only do so much to protect those that don't deserve to be dragged into it."

"But even then, what we do is so inadequate," Éliott said, despairingly.

"There are only so many of us that even want to come here and way more of *them*. We do the best that we can. And chin up. Now we've got one more."

"But what are we going to do about the demon?"

Honey hummed on that a little while. "At this point, nothing. We're going to watch him and see what she does."

"Do you think she would be able to send him back if it came to it?"

Honey beamed. "We'll just have to wait and see."

"Wonder what she's going to say when we tell her what is really going on?"

"Okay, that's enough, angel food. Let's get going." Honey made a shooing motion with her hands, indicating she expected him to take flight and get off the roof of the Wrightwood Ballroom.

"Will you stop calling me foodstuffs?" Éliott asked.

"Nope. Now hurry up, crumb cake. We have an escaped demon to find."

Helena opened her eyes but saw very little. They were gummy and filmy. She blinked rapidly to try to clear her vision, but it wasn't until she rubbed her eyes that they finally cleared.

She lay on the floor of her kitchen, the hard tile underneath pressing into her body, making it ache, like she had fallen asleep there and had never rolled over.

A rough tongue licked the back of her hand and Helena blinked to see her little black cat Pooka looking at her worried, though for a split second she thought she saw two of them.

"Hi, girl. I'm fine," she said, her voice croaky. She ran her fingers over Pooka's head, smoothing down her soft fur a couple of times, then rolled onto her back. Doing so made her bump into something on the other side.

"Rafferty?" she asked.

A man laid next to her on his side, his shoulder pointed up to the ceiling in a familiar round curve.

She rolled over and put her face into his dark hair, smelling his scent, spicy and masculine. No wings, no horns, no unhealthy pallor. Slipping her fingers under his arm, she pressed herself against him and held him tight.

His own fingers drifted up to lace through the back of hers and squeezed.

"Helena?" his voice croaked.

Pressing back, he turned over, cupping her face with his hand, and it was only then that she realized they were both naked. It didn't matter. Of course they would be, though she had no idea why she knew that.

"What the hell did you do?" he asked, looking around her kitchen.

"I have no idea," she said, laughing.

339

The circle beneath them was cold with no sense of wrongness or illusion. It just looked like someone had torched her floor as a stylistic choice.

"Are you alright?" she asked.

"Yes. Are you?"

She smiled. "Yes and no. We escaped." The sadness returned. "But Scarlet and Yosef..."

He closed his eyes and nodded. "We couldn't have stopped it. They messed with a demon."

Helena took that thought and applied it elsewhere. Sitting up, she set a hand on his very human chest. "Rafferty, can you...?"

"What?" he asked, unsure.

She lifted his hand up for him to see. "Look."

His confused silvery eyes shifted to his hand. Then went wide as he made it into a fist. Pushing himself up to sitting, he ran his hands all over his body. He was still too thin for his frame, but he wasn't emaciated like he had been before. His skin was a natural color and again, no wings or horns to speak of.

"Can you shift into it?" she asked.

He looked at her and then tensed all his muscles. Nothing happened. He stopped looking sheepish. "No," he said with a shake of his head.

"You're alive!" she said. She threw her arms around his neck and laughed.

"I don't deserve to be," he said, even though he held her back.

"Shut up. Yes, you do." She laughed and that was enough for both of them.

For the moment.

The Story
continues in
Baking and
Angels

Thank you to Autumn, Laura, and Kait,
you three keep me going.

Thank you to Michelle for upping my
foodie game.

Thank you to my friends and family who
put up with me with love.

Author Bio

Author Megan Mackie writes something for everyone—she's written cyberpunk, urban fantasy, paranormal demon romance, speculative fiction, post-post zombie apocalypse, steampunk, and mid-grade science fiction. She's also a contributing writer for RPGs Legendlore and Legendlore: Legacies by Onyx Path.

She's a popular figure at comic cons across the country, so if you come across her, ask about the Lucky Devil series and prepare to get your mind blown.

Whats the news, Barman?

Sign Up for Megan's Newsletter!

https://www.meganmackieauthor.com/newsletter

Also check out her free Wattpad novel!

https://www.wattpad.com/1423396171-i-can%27t-get-the-vampire-rogue-to-romance-me

**It was all fun, until she got
sucked into the game.**